Annie's Lights

by

Joe Pitts

Published by New Generation Publishing in 2015

Copyright © Joe Pitts 2015

First Edition

The author asserts the moral right under the Copyright, Designs and Patents Act 1988 to be identified as the author of this work.

All Rights reserved. No part of this publication may be reproduced, stored in a retrieval system or transmitted, in any form or by any means without the prior consent of the author, nor be otherwise circulated in any form of binding or cover other than that which it is published and without a similar condition being imposed on the subsequent purchaser.

www.newgeneration-publishing.com

 New Generation Publishing

This book is dedicated to Sharon Ann Brown for her inspiration and love, without which the book would never have been written.

John Egbert Junas

Professor John Egbert Junas was sat in the coffee lounge looking for one last time at his notes, he was the first speaker at the seminar on Quantum Communications and would be addressing some 700 delegates.

Egbert is a good-looking man in his mid-forties who keeps himself fit; he is clean shaven, with dark short hair, he is above average height and due to exercise has a manly chest and a slim waist. He is wearing his favourite plain black suit and a tailored white shirt.

He took one last look at the invite card for the event:-

Location: **Metropole Hotel, National Exhibition Centre, Birmingham**
Date: **25th May 2014**
Seminar: **Quantum Communications**
Speakers:
    Professor Egbert Junas – Leeds Metropolitan University
    Professor Chuck Stanton – Massachusetts Institute of Technology
    Doctor Linda Johnson – BT Research & Development

Egbert was signalled by the event director that they were ready for him and he got up out of his comfy leather chair and he walked into the packed conference theatre; he walked down the aisle through the audience towards the stage. The host for the event introduced Professor Egbert Junas to energetic applause from the audience. Egbert always got a buzz when he walked through the audience, it made him feel how he thought Elvis Presley, Freddie Mercury or Michael Jackson would have felt as they were coming out to perform in front of their audiences. When he heard the applause it made the hairs on the back of his neck stand up. He just had to block out the people in the audience thoughts as he walked forward, but he had now done it many times, so it was easy for him.

Egbert stood on the stage and he was dazzled by the spotlights shining in his face; he knew that there were up to 700 people out there looking at him, but the reality was that he could only see the first few rows due to the brightness of the lights. Egbert always used a roaming microphone as he preferred to be animated and to walk around the stage.

"Good Morning Ladies and Gentleman and honourable guests, my name is Professor Egbert Junas of Leeds Metropolitan University, I am here to talk to you about Quantum Communications and how its development will enhance the future of mankind. Science says that only a few thousand years ago men communicated by grunting, waving their arms around and by pulling faces; just imagine your teenage sons first thing in the morning and you will know what I mean."

Laughter from the audience helped Egbert to relax and he was feeling good about his presentation: he continued.

"Different grunts were used in different situations to mean different things and eventually these grunts became words, words from different tribes became languages and each tribe would develop its own language and learn to represent it by the use of different symbols and letters. As time went by man wrote down his words onto clay and slate, and then wood and then papyrus and paper and now those words could be sent to another location; the written words could be read and the recipient could write some words back to the sender. Letter post had been invented.

Now this wasn't a speedy process and it could take days and weeks to receive a letter, a bit like the UK Post Office at Christmas. I am only joking, if anybody in the audience works for the post office."

This caused the audience to laugh again and Egbert felt that he was getting his message across and that the audience were enjoying his performance, he continued.

"A new form of communication had been invented, but as it is today it was limited by time and distance, and although it was not conversation it was communication. There were other more instantaneous forms of communication for shorter distances, such as the beating of drums and the use of smoke signals and even runners, who would carry the message.

As time passed by new technologies were invented to make communication easier and faster such as the telegraph and Morse code. It really was now possible to send messages over a long distance in a timely manner, albeit somebody had to be able to translate the code at both ends. Along came Alexander Graham Bell and the telephone was invented and it was now possible to actually speak to somebody hundreds if not thousands of miles away; relatively quickly telephone communications were enhanced by undersea cables and satellite communication. Vast telephone networks across land, sea and air were established. Throw into the pot Telex and facsimile communication and it was all getting pretty sophisticated. It was inevitable that the telephone would become a cordless device and although initially it was only possible to use a handset a few metres away from a base station, people now had the freedom to talk and move around a room at the same time.

The next massive development was the mobile phone; no longer did a person have to be at one fixed location to make and receive telephone calls. The first mobile phones required a battery the size of a brick and the charge lasted for about 30 minutes; now we have very sophisticated mobile devices and the batteries for these devices are getting smaller and the charge now lasts for several hours.

The key point that I am trying to make is that technology and communication has moved forward by leaps and bounds since the earliest forms of communication and it has done so in a very small space of time, relative to mankind. In fact most of that development has happened in the last one hundred years. The growth of telephony has been remarkable, but what about the development of computers? At one time they would have taken up the whole floor of a building but now they are small enough to sit on a desk, or be carried in a handbag as a tablet or even in a pocket as a mobile device. Anyone today that is wearing a wristwatch has more computing power on their wrist than existed in those earliest room-filling computers."

Egbert paused for breath, as he had become more excited about his topic, he had watched the audience reaction and he could see that they were tuned into what he was saying, he carried on again.

"Then we have the internet, which is simply the largest library of information on the planet; it is accessible by everybody who has access to what is now a simple communication device via either wired or wireless technology. Not only has technology advanced in its own individual specialisms, but all of these are becoming inter-dependent on each other as well as becoming integrated. Ladies and Gentlemen and Honourable guests, what is there left for communications to advance to? We have come so far, surely there can be nothing else left to discover or invent?

Well, I believe that the most amazing discovery is still to come and everybody within this room will be capable of discovering it for themselves. That amazing discovery will be telepathy. I believe that we are almost there; just imagine for one moment, if we had a world where we could read each other's thoughts, there would be no more lies or deceit, wars would stop and we would live in peace: could it really happen? I believe that we all have the gift of telepathy but that it is currently locked away in our brain and it needs an unlock key, very similar to a piece of software that you might install on your computer, when you have to enter a key code to make it work. If this ability is within our brains, surely we can find a way to unlock it."

The audience were captivated by this and they were clearly hungry to learn more as Egbert continued to speak.

"Now we all know that the brain is very complex, but we still do not fully understand it; if we did we might have created an artificial one by now, or found cures for diseases of the brain. Within it there are over 100 billion nerve cells called neurons, yet the brain itself cannot feel pain as there are no pain receptors in the brain. The brain is broken down into 5 main parts:-

"The frontal lobe controls cognitive ability, memory, behaviour and the ability to speak and write; the parietal lobe controls sensory discrimination and body orientation, spatial disorders, seizures and language disturbances; the temporal lobe controls a person's ability to hear and also to understand the spoken word; the occipital lobe is for seeing and understanding visual images; the cerebrum has two hemispheres and each hemisphere contains the above 4 lobes. The right hemisphere controls the left side of the body and the left hemisphere controls the right side of the body; tucked within the brain is the pineal gland and this has been described as the 3rd eye, which is where the experts believe that additional senses can be developed. If I told you that it was already possible to read minds, would you believe me? I will demonstrate this ability to you and prove to you that I can read minds."

Egbert took time before speaking again to look at the audience to judge their reaction to what he had just said and also to allow his last statement to sink in.

"If one person can read a person's mind, then it must be possible that there are other people who can also read minds. If there are two people that can read minds, then we only need to master sending our thoughts to each other and we have telepathy."

Egbert asked for the spotlights to be dimmed and the house lights to be turned on; he wanted to be able to see the whole audience, not just the few front rows.

"Let me show you the power of mind reading: could I have three volunteers to come on to the stage, please? Yes, the lady over there, in the red dress, and the gentleman wearing glasses on the very back row, I am sorry you have so far to walk, finally and last but not least the gentleman with the blue jacket, 5 rows back from the front. Thank you and welcome, have I met with any of you before?"

The three people shook their heads and confirmed that they had not met Egbert before.

"That's good news, it saves me from picking three other victims, I am sorry, and I meant to say volunteers."

Egbert knows that the mood in the audience is good and enjoys hearing them laugh each time that he introduces his humour.

"Could you introduce yourselves to the audience please?"

The man with the glasses from the back row went first.

"I am Geoff, from Wolverhampton."

Then the lady in the red dress introduced herself.

"I am Linda, from London."

Finally the man in the blue jacket made his introduction.

"Hi, and I am Matthew, from Leicester."

Egbert smiled at the three of them and then he continued.

"Do you see the blank sheets of paper sat there on the table, please would you each select one and bring it back with you, select any sheet from anywhere in the ream, pick up a pen also; they are only cheap, but you can keep the pen as a memento. Thank you, I would like you all to write something down on your piece of paper, something that only you could know and something that you don't mind sharing with the audience, I don't want to embarrass anybody."

There is laughter from the audience.

"Geoff, would you go first please and after you have written the question and the answer please fold the paper in half and hold it in your right hand; Linda if you could do the same and if you could also do the same Matthew."

Egbert gave them a few moments to do this, the audience laughed when Linda, tore her sheet of paper up and went back to get another one— she had obviously written something down that she decided she did not want to share. Egbert smiled her when she did this and said, "I agree Linda. You probably shouldn't share that."

This caused Linda to blush and smile at the same time; after Linda had written on her second piece of paper, Egbert turned to Geoff and said. "Geoff, could I ask you to look at me and think about the answer you have given and I will tell you what it is? Geoff, the answer is Jenna and now if you could think about what the question was; Geoff, she was your first girlfriend, please pass your paper to Linda. Was I correct, Linda?"

Linda replied, "Yes, one hundred percent."

The audience applauded and Egbert then looked at Linda and said, "Linda, please would you face me and think about your answer, but do not tell me it. The answer is 16th August 2014, now think about the question Linda. Yes, that is the day you are flying out on holiday to Spain; please pass your piece of paper to Matthew. Was I correct, Matthew?"

Matthew replied; "Yes, spot on."

The audience again gave another round of applause and a smiling Egbert then looked at Matthew again and said. "Matthew, if you could kindly look at me and think about the answer. Matthew, the answer is Walton, now think about the question. Matthew, the answer is, it is your mother's maiden name, please pass the paper to Geoff."

"Was I correct, Geoff?"

Geoff looked at the paper and smiled and replied "Yes, bang on again!"

The audience applauded loudly and as it quietened Egbert faced the three of them and asked them. "Linda, Matthew and Geoff, is there any way that I could have seen what was written on those pieces of paper?"

The three of them shook their heads and replied, "No they were folded up and held in our right hands."

Egbert looked at the audience and then said; "Thank you, to all three of you now please return to your seats, please could I have a round of applause for these brave people." The audience applauded loudly again.

"Ladies and Gentlemen and honourable guests, as you can see I can read minds and I believe that before long we will be able to have telepathic conversations, with all of the benefits which that will bring to mankind."

The audience applaud again. When it quietens Egbert continues to speak.

"Now, I am in this large room full of people and you are all thinking your thoughts, if I tuned into you all at the same time, it would drive me crazy, so I have had to train my mind to be selective; I have had to learn how to shut off and to switch on my mind-reading senses. I have learned to control my senses, just as if I have locked and unlocked them. Now if I can open and shut my mind at will, then in reverse it must be possible to unlock the parts of our brain that we currently under utilise. I would now like to throw this session open to the audience, I am sure that you have some questions for me, just call for the roaming microphones and then ask your question."

A lady called for the roaming microphone, which was passed to her.

"Hi, I am Jane from Telford, how long have you been able to do this?"

Egbert replied to her question. "Hello Jane, I have been able to do it for as long as I can remember, but when I was younger it did cause me some problems and my father, who was a hypnotist used his skills to help me to control it."

Another man called for the microphone and it was taken to him, he then asked; "Professor, I am Norman from Wigan: how far away from a person can you be and still be able to read their thoughts?"

Egbert looked at the man and then he answered his question. "Norman you are about 20 rows back from the front, so I guess that is about 70 feet, would you agree?"

Norman nodded and then Egbert continued. "Norman, what I can tell you after reading your thoughts is that I am not a fraud and you can't catch me out, because this is not a trick, and am I right to say that this is what you were thinking?"

Norman looked sheepish and replied. "Yes, I am embarrassed now."

A smile came over Egbert's face and he spoke to Norman. "Ha, ha, ha, don't be embarrassed Norman, you have just helped me to prove my ability, and to answer your original question I can read minds which are at least 70 to 100 feet away, maybe even further."

An older man raised his hand and requested the microphone, which was passed to him, he asked Egbert his question. "Professor Egbert, are there other people who are able to read minds? I am James Pilkington, a civil servant from London."

Egbert looked at this man and his face was familiar, but he could not put a name to him or think why he might recognise him, but he then replied, "Well James, as I said earlier I believe that we all have it within us to be able to communicate telepathically and I therefore must come to the conclusion that there are most certainly other people out there who are able to read minds."

James looked back at Egbert and asked a follow-up question. "Professor Egbert, how easy is it to lock your mind?"

Egbert smiled and replied, "James it is a technique that I have developed through the use of hypnosis and concentration techniques and now I find it easy to switch it on and switch it off."

James was clearly engaged with Egbert and would not let go of the microphone when the girl asked for it back; instead he asked another question. "Professor, surely your ability could be used for evil as well as for good, should we be worried about that?"

Egbert was taken aback by this question and looked at James Pilkington, he was desperate to read his mind and he did. James Pilkington was thinking over and over;

"Professor, I would like to meet you after the seminar, do you agree?" "Professor, I would like to meet you after the seminar, do you agree?"

Egbert nodded to acknowledge what James had said and then he replied. "James, all skills and talents can be used for good or evil, but that depends on whether the person with that skill or talent is good or evil; it has nothing to do with the skill or the talent." Egbert then looked directly at James and said, "I am, though very interested in your last question and I wonder can we meet for a short while after the seminar as finished?"

James Pilkington looked back at Egbert and nodded and then thought;

"I will see you in the reception bar in the hotel after the seminar."

Egbert smiled and nodded back to Pilkington; he then looked back out into the audience and asked; "Ladies and Gentlemen, we have now come to the end of my section, but the good news is that I will be followed by Professor Chuck Stanton from the Massachusetts Institute of Technology (MIT) and if you enjoyed my session, you will love what he has to say."

The host came back onto the stage and he shook hands with Egbert and at the same time the audience applauded loudly, Egbert gave a friendly wave as he left the stage. He walked down the aisle to the applause and he went to the reception bar to meet James Pilkington.

The Meeting

James Pilkington was sat in a comfortable red leather chair in the bar area and had ordered himself a gin and tonic. Egbert thought to himself, *"It must be good to be on expenses."* Pilkington thanked Egbert for coming and asked him if he would like to have a drink; Egbert asked for a plain American coffee.

Pilkington was in his 60's, he was around five feet and nine inches. He had kept himself fit, and he was smartly dressed, he looked like he could have been a solicitor or a barrister with his sharp charcoal pinstripe suit, white shirt and white hankie in the breast pocket of his jacket. Prior to Egbert's coffee arriving, pleasantries were exchanged and as soon as it arrived and the waitress had left Egbert asked Pilkington directly why he had asked for the meeting.

Pilkington smiled and then commented, "Typical Yorkshire man, no beating around the bush; can I call you Egbert, or do you prefer John?"

Egbert smiled and replied, "I stopped using the name John when I became a Professor, I thought that Egbert carried more gravitas, so of course you can call me Egbert, shall I call you James?"

Pilkington replied, "Of course you can, now let me get straight to the point: we would like you to use your skills and senses to help us to get some information, you do actually know the person that we need the information from, but probably you don't remember her; she used to be at the Unit at the same time that you were there with your mother and father. Your father used to hypnotise her and use regression techniques on her, just as he did with you and the unfortunate soldiers that were there at the time."

Egbert looked at Pilkington and replied, "So you know about my time at the Unit?"

Pilkington continued; "Yes, your father was working for us at the time, the British government, that is; and it was his job initially to work with the soldiers who had come back from action and who had been traumatised by their experiences, by the use of regression techniques he helped to heal them from their mental trauma which they had suffered. I saw you a few times when I visited your father at the Unit, do you remember my face at all?"

Egbert smiled and said that he did vaguely remember him, but that obviously James had aged since then and that was why he hadn't remembered straightaway when James had asked the questions at the seminar.

Pilkington went on to say, "Incidentally Egbert, I was sorry to hear that your parents had died in a traffic accident; they were good people, it must have been very difficult for you after they had died, especially after all your father had done to help you with the control of your reading minds and not forgetting how he taught you how to use hypnosis."

Egbert took in a sharp breath and replied, "Yes, I still miss them even now and it was hard to lose my parents at 16, but my Aunty Linda and my cousin John looked after me well, and if anything it has made me even more determined to develop my understanding of Quantum Communications and the benefits that it will deliver; you could say that it will be a lasting legacy to my father."

Pilkington nodded and then continued. "Whilst you were being educated at the unit and before you went back into mainstream education, your father had some other guests that he hypnotised and regressed. They were all children and they were there because they had a fear or phobia of going to school, at least that was the official reason that we gave. You were allowed to study at the Unit so that your father could fulfil his role with the other children, but at the same time he could help you to develop your mind-reading skills by the use of regression techniques and hypnosis. Without your father's help it would have been very difficult for you as a child to grow up and develop in the right way, you would probably have become very insular and even reclusive as the gift which you clearly have could have become a nightmare for you. In any case the tutors at the Unit were very good as they had received specialist training for dealing with special children. After your two years there you were able to go back into mainstream education, with your Mind Reading skill under control."

Egbert then asked, "James, you mentioned that the girl was at the Unit, was she the same age as me?"

Pilkington replied; "She was a few years younger than you, but she had a very different background to you, which we will go into later. All of the children that attended the Unit had great intelligence and yet none of them would attend school; individually all of their IQs were higher than anybody of a similar age in mainstream education. They all had another thing in common; they were all suffering post-traumatic stress disorder, some had no confidence whatsoever and all had a memory of being visited by something not human. Whatever it was that investigated them, I will call NHB's: None Human Beings."

Egbert's eyes had lit up; this was a topic that he was very interested in. "James, this is amazing, but I can understand how it could happen, my beliefs tell me that there has to be life on other planets in our universe or beyond, we are only just developing our thoughts about Quantum Communications, but if another planet was born only one thousand years before ours and if its life had developed at the same rate as ours, just imagine how technologically advanced it would be?"

Pilkington could tell that Egbert was interested and asked him; "Are you interested in knowing more Egbert? Will you help us? I cannot tell you anything more until you agree, and then once you agree you might just find that all kinds of opportunities open up for you especially in relation to brain control and the opening up of new senses, as well as furthering your knowledge of Quantum Communications."

Egbert did not even hesitate before replying, "Yes James, without doubt, I want to know more, but first will you tell me how long have you known about me being able to read minds?"

Pilkington nodded and then replied; "We have known about it since you were a child and we have watched you develop and grow into a man; we always knew that there would be a time that you could help us and that now is that time. I am sure that you make a good living from your seminars, especially when people are paying £750 per head to hear you and your colleagues speak at the many different locations across the Globe, but Egbert, does it really help you move forward with your research to master the art of Telepathy? I don't think that it does, but your involvement with us will open up all kinds of research and scientific knowledge to help you move forward."

Egbert looked at Pilkington and he felt very excited about the prospect which had been placed in front of him and he then replied, "James, I have to admit it all sounds very interesting and I think you already know that I am going to accept your offer at least to understand more of what you want me to do but why did you come here today, surely you could have just arranged a meeting for me at your office?"

Pilkington nodded and then replied; "Egbert, I wanted to hear and see your performance for myself— I have heard so much about what you can do and the time for using your unique skills has never been better. You may well be the only person in the world who can do what we need, we are certainly not aware of anybody else and the greatest advantage is that you were at the Unit at the same time as the girl, which we believe will help."

In truth Pilkington knew that Egbert would be pumped up on adrenalin after his performance at the conference and that this would be a good time to ask for and to obtain his services; he also had taken a calculated risk in telling

Egbert about the NHBs, but he knew that this would spark Egbert's interest and that the gamble was worth it if he could get Egbert on board. He then asked Egbert, "Can you come to my offices in London tomorrow at 11.00? It is in the SIS Building, 85 Albert Embankment, Lambeth, London, SE1 7TP. We used to be known better as MI6."

When Egbert heard Pilkington refer to MI6 he frowned and then replied; "MI6, I am no James Bond."

Pilkington smiled and reassured Egbert; "Don't worry Egbert, SIS stands for the 'Secret Intelligence Service', it is an information-gathering department manned by civil servants. Most of our work is carried out on PCs and sitting at desks— James Bond is purely for the movies. We are responsible for National Security, but that takes many forms and as yet the government doesn't have a specialist department called "Investigation of Non-Human Beings" so we have the delight of dealing with any such investigations."

Both men laughed and then shook hands. As Pilkington left Egbert wondered just what he was getting himself into, but he also felt a tinge of excitement at the thought of how all of this could develop.

Ivan the Russian

May in Latvia is a good time to visit, at that time the severe Baltic winter has eased, the shoots of the spring flowers are starting to grow and the sun is getting warmer. The harshness of the winter, which often drops to temperatures of -20C, contrasts with the summer when it can reach temperatures of +40C; this might explain why they are a resilient and hardy race of people. They have had to be resilient in the past; they were ruled by the iron fist of the Russians and then freed from the Russians by the Germans during the Second World War, only then to have their German saviours send the Jewish Latvians off to the dreaded Nazi gas chambers. Towards the end of the Second World War the Russians came back and threw out the Germans, but they did not like how the Latvians had become Westernised and Capitalistic; why should a restaurant owner want to own a hotel as well as his restaurant, or the baker have more than one bakery? It could only be to make more money, which did not conform to the communist ideology and these unfortunate entrepreneurs were shipped off with their families to appreciate the other states of the USSR such as Siberia. The Russians did not stop there they realised that there would now be a lack of skills in Latvia, so they shipped in skilled people from other parts of the USSR to fill that gap. This also meant that the Latvian population was now more than 50% Russian and would ensure that the Latvians would never rise up against Russian rule.

The states of Russia broke up and Latvia is now independent and is also part of the European Union; however, there is still an uneasy split in the country between Latvian citizens and Russians. This becomes even more confusing to Westernised thinking; a child born in Latvia from Russian parents is classed as Russian and has to apply to become a Latvian citizen and pass the test. A Russian Latvian cannot travel on an EU passport and has to apply for a visa to travel, whereas once the citizen test is passed, an EU passport can be applied for. When is a Latvian not a Latvian? The answer is when he is a Russian, but as far as Russia is concerned he is not a Russian either, so you can see how these people are confused from birth and feel like they do not belong anywhere.

Ivan Niklai is such a Russian; he was born of Russian parents, so in Latvia was classed as Russian, but he passed the citizen test and now holds an EU Passport which means that he can travel freely within the European Union and wider afield. Brought up by his Babushka (grandmother), Ivan hates the Russian rulers who sent his father to a Gulag in Siberia, his mother died not long afterwards and he believes that it was from a broken heart as her husband had been taken from her, so he hates them for that as well. Ivan also hates the Latvian government, because his Babushka was not cared for well enough when she caught pneumonia, which had been brought on by the severe Latvian winter and she subsequently died in a ward of the general hospital in Riga. Ivan hates the West just because they have a better lifestyle than people in the East, but he does sympathise with the rebels of Chechnya because at least they are trying to do something about it. He cares for nobody apart from himself and for him his God is Money; he is a professional assassin and he is very good at what he does. His CV, if he had one, would include working for extremists from around the world as well as the Russian mafia who are much closer to home and are able to provide him with plenty of work. Ivan has one motto: "Kill and enjoy it" and he does it as often as he can. Ivan's idea of compassion is to kill a victim quickly. He does accept none killing work, but only if the money is good and only if he has done work for that employer before. He speaks Russian, Latvian, German and English and his talents are in regular demand.

It was late in the evening and Ivan was watching Alexander, the son of a local nightclub owner spending some of his father's profits in the Reval Hotel on Elizabetes Street in Riga. He was drinking the local champagne like it was going to be rationed the next day and he was showing off to his friends and the women that were in his party. Alexander's father had angered the Russian mafia; he had taken a baseball bat to one of their income collectors. The collector ended up in Hospital with a fractured skull and it was still not clear whether he would survive. Ivan had been given the job of delivering revenge. The mafia boss had decided that the nightclub owner was still of value to him, as long as he could learn the error of his ways, but for the nightclub owner to survive, he had to be seen to be punished and to accept that punishment, it was decided that the punishment would be that his son must die.

The mafia saw the value of the nightclub owner because his nightclub contributed well to their coffers through the kidnapping and trafficking of the pretty Eastern European women that visited the nightclub. The beautiful and sexy women were in high demand throughout the Western world. The decision to exact revenge on the man's son might be seen as harsh, but reputations and credibility, and last but not least power and control had to be maintained.

Ivan sat in the bar and watched Alexander and his friends; Ivan was dressed in black trousers, a black top and a black leather jacket but didn't look out of place in the bar area of the hotel, this is a typical male fashion in Latvia. It was getting late and everybody was merry and drinking the local vodka, beer and champagne. Ivan was in no rush; he would time his moment well. People would start drifting out of the hotel soon to go to the nightclubs where sex and more drink and maybe even something stronger would be on offer. Ivan was steely-eyed and kept watch on the party, like a lion watching and waiting for the right time to make its kill. He sipped at his sweetened, strong black coffee and then he took out of his inside jacket pocket a post-it pad and a pen and he wrote on the top sheet of the pad. Alexander stood up and made his way to the Gents' room and he was going alone; Alexander held the door open for the man who was walking closely behind him, without any idea what was in the man's thoughts. As Ivan followed Alexander into the room, he stuck a simple post-it note on the door which came from his inside jacket pocket; it said "Out of Order." Alexander walked over to the urinals and started to urinate, Ivan turned the lock on the inside of the door and then went and stood at the wash basins and waited until Alexander had finished; he didn't want the man's urine all over him. Alexander started to shake himself dry, at that point Ivan went up behind him and struck him on the back of his neck with his fist, Alexander fell heavily to the floor, and he was dazed but still conscious. Alexander looked up and he could see Ivan standing above him but he did not have time to do anything before Ivan grasped him with one hand around his throat and started to squeeze, Alexander was gasping and was trying to get some air into his lungs, but then he suddenly felt a sharp pain in his side where Ivan had pushed a sharp blade into him. Ivan looked into Alexander's eyes; he loved this part when he could see the terror and the panic of his victim, followed by the hopelessness that his victim was feeling. It is said that the eyes are the gateway to the soul and it was this that Ivan loved. Ivan pulled the blade out of Alexander's side and then put the blade to the man's throat and he pressed it hard and it sliced through Alexander's windpipe until he felt the resistance of the bone, he drew the blade slowly to his right and the eyes showed that Alexander had accepted his fate, within seconds Alexander had slumped down with a gurgling noise coming from his throat, his eyes had closed. Ivan had warm blood on his hand, a feeling that he enjoyed and as the blood seeped from the open wound in Alexander's throat, he licked the warm blood off the back of his hand and he smiled. Ivan wiped his blade on

Alexander's suit jacket and checked his own clothing for blood splatter. There was some on his black leather jacket but he quickly cleaned this off at the basin, he washed the blood from his hand and then left the room, he knew that his work was done and that the Russian mafia would be pleased with him. Ivan left the hotel and was four blocks away before he heard the wailing noise of police sirens and the ambulance. He knew that there was nothing that either the police or ambulance could do; he was a professional, he had done his job well.

By this time it was about 22.30 and Ivan called into a bar to quietly celebrate the kill, he drank a large glass of ice cold vodka and then went back outside where he shouted for a taxi that was coming towards him and the taxi stopped. Ivan told the driver to take him to the Maxima Supermarket at Plavnieku, just out of the Centre. It cost him €10, but that evening he was not worried about the cost of the taxi, he went to an ATM on the outside wall of the Supermarket and he saw that €50,000 had been deposited into his account. Ivan then walked the short distance to his apartment. He lived in a typical Russian apartment block which always look as if they are about to fall down and they remind us of the Communist rule by the Russians. Ivan walked up the 5 flights of stairs to his apartment; he didn't want to risk going up in the lift at that time of night, as it was so unreliable and he didn't want to get stuck in the lift all night. Ivan opened his door, and then locked it behind him, as he entered his apartment he took a bottle of ice-cold vodka from his fridge and he saw that he had a message on his answering machine. With his glass of vodka in his hand he sat next to the answering machine and played the message. The message was in Russian and it said, "Ivan, it is Hanif from Chechnya, we would like you to transport some goods for us from England. I will send you the purchase order and details via email, but I need you to fly from Riga to Leeds/Bradford Airport, I will advise you of the date soon. We would like the goods to be packed safely and securely, but if in your opinion they are not good enough, dispose of them in England. Your fee will be in the email." Ivan understood the message completely; he was to bring some people from England to Latvia or wherever it was they wanted them taking, and he should aim to bring them in good health, but if he couldn't get them back safely he was to eliminate them. Ivan went to his PC and switched it on. He opened the email account of his Babushka who had been dead a number of years now, there was virtually no chance of anybody ever checking into this account and he saw on Outlook that he had one email waiting; he could see it was from Hanif. He started to read the email; "Ivan, you will work with Aivars to bring to us Professor Egbert Junas and his female friend, who we only know as Annie; he lives in Bridgewater Place, Leeds and she lives in the Bradford area. Once you find him you will be able to find her. We need them both in healthy condition. When in England Aivars will meet you; he is already staying in Bradford, he has the transport and he will assist you in securing the two of them and getting them to Marbella in Spain. Once in Spain we will take over. Aivars has a team of men that will also be involved but only to ensure that British agents do not get in your way. You may need to sedate the professor and the woman and restrain them in the transporter; they are important to our cause and we would like them delivered to us in a healthy condition, but if you cannot get them to us, do not leave them for the British government, you must dispose of them. Ivan, Junas is not dangerous and as far as we know he has had no training, so he will not put up much of a fight, but we understand that he can read minds, I am sure that for a man of your skills that will not be a problem; the woman Annie lives a reclusive life and she will not fight either. It is important that you take them both and that we get them both together, if you can only bring one, bring the woman and kill the man. I must stress, though that we would like them both healthy. If you complete the task fully you will receive €500,000 and anything less than 100% success will see a reduction in that fee. The day before you fly to England we will deposit €20,000 into your account; you will get the rest on completion of the task, and if you are not successful you are already aware of how we will deal with failure."

Ivan knew what the email meant and he knew that if he failed he would be killed himself. They would not ask for the €20,000 back, however he would not be in a position to spend it. But Ivan never failed and he would make sure that he would complete the task. Ivan then thought about the fact that Junas could read minds and thought to himself that he wished that he could read minds; he loves to look into somebody's eyes as their life drains away; how fantastic would it be to read their minds as they were dying? He again thought to himself that if he had a blade at the professor's throat his mind reading skills would not help him very much.

Ivan had enjoyed a good day; he had just returned from a kill, he was going to earn himself up to €500,000 and he had a glass of ice-cold vodka in his hand; he would finish the bottle and go to sleep.

SIS Building

Egbert decided to catch the train from Birmingham to London that evening and he checked in at the Ramada Hotel in Regents Park, where he had stayed previously on a number of occasions. None of the staff recognised him, but that was normal; there is always a large turnover of staff at London hotels. He had a couple of drinks in the bar and a meal in the restaurant and took himself off to bed. He tossed and turned all night, his excitement about the meeting the next day was getting the better of him.

Next morning he woke and had a full English breakfast in his room, he got himself ready and checked out. He knew that he could always check in again later if he needed to stay down in London. He went outside and he hailed a taxi which was there within seconds and gave the address as the SIS building at Albert Embankment. He felt a bit like James Bond as the taxi took him there; the taxi driver tried to pass the time of day with Egbert, but Egbert had a lot on his mind and although he was polite he did not really want to get into a conversation.

They arrived at the SIS building and Egbert paid for the taxi and went inside, he was met by a security officer as he entered the building and he had to walk through a metal detector, after which he was scanned with a portable scanner, all was ok, he gave his name and he was told to wait in the waiting area as somebody would be coming down to collect him. While waiting he couldn't help but notice the several CCTV cameras around the area as well as the security officers on the door; he was sure that he had several pairs of eyes watching his every movement.

Within a few minutes an attractive girl had come to collect him, she had shoulder-length, auburn hair, a slim figure and a friendly, smiley face. Egbert instantly liked her and she seemed approachable. She asked him to follow her and as she wiggled her bottom as she walked towards the lift, he thought to himself; *"Yes indeed I will."* When they were in the lift she told him that her name was Joanne and that she worked for James Pilkington. Egbert could not see which floor they were going to, as Joanne was stood in front of the lift buttons, but he felt that it was going up as opposed to down. They got out of the lift and went along the corridor to an office with an open door; Joanne knocked politely and they both entered, Pilkington was sat behind an old oak desk and he invited them both to sit down. Egbert wondered why Joanne was in the meeting but he did not mention it.

Pilkington told Egbert that Joanne was there just to take notes, but Egbert decided to do his own investigation on Joanne's mind and he worked out from what she was thinking that she was actually there to study his body language, she had already thought and written down; *"Relaxed, confident, legs crossed and right toe pointing towards me."* This apparently meant that Egbert fancied her, which was not wrong.

She also thought; *"He is open and keen to hear what was to be said."* Egbert thought about asking Pilkington why he was being analysed, but decided to leave it for now. Pilkington looked at Egbert and said "Egbert, I remember your response to our chat about NHBs, you clearly believe that they could be other forms of life?"

Egbert thought for a moment and responded;

"I am very open-minded on the subject, I believe that we are such a small planet in such a large universe that there must be other forms of life out there and just as we are looking for them, why would they not look for us?"

Pilkington smiled and looked at Egbert; "Yes, you are right we know that there are such things as NHBs, we know that they have communicated with us in the past and that some of those occasions are well-documented albeit held in secret official files." There have been events such as Roswell and the many possible UFO sightings that the public know about, but there are also other occasions where people have speculated but where we have no concrete evidence. To add some balance to this, though not all UFO sightings are genuine and if you believed every conspiracy theory on the Internet, we wouldn't be able to fly our commercial flights due to all the UFOs that would be blocking our airspace. We believe that NHBs have visited Earth for thousands of years; it could explain how man built the pyramids on several different continents, all around the same time, when only a few centuries earlier they had been living in caves. Do you know where Hitler got the technology from for some of his advanced weaponry; which fortunately he never got the chance to use? "We believe that it was NHBs that helped him and that either they made contact with Hitler or that he found a way of making contact with them; maybe it was evil frequencies that were being given off and received. How are crop circles formed? By a man and his tractor in the dead of night; over large fields and to very detailed specifications, or could they be created by NHBs who are trying to send us a message?" Egbert, we believe that there are good NHBs and bad NHBs just like there are good humans and bad humans. We believe that the NHB's helping Hitler were bad ones and that the ones making the crop circles are good ones who are trying to communicate peacefully with us, but in all honesty we don't really know. What we do know is that we would like to have contact with NHBs and that it is becoming of paramount importance. The world has never been in a more vulnerable position; we seem to be having near misses with asteroids on a regular basis, tsunamis, earthquakes, flooding, not to mention terrorist threats. We are living in a world where our energy resources are being used at an alarming rate and oil and gas supplies are running out as well as all of the problems that they create with global warming and the ozone layer. We have new diseases, each which is stronger and more deadly than the previous disease and we need to find ways to tackle them. We believe that the NHBs have a far superior knowledge and technology than us and that they can help us to overcome our problems. We need to find a way to communicate with both the good and the bad NHBs, we need to make friends with both if we can, but if not we need to understand any weaknesses that they might have in case we ever have to defend against them. If the NHBs have the advanced technology that we think they have, they should be able to help us through the myriad of problems that we face. That is where we think you can help."

Pilkington paused for a moment or two, he was well-aware that he had just thrown a lot of information at Egbert and he wanted to make sure that Egbert had time to take it all in. He then began speaking again.

"We believe and hope that the key lies with the children who were at the Unit and that were examined by NHBs. The children have clearly captured the interest of the NHBs, and we believe one child in particular. We believe that this child can help to provide a pathway which will enable contact with NHBs. We know that from some of the regression work that your father carried out with the children that each and all of their stories are consistent with each other, with one exception: a girl called Annie. You might remember her, she was a couple of years younger than you, skinny, short, wore glasses and had dark hair. She also swore like a trooper?"

Egbert laughed and then replied, "Yes I do remember her; all of the children kept themselves to themselves and I didn't really mix with them, but as you know I lived at the House with my parents within the grounds of the Highlands Military Hospital and the children stayed in dormitories within our house, it was known as the Unit. I used to see some of the children out in the grounds as well as in the house. I remember Annie because she had a real attitude about her; she used to strop around everywhere and she used to always be exploring, I remember going into my bedroom one time and I opened a cupboard, she jumped out and she frightened the life out of me. She told me to fuck off and then ran off."

Pilkington smiled and then replied, "Yes, that sounds like Annie, yet she could also be so kind; I remember she was only 10 years' old, but there was another girl there who hadn't spoken for 4 years and Annie by showing her kindness had her speaking again within a matter of weeks. I am not sure whether or not she taught her any of her choice language though."

Egbert replied, "I never really got to know her, but I liked her attitude and she did seem different to the rest, they were all fairly quiet and subdued, they didn't really seem like they wanted to be there, but Annie didn't seemed to mind too much and although she had sworn at me, when she saw me she usually smiled at me. You said that Annie was different from the others, why was that?"

Pilkington replied; "She was different because although her answers were consistent with the other children when under hypnosis, she would only tell so much and then it was as if her brain automatically locked and she would give no more, we believe that there is more for her to tell and we also believe that it could be the key to communicating with NHBs. All of the other children had been broken by their experience with the NHBs; they were almost like empty shells with no spark or fight left in them, but as you know from your own experience of Annie, she had plenty of fight still in her."

Egbert nodded in agreement and then he said, "But why now, she must be almost in her 40's, haven't you tried to get the information from her over the previous 30 years?"

Pilkington replied; "We have tried, Egbert and we have completely drawn a blank, she had some health problems about 10 years ago after experimenting with whisky and pills and we used the opportunity to section her into a psychiatric hospital in Bradford. We carried out further regression on her, but all we got was exactly the same information as we had got previously. It was like listening to the tape recording from all those years before, we prescribed her with mind-altering drugs like Lithium, which we thought would lower any resistance that she had, but we still could not get any more from her. We don't know if she is controlling her own mind or if it is being controlled by NHBs; either way we still believe that she is the best chance we have got of unlocking the key to the mystery. We need your skills to find a way into her mind and to unlock what we need to know, and then hopefully our scientists can use that to then find a way to communicate with the NHBs."

Egbert sat and pondered for a moment or two and then he asked, "James, what about the other children, you must have tried questioning them?"

Pilkington nodded and replied, "We have on many occasions, but they have nothing that they can tell us that we don't already know, and believe me we have pushed them as far as we dare, any further and we could cause them permanent damage. They are so different to Annie though; it is as though they would tell us more if they could, but they just can't, whereas Annie can tell more but won't and we don't know why that is."

Egbert then asked, "So how do we go about this James, are you going to bring her in so that I can talk to her?"

Pilkington shook his head and he replied, "Not a chance Egbert, she would just close up shop and we would get nothing. You need to win her trust and then gently extract the information from her. If she were to go into her shell, we would get nothing from her, which is why we have left her alone for so long, albeit we have constantly kept an eye on her, to make sure that she was generally safe."

Egbert thought about this and then replied, "Well, you didn't do too good a job if she experimented with pills and whisky, did you?"

Pilkington didn't like Egbert levelling criticism at his department, but he answered, "That was unfortunate, we never saw it coming, we have had to keep a fine balance between monitoring her and controlling her and on that occasion we messed up, although it did give us the chance to examine her again."

Egbert was feeling a little agitated and he replied; "Well, it sounds to me that you don't really give a damn about Annie, only about what she might be able to tell you."

Pilkington replied, "Egbert, you have to put this in context, she is one life on this planet and she could provide the solution to save millions of lives."

Egbert asked Pilkington a direct question. "Why me? I can't believe that there are no other people in the world who have the same skills as me; there must be another way, a safer way and a surer way for you to tap into her knowledge?"

Pilkington replied back to Egbert, "I assure you that we have tried everything reasonably possible with Annie and the others, and yes there are other people that claim to be able to read minds, but none yet with your success rate. Even the Russians and the Americans agree that we need somebody close to her who she can trust if we are to succeed."

Egbert shook his head, he was not feeling at all comfortable, and he replied to Pilkington, "Bloody Hell James, I don't like the sound of that, I don't like lying to the poor woman, she has done nothing wrong and it sounds like she has been through enough already!"

Pilkington tried to reassure Egbert. "As I have said, there is no other way we have tried everything else, but before she opens up she needs to trust you and even then we don't know if it will work. If you can find anything though, you would be doing your country and the world a great service. What we have learned about Annie is that she will give nothing under duress; in fact we believe that duress would actually be like double-locking her brain, she is a tough little cookie and stubborn. In return for your services, Egbert we will give you access to some of the greatest brains in the world to help you with your quest for telepathy through Quantum Communication and if only for the advancement of science that has got to be of interest to you."

Egbert was pensive for a time; on one hand he did not like the idea of not being straight with Annie, but on the other hand he could see the importance of the task and he came to his decision and then he asked, "How do I set about contacting Annie?"

Pilkington was pleased that he got that reply from Egbert and he in turn replied, "That is easy she has a Facebook identity 'Annie Brown' and she is a member of the Highlands Unit Group, you can contact her through there and then arrange to meet with her when the time is right. We have already made her a friend under our pseudonym "Star Watcher". You become a friend of Star Watcher and you are in. She lives in Bradford, only about 15 miles from your Leeds home; you need to become her friend, don't forget you were at the Unit at the same time so you do have some important common ground. We will be transferring a regular monthly amount of funds into your account to compensate you for your lost income from the speaking circuit, but I am sure that after all of this and with the newfound knowledge and skills that you will discover you will become a very wealthy man."

Egbert nodded his head and replied, "James the money will help and I will do everything I can to get what you need, but I do not want to lie to Annie, so you will just have to trust me to do it my way."

Egbert then turned to Joanne and asked "Did I pass the body language test?"

Joanne blushed but responded, "Well, you said nothing that would give me any major reason for concern."

Pilkington interrupted and said, "I am sorry Egbert but we had to be sure about your feelings about all of this, but once again you have displayed your skill and you have read Joanne's mind and all we have done was read your body language, hardly a fair comparison."

Egbert replied; "Fair enough and by the way Joanne I have a 44-inch chest, a 36-inch waist, size 10 shoes, I am 5 feet 11 inches tall and my manhood is all in proportion. Ha, ha, ha, I read your mind, sorry to embarrass you though."

Joanne blushed again, but also smiled.

Egbert turned back to James and said that he needed to know much more about the children's experience with the NHBs as well as some more background information on Annie. Pilkington told him that Joanne would give him a tablet with all the files on it that he would need and would also give him a mobile phone with Joanne's number already programmed into it should he have any further questions. He then said, "The files of the children have no names attached, but you will very quickly work out which one is Annie; we withhold the names due to data protection and clearly it is sensitive information".

Egbert stood and as he and Joanne were walking out of the office, he turned back and asked James a question. "James, are you sure that there is no danger involved in what I am doing, I do not want to sign up to being a spy?"

James replied back, "None whatsoever Egbert, you are simply using your skills to information gather; you are not really working for us, more like we are paying you as we would a contractor who was providing us with a service."

Joanne stood and then turned to lead Egbert back down towards the lift and to reception; she called into her office on the way and collected the tablet and the mobile phone which she then handed over to Egbert.

They got into the lift and travelled down to Reception in no time at all and Egbert was then signed out through security. Joanne said nothing all the way down in the lift, but her face was smiling and friendly; as Egbert was leaving Joanne smiled and told Egbert to stay in touch. Egbert smiled back and said, "Goodbye, for now." He then went outside to hail a taxi. There was nothing to keep him in London, so the next stop was King's Cross Station and a train north to Leeds and then to his home.

Post Meeting

Joanne went back in to the lift and returned to Pilkington's office, he was still sat in his leather chair, he stood and offered Joanne a coffee and then they both sat together on the sofa in his office. "So Joanne, what do you think about our man, is he up to the task?"

Joanne replied; "I am not sure sir, he certainly demonstrated that he can read minds and his body language was very positive, but he is clearly not comfortable about lying to Annie; I am sure that at some stage he will tell her what he is doing

Pilkington pondered and then replied; "I agree Joanne, but I am not sure that it will be a problem. He has good integrity and it may just work in our favour if he can build the right kind of relationship with Annie, it may even make her trust him more when he tells her, in any case nothing else has worked."

Joanne took a drink of her coffee and thought for a moment, she then replied, "Sir, he asked you if there was any danger to him and you told him that there wasn't; can you be sure about that?"

"Joanne, both he and Annie are in danger— there are people out there who want to make contact with NHBs as well, but for different reasons. Their intelligence will have told them the same as ours and they have played a waiting game hoping that Egbert or somebody like him would come along and find a way into Annie's mind, and once that happens they will strike. We know that Egbert has been attracting attention from these people for a while, but we are confident that they have not yet contacted him, because we have been watching Egbert as well. We need to make sure that our timing is spot on and that we strike at precisely the right time, before these other people do."

Joanne took on board what Pilkington had told her and then she replied; "Sir, he also asked you earlier why we were doing this now and not sooner, which you answered and he seemed happy to accept it, is there another reason?"

Pilkington nodded and then responded to the question. "Well Joanne, Professor Junas has been delivering his lectures for about 18 months now and we have continually monitored his performance for accuracy and consistency; we have spoken to the Russians who are experts in this subject and they have compared his results against other people who claim to be able to read minds and they have confirmed that he is 100% accurate and consistent. In their tests with other people that claim to be able to mind read they say that the average is around 60% accuracy, which is still exceptionally good, but based on the importance of what he is undertaking only 100% will be acceptable."

Joanne replied, "So Sir, we are working with the Russians on this."

Egbert nodded again and then said, "Yes we are, the Russians are the experts in this area, they have been working on the additional senses for decades and they are also great researchers into NHBs. After the Second World War, half of the German scientists went to the USA and the other half went to Russia; they know exactly where Hitler was getting his knowledge from to help develop highly-advanced technical weapons and you can bet your bottom dollar that Russia got their pound of flesh out of these German scientists. They could not find out, though how Hitler was in contact with the NHBs, otherwise we would not need Annie."

Joanne still had questions in her mind and she asked; "Sir, are there other people like Annie?"

Pilkington smiled at Joanne's questions and answered her, "There are people all over the world who have had similar experiences to Annie; both the Russians and the Americans have worked on them, but with no success, the problem has been that once the NHBs have finished with these people there is not much left to work with and the people just seem to be surviving, but without any spark. Certainly any of the techniques that we have used on these people to date have failed. Annie is different, maybe even unique and that's why we believe that we might get something from her."

Joanne was still not satisfied and she continued to push Pilkington for more explanations; "I can't believe that the Russians have been happy to play this waiting game for so long, I would have thought that by now that they would have had Annie wired up to some computer and got what they wanted or fried her brain?"

Pilkington explained. "During the 'Cold War' I am sure that they would have been much more impatient and the Americans also, for that matter, but we are in a different world now and there is, believe it or not, much more collaboration between our nations. At the moment we work together and we give the impression that we trust each other."

Joanne put down her coffee on the table and asked another question. "What if something had happened to Annie during this time shouldn't we have brought her in so that we could protect her like the valuable asset that she is?"

"Joanne these are all good questions and it is what I expected from you, we have debated this many times and we eventually decided that if we brought her in she would just lock her brain as she has done in the past and again we would get nothing from her; she would be safe but of absolutely no value to us. We decided to leave her out there to lead her normal life, but at the same time she has been under constant observation from us, you could say that we have acted like her Guardian Angel, not interfering, but there to protect her if and when we needed to."

Joanne replied, "And have we ever had to protect her?"

Pilkington replied, "There was one time when one of her boyfriends was getting a little too aggressive with her and we stepped in and sorted him out. Annie does seem to pick the wrong men and although she is pretty good at looking after herself, this one was a vicious bully; we did some research on him and it turned out that he had put a few of his previous girlfriends in hospital with his nasty behaviour. He got into the habit of slapping Annie around and it was only a matter of time before he was going to give her a worse beating or Annie was going to stab him with the kitchen knife, which we didn't want to have to deal with, so we decided that the boyfriend needed to be dealt with. We got one of our boys to give him a good sorting out and he told him that he was Annie's cousin and that if he didn't disappear out of her life, the next time the sorting out would be much worse. The bully saw the error of his ways and he never even went back to Annie's apartment to pick up his clothes. You asked me a few moments ago why now, and I would like to answer that question further; whilst we and the Russians and the Americans have been collaborating, everything has been under control. As well as with Annie, we have also jointly been working on other ways of making contact with the NHBs; we have used beacon transmitters to send out different frequencies into space to see if we can get a response. We also use the space stations and satellites to emit all kinds of signals, hoping to make contact, but so far there has still been no success. The truth is we have been trying to make contact with the NHBs for 100 years, the BBC in fact have been transmitting signals since they came into being. We are receiving new information all of the time from researchers and experts who are investigating into the possibility of NHBs. Recently we were told by Senior Astronomer Seth Shostak of the SETI Institute in California that it is most likely that within the near future we will identify extra-terrestrial intelligence; we are confident that the SETI Institute is very credible, the abbreviation stands for the Search for Extra Terrestrial Intelligence. It was co- founded by the world-renowned astronomer and author Carl Sagan, there are even a number of Nobel Prize winners who work there. They have already discovered 960 planets by using the massive power of the Hubble Space Telescope, as well as the Kepler Space Observatory, and there are a further 2900 possible detections which have yet to be confirmed, and what is most impressive is that they have done all of this in only a few years since the Kepler Telescope was introduced in 2009. There is every possibility of life-supporting planets out there which could be home to NHBs. I am telling you all of this to add credence to some of the things that I have already said about NHBs and that NHBs are now being regarded as more likely to be fact than fiction by the powers that be."

Joanne looked at Pilkington and smiled and then said, "Sir, I appreciate you going into so much detail with me; it does help my understanding. You also said that other people are watching both Annie and Egbert, but who are they and why?"

Pilkington replied; "That's my pleasure, it is important for you to understand. Obviously, it is not the Americans or the Russians because they are working with us, but there are powerful groups of people in the world who even sit above governments, more powerful than you can start to imagine. If they could make contact with the NHBs they could really gain control of the world and governments would pretty much become powerless. When you consider some of the actions of world governments over the years, it wouldn't be difficult for these powerful people to gain favour with NHBs."

Joanne was becoming very absorbed in the conversation and she was starting to forget about the time that was passing by; she continued to ask her questions. "Is it the Illuminati that you refer to, I have seen information about them on the Internet?"

Pilkington looked at Joanne and replied, "The Illuminati is a word that has been used for hundreds if not thousands of years, and yes they have been called that, but they are a very secretive group; you will never find anything written down or confirmed by them, but I am pretty sure that they do exist in some form, there are certainly lots of conspiracy theories about them which you will have read on the Internet."

Joanne then moved her questions to another subject. "What about the NHBs, could Egbert or Annie be in danger from them?"

Pilkington smiled again and answered; "Joanne, right now, we have no idea, but of course there could be a risk, they might decide that they don't want us making contact with them and they might put a stop to it altogether, but I don't think so; I think they want to make contact with us safely and in the right way. We do believe that they generally want to help us and not destroy us, otherwise why would they have made contact with Annie and the others, in the first place? I took the decision not to tell Egbert any of this, I decided that if he knew too much it could make him less effective, I don't want him being nervous and looking over his shoulder every two minutes; his mind needs to be clear. In any case, he now has our people watching him from a safe distance to make sure that he comes to no harm, if there is any problem, both he and Annie will be pulled out and made safe. Now I need to bring our meeting to a close, I have lots to do; I want you to act as the interface between Egbert and the SIS, which is why I have told you all of this. Do not tell Egbert any more than he needs to know. I did not tell you any of this earlier because I did not want you giving anything away in case Egbert decided to read your thoughts. I kept my mind focussed on exactly what I was saying, in case he tried to read mine. Mind-reading is not infallible Joanne, but it is damn good if you can do it and the other person does not know you are doing it."

Joanne nodded and although the meeting was coming to an end, she did want to ask more questions; "Do you know where the leak about Annie and Egbert came from, by the way?"

Pilkington was starting to feel like he was being interrogated and was getting a little annoyed, but he answered the question. "Yes, it came from Russia; one of their scientists on the joint team decided that Putin was not for him and he took the information to the Chechnya rebels, Russia is embarrassed about it as you can imagine and Putin is beating his drum about what he will do, but Chechnya has been a thorn in his side for years and he still hasn't been able to do anything about them. We believe that Chechnya rebels are being orchestrated by the powerful people that I told you about earlier and if it serves their purpose they would work with Chechnya rebels, Al Qaeda and in fact anybody who can provide them with a means to an end. So now you see why we need to make contact first, these people are ruthless and are only interested in control and power; they have no concerns about social responsibility which governments provide to a greater or lesser degree. It may seem strange to have these terrorist groups working together and we still cannot be sure to what extent, but we have intelligence information that would support our theory. We have good agents looking after both Annie and Egbert and once I hit the send button on my PC you will have all the files on your PC so that you can see who and where they are and all of the contingencies that we have in place. There are two teams of three watching both Annie and Egbert round the clock, and in each team there will always be at least two of them active while the other one rests. Now the meeting is over, so go and read the files."

Joanne thanked Pilkington and stood up and left his office, to go back to her own, she knew that it was important to be fully-briefed on all matters involving national security and she had a thirst for knowledge, which for now had been satisfied.

The Train Journey

Egbert had managed to catch the 13.05 from platform 4 at King's Cross and he decided to treat himself to a First Class Ticket, he wanted to make sure that he could read the file in peace and he also thought that he might get a meal on the train at the same time; it would save him calling out for a takeaway when he got home. The train was generally quiet and particularly quiet in First Class; he had a seat of 4 all to himself. The train pulled out and before long a steward asked Egbert if he wanted a drink, he had left his car at home and he didn't have to drive at the other end so he ordered a large gin and tonic and a half-bottle of Shiraz to go with the peppered fillet steak that he had ordered for his meal.

Egbert resisted the urge to power up the tablet that Joanne had given him and he sat quietly, just thinking to himself about the last 24 hours which had been quite amazing even by his own standards. Yesterday he was a lecturer doing the circuit and giving his presentation on Quantum Communications and today he was working for the SIS, he was almost a spy which made him laugh out loud. He thought to himself; *"I hope nobody is reading my mind at the moment, or they would get a shock."* This made him laugh out loud again and made the steward smile when he brought Egbert his large gin and tonic. Egbert thanked the steward and apologised for laughing, he said it was something that somebody had said to him earlier. The steward continued smiling and said he would return with the Shiraz when Egbert's steak was ready, unless he wanted it sooner. Egbert said; "Later would be absolutely fine." Egbert picked up his gin and tonic and raised his glass to himself, and he thought, *"It is not every day you work for 'Her Majesty's Secret Service."* He knew that his father would be very proud of him and it was one of those moments that happens when you have lost somebody when you just want to pick up the phone and tell them, but then you realise that you can't and you feel the momentary sadness that the realisation brings with it.

Egbert's steak and wine arrived and he started to eat it quickly because he wanted to fire up the tablet and get on with reading the file. Egbert enjoyed his meal and his wine, but now he was ready to read the file; he switched the tablet on and he opened the file. The file was titled "The Unit" and when Egbert opened it, he could see that it was not a large file; it had a covering general summary with 10 separate sections for each of the children that had been at the Unit. It was as Pilkington had told him there were no children's names or addresses, just letters of the alphabet from A to J. Egbert read the covering summary, which he noted had been prepared by his father Edwin Junas all those years ago, he therefore assumed that all of the individual children's information had also been prepared by his father.

Classified Information
For Your Eyes Only
Dated: 18th June 1984

Non Humanoid Visits and the Effects

The project started in 1983 when we were made aware of a phenomenon around the world of children being targeted by what would appear to be aliens or Non-Human Beings "NHBs." There are recorded cases in the USA, Russia, and Australia, and in the UK there were several reported cases mainly in West and North Yorkshire. How many of the cases reported are legitimate we are not sure, but from early investigations it would appear that 50% of all cases can be substantiated. For this report we are concentrating on the children in the United Kingdom.

The Children

The children come from differing backgrounds and from different areas of Yorkshire. They are in the age ranges of 9 to 11.

Children A, D, E, I and J have talked about possible visitations, but under hypnosis and regression techniques there is nothing to substantiate the accuracy of their claims and it is felt that these children are genuinely suffering from a phobia of school and having associated hallucinatory experiences which in their own right need to be examined, their descriptions of what has happened could be read in any superhero comic. It is proposed that these children should continue to receive psychiatric support.

Children B, C, F and H do appear to have had NHB visits and are genuinely traumatised by the experience; their experience is consistent with the reports which we have received from other countries. Each child has been left like a shell and appears to have had some minor brain damage, similar to what would happen when suffering a mild stroke.

Child G is the anomaly; when under hypnosis and when using regression techniques her report of what happened is consistent with the other children who also appear to be genuine, the main difference is that she is very alert and does not appear to have suffered any brain damage. In fact she is a very strong and spirited child who under hypnosis and regression refuses to tell any more than she is prepared to and literally "closes up the shop" with a knowing smile on her face.

Conclusion

The children have all been traumatised, but the first 5 mentioned appear to have been traumatised by a simple fear of school; the second 5 all appear to have had an experience with a NHB, with child G being the one where there appears to be most potential for learning more.

At this stage we do not have the technology to delve any more into child G's experience, but we should continually monitor her until we are able to investigate her further.

At this stage she should be classified as a major asset to our investigation of making contact with NHBs and given the necessary protection and whether that is in an institution or by surveillance, will need to be examined further and then a decision made.

Egbert was fascinated by what he had read so far and decided to scan through the reports of each child. When he looked at A, D, E, I and J it was fairly clear that the children had not been genuinely visited by NHBs; they had talked about NHBs with large green heads, ray guns and some with letters on their chest like Superman or Batman, under hypnosis they were asked to tell about what had happened, but they were not able to and it was decided that although they were traumatised it was not caused by NHBs and that there was some other reason. It was felt that each of these five children may have suffered from bullying or some other form of abuse. They had likened their abuser to an NHB for it was easier for them to rationalise that an NHB might treat them badly rather than somebody that they knew.

The individual reports of B, C, F and H gave a clear description under hypnosis of what these children had seen and were consistent; generally the wording was as follows:

"I lay in my bed and as I was falling asleep I saw a light in the corner of the room, it was the size of a pin head, but started to get bigger, it grew bigger and bigger from a pin head to a tennis ball, to a football until the light filled the corner of the room and it started to come towards me, as it did I could not move because of fear and I tried to shout out, but no words would come, the light was now over the top of me and it shone down on me. The light started to weigh heavy on me as if I was covered by water and I could not breathe, the pressure and weight of the light was so intense that I was paralysed and then everything went black and I woke up covered in sweat and I felt terrified and so weak, but thankfully the light is no longer there." In each case these children appear to have passed out and woken up some time later and are not able to explain what the NHB was doing.

Egbert then read child G's report. "I lay in my bed and I looked in the corner and saw a bright light the size of pin, it grew bigger and bigger until it was the size of a balloon and then a beach ball and it continued to grow until it filled the corner of the room, the light came towards me and then it was above me, it was weighing me down so I shouted at it and told it to fuck off and leave me alone. I felt its thoughts come into my head and it was saying; *"You pathetic Earth Child do not shout at me, or I will destroy you in one flash."* I shouted at it and told it to fuck off again and I tried to kick out at it, but I could not move my legs, I felt it pressing down on my body like it was trying to crush me and I could not breathe, but I was not going to give into it, I stopped being able to talk and I could not move, but my eyes stared at the light and if my eyes could have talked, it would have known, that if I could move I would kill it. I heard it again in my head, it was like it was laughing at me and then I felt a pain all the way through my body, like I have never felt before, it was like heat and ice surging through my veins all at the same time, it felt like the thing was inside me, I knew that if I closed my eyes now I would die and I was not going to let it kill me. I wanted to shout at it, but I couldn't, but I kept my eyes angry and I thought in my mind; *"Fuck off, you fucking Monster, I will fucking kill you."* It was inside me and it felt like a photocopier taking pictures of the inside of me, from top to bottom and then from side to side. I concentrated with all my might and kept thinking; "Fuck off, fuck off! I could hear it in my mind laughing, but suddenly I felt a peace and a calmness like I cannot explain, all of the pain had gone and it had left my body and as it did it shrunk to the size of a pin head and then disappeared. I felt absolutely shattered, I felt almost dead, but I was not, I was alive, I wanted to go after it and kick it and jump on it, but I couldn't I was too weak, I just lay there feeling exhausted and I went to sleep. I woke the next morning and I tried to tell my mum what had happened but she said that it was just a bad dream, but I knew that it wasn't."

Egbert got to the end of the report that his father Edwin Junas had written and he read; "This was one of the strangest hypnotisms that I have ever carried out, when Child G was relating this to me it was like she was fully-awake and not under hypnosis and I felt frightened, almost as if the light was in the room with us, I almost felt like she was controlling me and not the other way around."

Egbert put the tablet down onto the table and he was excited and amazed by what he had just read; he needed to fully absorb the information. He could see now why it was felt that Annie could tell them more about the NHBs and he was looking forward to meeting her, irrespective of the secrets she held, she sounded to be a real character and a challenge. Egbert's train arrived on time and he quickly got off the train at Leeds Station and then took the short walk to his apartment in Bridgewater Place, Leeds.

The Highlands Unit Group

Egbert had slept well and when he woke the next morning at just after 09.00, he made himself a coffee and a bowl of porridge from a packet, which he added milk to and then popped into the microwave. He sat at his table and decided to have a look on Facebook, he found the user group "The Highlands Unit Group" and he requested that "Star Watcher" should make him a friend; that friend request was accepted within only a few minutes and then he made a subsequent request to join "The Highlands Unit Group" which was also accepted within the hour. By 10.00 Egbert was in! He looked through the feeds of the group and noticed that Annie had posted an article on crop circles in Wiltshire; he decided to comment on the feed and he commented on the absolute preciseness of the angles in the photograph of the crop circle. It was now just a matter of time to wait and see if Annie took the bait. He didn't have to wait long, at lunchtime he checked Facebook again and he saw that Annie had replied to his comment as follows: "I know, it's amazing and apart from the fakes that appear from time to time all of the crop circles that we see are very precise in their appearance, they are a wonder of the modern day, he, he, he."

Ten minutes later there was another post from Annie; "Egbert, when were you at the Unit?" Egbert decided to leave it an hour or so before responding, he didn't want it to seem too staged. An hour later he replied; "Hi Annie I was at the Unit from around 1981 to 1984, my father worked there with the children and also the soldiers who had returned from combat. I didn't go to school at that time and I had all of my lessons from the teachers at the Unit."

When Annie read this she thought that Egbert must have been at the Unit for the same reason as she had been, so she asked him, "Did they say that you had a phobia about school, is that why you were there?"

Egbert sent a reply; "No Annie, it was just because my father was working there and I was allowed to be educated there, that's all." He could tell from her messages that she was intrigued and he sent another message; "Would you like me to call you on the telephone and we can talk about it?" He was hoping for a quick reply, but there was no response, he waited 30 minutes, 1 hour, 2 hours and there was still no response, he was beginning to think that he might have frightened Annie off and he was a little worried, but then he decided that he would just wait, hope that she responded and if she didn't he would wait until she posted something again and make another comment on it and take it more slowly.

That evening after Egbert had eaten his dinner, he logged into Facebook again and his heart started to beat faster when he saw a reply from Annie. It said, call me on 07945 195695. He was elated and he sent her a message back saying that he would call her at around 20.00 and hoped that she would be free, he got a message back and it simply said OK. When 20.00 arrived Egbert felt nervous, but also excited at last he was going to speak with this special lady who might have some knowledge that would turn the world upside down. Egbert wondered what he was going to say and he decided that he would just be himself; he got on pretty well with people anyway and he was sure that he would be better at being himself than trying to be somebody that he wasn't.

When 20.00 arrived he called the number and it rang once, twice, three.....six times and then there was an answer, but it had gone to voicemail and he listened to the recorded announcement, "Hi, this is Annie, please leave your message and I will get back to you."

Egbert was frustrated that she hadn't answered his call, but he replied to the message, "Hi Annie, this is Egbert, I will call you back in a while."

Annie's Lights/Pitts

Annie had sat and listened to her phone ringing: it played the Star Wars theme tune, she had let it ring until it went to voicemail, she gave time for a message to be left and then she picked the phone up and called in to listen to the message that had been left and she thought to herself; *"Yes, he sounds friendly enough, I will talk to him, when he calls again."* Annie stored the number in her contact list; she wanted to recognise the number next time it called.

Egbert called again about 30 minutes later, one ring, two rings and then the call was answered by Annie, she said, "Hello Egbert, it's Annie."

Egbert replied; "Hi Annie, how are you?"

Annie smiled and then she replied, "I am fine, I am sorry I missed your call earlier I was in the bathroom." She had decided to tell him a little white lie; it couldn't do any harm, she thought to herself.

Egbert was relieved. "No problem Annie, you are here now. Have you spoken with many of the people who were at the Unit at the same time as you, the Facebook group looked to have quite a few members?"

Annie replied, "Not really Egbert, they keep themselves pretty much to themselves. I have only swapped a few short messages, they don't seem to want to be in contact or discuss their time at the Unit, I don't even know who set the group up, it's a shame really because I bet they have some interesting things that they could say. It was nice when you commented on my post, I don't usually get any comments, but sometimes I might get a couple of likes."

Egbert laughed and then replied, "Well, I find crop circles interesting and I am sure that they are not man-made, they just seem to appear overnight and they have such marvellous shapes and are so precise."

Annie replied confidently; "Egbert, you are so right, they are not made by humans."

This made Egbert's ears prick up and he replied, "How can you be so sure Annie?"

Annie simply replied, "Because, I just know that they are not."

Egbert was getting excited and he wanted to keep this conversation going, he wondered if Annie was going to tell him something important at this early stage, and he said, "Wow, that's quite a statement to make!"

Annie laughed and replied to Egbert; "Yes, you are right, I got carried away." Annie decided to change the subject and she asked, "So, what do you do Egbert?"

Egbert realised that he needed to be patient and not push it, or he might spoil it and so he replied, "I am a Professor, Annie. I work in Quantum Communications and until recently I have been giving talks at different venues around the world, but my main job is at Leeds Met University, where I give talks to the students."

Annie sounded excited and replied, "So I am talking with somebody famous?"

Egbert laughed and said, "Well, I am well-known in my specialist field, but I wouldn't say that I was famous, I don't get asked for my autographs or anything like that. What about you, do you work?"

The conversation was going well and both Egbert and Annie were feeling comfortable speaking with each other, it was very natural. Annie replied, "Well Egbert, I am a Professor of research, I specialise in researching the Internet and sitting on my sofa and drinking cups of tea. I am very interested in spiritual things and I like reading about things that most people don't understand." Annie laughed and then continued; "I am not a Professor really, Egbert, I am just me."

Egbert laughed with her and replied, "Well, I think you should continue being you, because you sound lovely."

Annie enjoyed the flattery and responded, "Awww bless you Egbert that is a nice thing to say."

Egbert was very pleased with how the conversation was going and he then asked; "I wonder, if would you like to meet for a drink or maybe something to eat and we could have a chat about our times at the Unit and you could tell me about some of the things which you have researched on the Internet."

Annie replied, "I don't know about that Egbert, I don't really go out much and what if we meet and we don't like each other."

"Annie, I am sure that even if we didn't like each other, we could be civil to each other for at least half an hour, in any case it would make a change for me and not eating out of my microwave would be nice. In any case I am enjoying talking with you and I am sure we will get on ok."

Annie paused for a few seconds and then replied; "Yeah, go on then, you don't sound like an axe murderer, not that I know what an axe murderer sounds like!"

They both laughed and Egbert replied, "That's great, when would you like to meet?"

Annie replied; "Do you know the pub at the Chain Bar, near the M62 and M606 junction, it is on the left when you go up towards the fire station, we could meet next Monday about 18.30?"

Egbert replied, "Yes, I know it, how will I recognise you Annie?"

Annie replied, "I will be carrying an axe." Annie laughed and then continued; I have a silver old-type Rover, I can't remember the registration without going outside to look at it, but I will be watching out for you, what car will you have?"

Egbert responded; "I will be in a silver Jaguar registration number EJJ 600."

Annie laughed again and said; "Oooh, look at you, your own personal plate and driving a Jaguar, I hope you aren't too posh?"

They were both laughing and then Egbert replied, "Don't worry Annie, you will find that I am just a normal bloke. It's a date, I will see you next Monday."

Annie replied; "Yes, it should be good, I am looking forward to it already, bye for now."

The call ended and Egbert was smiling, he had liked Annie's humour and he was glad that he hadn't lied about anything, he felt that they would meet and have a good time. He was looking forward to it, he had almost forgotten that he had a task to complete and that this wasn't just a social meet.

Annie Brown

Annie lives in a two-bedroom apartment in a suburb of Bradford which she rents from a local landlord; she has not worked for a few years due to her having back problems caused by a curvature in her spine which she appears to have had from birth. She receives state benefits which enable her to live modestly, but she rarely has spare money for luxuries. Annie is a good-looking lady with a slim figure and long dark hair; she stands around 5 feet 1 inch tall, and she has a lovely, friendly smile. On the rare occasions that she dresses to go out Annie looks stunning and always turns the heads of potential admirers, she is a friendly person, but does not have many friends, although the friends that she has are extremely loyal to her. Although Annie did not have a good record of attending school she is a very intelligent lady and in fact gained a Higher National Diploma at college as a mature student. She took the diploma to push her own boundaries, not so much on the intellectual side, but more to do with actually going out and socialising with others.

Annie is a very spiritual person and she is more than capable of discussing most spiritual topics at a very high level, she regularly meditates to relax herself and she has always dreamt about visiting a retreat so that she could relax into that lifestyle, if only she could afford it. Annie has had a number of boyfriends and one failed marriage over the years; her choice in men has not always been the best and she has suffered many beatings because of it, although it has to be said that whoever gave her the beatings did not have it all their own way.

For a while Annie worked behind the bar at a local pub, The Beacon which is in the Buttershaw district of Bradford. Saturday night in the Beacon used to be like a night at the saloon in Dodge City out in the wild west of

America all of those years ago. It was common for there to be several fights happening throughout the evening and despite her small frame Annie was often seen in the middle of those fights and was responsible for breaking them up. She certainly commanded the respect of the regulars and she was not one to be taken lightly. Annie is interested in all things technical and she has built several computers from scratch at a fraction of the price it would cost to buy them on the High Street, she has spent many an hour building these for her friends and her family. She would love to travel, but has never really been able to afford to go abroad; she has said in the past that when she has her own spaceship she will go wherever she wants to. Her friends have never been sure whether she was joking or not.

Hunting Wild Boar

Ivan woke up and he felt the need to get some fresh air, he had the urge to hunt and kill and he chose to travel to his favourite forest to hunt for wild boar; the forest was less than one hour away from Riga but it was like a different world, the air was fresh and there were few people, he would not be bothered by the amateur hunters who came to Latvia to hunt the abundant wildlife, those people went to the commercialised wildlife parks where everything was organised. Ivan had been hunting in this forest for many years now and he knew instinctively where the best wild boar would be. In the wildlife parks the hunters had to use high velocity rifles, but this was not for Ivan; he liked to hunt the wild boar with his hunting knife, then it was a true test of his skill against the animal's skill for survival.

The wild boar is a ferocious animal and when they feel they are in danger they have no hesitation in trying to kill who or whatever threatens them. They only have short legs, but they have a strong and muscular body and can outrun a man. The best ones to hunt are the ones that have young to protect; this makes them even more dangerous and unpredictable, Ivan liked this greater sense of danger, he knew that the boar would always put up a fight and would test him more than any man could. The reason that wild boar are hunted with a rifle using high velocity bullets is due to the thickness of their skulls, which a normal bullet will not penetrate.

Ivan had been in the forest for more than one hour, he had heard a group of wild boars foraging in the undergrowth and he had slowly crept through the forest so that he was within thirty metres of them. He spotted the one that he wanted to kill, it was bigger than the rest and its tusks were almost six inches in length as they curved away from its mouth, this boar was in the prime of its life and Ivan would enjoy the battle that it would give him. Ivan stayed close to the ground, downwind of the beast; the forest was thick with trees and there were plenty of hiding places for him, he would be able to get close to his prey before the beast would even be aware of him. Ivan was an excellent hunter and he knew to approach it slowly; he walked carefully so as not to make a sound, the closer he could get before the beast charged at him would mean that the beast would have less time to build up any running momentum. At twenty metres the beast had still not sensed him and he carried on creeping slowly towards it, but Ivan could now smell the animal, which meant that he was within a distance where the boar would also be able to smell him. He knew that his timing had to be perfect because he would only have one chance to kill it, if he mistimed his attack on the animal the tables would be turned and Ivan could be badly injured or even killed; but this was the danger that Ivan liked, the adrenalin of the hunt and the kill was like a drug to him. He took his long hunting knife from his belt and he held it at the ready in his right hand, he was now only fifteen metres away from the boar. The boar's snout started to twitch and it looked up from its foraging, at this moment Ivan knew that the beast was aware of him and that now it was at its most dangerous. Ivan stood up so that the boar could see him and then he dropped down to his knees with his knife held in both hands with the blade resting on the ground, the boar, after seeing Ivan started to run towards him, its small legs very quickly built up some speed and its large frame looked impressive as it ran towards him with its head bobbing up and down and twisting from side to side to make sure that its curved tusks would rip into anything that got in its way and that it would cause maximum damage. Ivan could see the glaring eyes of the beast and it was foaming from its mouth, heading straight towards him; this was a time when Ivan had to be completely focussed, it was coming towards him like an express train. Ivan's muscles went tight as he crouched in front of it with his knife held at the ready, the animal continued twisting its head as it planned to slash Ivan with its tusks and bring him down to the floor where it could then get its powerful jaws to finish the job off. The animal was almost on Ivan and he felt the mucous from its mouth splash onto his face, Ivan had to be perfect with the knife; the animal lifted its head in one motion to rip into Ivan and as it did Ivan brought the knife up with all of his strength into the soft throat of the boar, his force lifted the animal off of the ground. Ivan felt the knife go through the skin and muscle and then he twisted the knife as it entered the boar's brain. At exactly that time Ivan threw himself to his right-hand side to make sure that the animal's tusk did not slice into him; for the boar the fight was over.

Ivan lay on the floor next to the animal, his heart was pounding from the excitement and he had sweat running down his face and blood on his hands from where the animal had bled out. He looked at the dead boar and he felt a sense of achievement, he licked its blood off of his hands and shouted out an animal-type roar of satisfaction and success; at that moment Ivan was the king of the forest just as the boar had been. After a few minutes Ivan got his breath back and then he set about dragging his kill back to his vehicle, he wanted to get it back to his home to butcher it in readiness for it to be cooked and eaten; its tusks would go on his mantelpiece next to the others to remind Ivan of what a great hunter he was. Ivan was happy and content, already thinking about his journey to England and he wondered how many people he might enjoy killing before the job was complete.

The Date

Egbert arrived in the pub car park and he sat and he waited, it was only 18.15 and he was early, he had given himself plenty of time because it is not always easy to gauge the traffic when coming out of Leeds at that time. After about 10 minutes a silver car pulled up nearby to where he was parked and he saw a dark-haired, attractive lady sat in the driver's seat; he couldn't make out what kind of car it was, but he wondered if this could be Annie. However, he decided that he couldn't be that lucky, so he carried on waiting. Next there came a tap on his driver's side window and he saw dark, pretty young lady smiling at him, he couldn't believe it, it was Annie after all. Egbert opened the door and got out, he didn't know whether to shake her hand, hug her, or kiss her on her cheek, he decided that he would take her right hand and give her a kiss on her cheek. She beamed and said to him, "Where I come from, you are more likely to get a punch and not a kiss on the cheek, thank you very much."

They both laughed and Egbert said to her, "Annie, you look lovely." She replied; "You are not too bad yourself, Professor." Annie then held out her hand and she gave Egbert a small box. Egbert said; "What is this Annie?" She told him to open it, which he did and inside was a small crystal-glass pyramid. Annie said, "I liked you from when we chatted Egbert, and I thought you deserved the gift of the crystal, its healing powers will come to you whenever you might need them."

Egbert was genuinely speechless and he smiled and leaned over towards Annie and he gave her another kiss on her cheek and said, "Thank you, I really appreciate it, what a kind and lovely lady you are." They both smiled and then went inside the pub.

Egbert asked Annie what she wanted to drink and she asked for a Bacardi and lemonade with no ice, Egbert ordered himself a pint of the local brew and they then sat down at a table away from the bar and near a window looking out over the car park.

Egbert lifted his glass and then he spoke; "Here's to you, how nice it is to meet you and thank you once again for the lovely gift."

Annie lifted her glass and raised it back to Egbert and then said, "That is my pleasure Egbert and here's to you." They chinked glasses and both had a drink.

Annie then looked at Egbert and said, "Now tell me Egbert, why does a famous Professor really want to see little Annie Brown?"

Egbert replied; "Well, apart from you being a beautiful lady and intelligent and easy to talk to, I can't think of one good reason." Egbert was taken aback by the directness of the questions, so he decided that he needed to know more about what Annie was thinking; he looked at her and he smiled, but at the same time he was tuning into her mind. He focussed in on her thoughts, but he was receiving nothing; this had never happened to him before and he could not understand it. He was worried and felt a little panicky. He got nothing at all from her thoughts and he continued speaking. "Annie, I was at the Unit at the same time as you, albeit for different reasons, my father used to talk with you, I know that, because he talked with all of the children. My father unfortunately died not long after you were there and I just felt like I wanted to try and make contact with anybody who was at the Unit at the same time as me. It is a bit like 'Friends Reunited', I simply want to reunite with my past."

Annie looked at him for a moment or two and said; "Why do you think I agreed to meet you? Egbert when we spoke on the phone, I was intrigued as to why a Professor would want to make contact with me, I also had the same thoughts about the 'Friends Reunited' thing and……..I like your voice, it is sexy."

Egbert looked at her and then burst out into laughter and then said, "Well I don't know about that, but you are here and I am pleased." They both laughed.

They looked at the menu and Egbert ordered a Chicken Caesar Salad for each of them and the originally planned 30-minute meeting lasted over 3 hours, but because they were both driving they did only have a couple of drinks each. The conversation flowed easily and before they knew it, it was time to leave. Egbert went to the bar to settle the bill and Annie went to the Ladies' toilet. While Egbert was at the bar he decided to test his mind reading and he tuned into the barmaid's thoughts; *"When I go to that table over there, if that bastard touches my arse again, I am going to punch him, and I don't care if he is a customer."*

Egbert was pleased that he hadn't lost his skill, but he couldn't understand why he had not been able to read Annie's thoughts and he was a little concerned about that, he thought to himself; *"Maybe she is on a different frequency, maybe the NHBs have completely locked her mind?* He decided though, that at this stage he would not mention it to Pilkington or Joanne; it might just be a blip and maybe it would work the next time.

When Annie came back to Egbert he had paid the bill and they were just about to leave the bar when they heard a commotion in the corner; apparently one of the barmaids had punched one of the customers and there was all hell going on. Egbert and Annie went out into the car park and Egbert walked Annie to her car, she stopped and said to him; "I don't want to go home just yet Egbert, can I sit in your car with you for a bit?"

Egbert said; "Of course Annie, I will pull out of this car park and round the corner, to the one at the rear; I don't want us to get caught up in that trouble that was going on in the pub as we left."

Annie said; "Yeah I agree, very wise." They got into Egbert's car and he drove round the corner and parked in the rear car park. Annie sat in the passenger seat of the car and she said, "Egbert, I have had a fantastic evening, I would like to do it again, if you would?"

Egbert looked at Annie and he said; "I have had a fantastic time too and I would love to do it again, are you free on Saturday?"

Without hesitation Annie said; "Yes, pick me up at 19.00 at mine, this is the address." She passed him a piece of paper which she had written her address on. They both smiled at each other and there was genuine warmth that had developed between them in such a short period of time.

Annie was still smiling and she was looking at Egbert when she said; "Egbert, I am not trying to give you any wrong ideas but, would you mind kissing me?"

Egbert smiled and said, "Well, I don't usually do anything like that on the first date, I have my reputation to think of, but I don't mind if I do." He then burst into laughter and he took Annie in his arms, he stroked her cheek and he moved his mouth to hers, their lips touched and they kissed gently, until Annie responded more passionately and her tongue licked against his lips. Egbert returned the passionate kiss and they were locked together for an enjoyable few minutes. Egbert was the first to speak. "I wasn't expecting that, that was very nice."

Annie smiled back and replied, "Neither was I, but I am glad it happened. I better go now if you don't mind, so take me back to my car and I'll see you on Saturday."

Egbert started his car and pulled round the corner and he parked next to Annie's Rover and then Annie got out, he also got out and he followed her. He opened her car door to let her in and gave her another kiss and a hug and then said; "I will see you on Saturday, Annie."

Annie smiled and then got in her car and then she drove off.

Egbert got back in to his car and sat for a few minutes and reflected on the evening; is that what was supposed to happen, should he tell Pilkington or Joanne, had he compromised himself and then he thought to himself; *"To hell with them, I bloody enjoyed it and I like Annie, I will find out what they need, but I will do it my way and that way is by me being honest with Annie."* Egbert then started his car and drove the short distance along the M62 and onto the M621 and then to his home in Leeds. Egbert drove into the underground car park at Bridgewater Place. For the first time he looked around the car park and felt the darkness and the shadows, he had never thought about it before, but for some reason he felt like he was being watched; however he couldn't see anybody and he was not picking up anybody's thoughts, he put it down to the excitement of being involved with the SIS and decided that his imagination was getting the better of him.

Egbert got out of his car, and walked to the lift and then went in that up to the floor of his apartment, he opened his door and then closed it behind him, he poured himself a malt whisky and sat down to enjoy his nightcap before going to bed.

After Egbert went into the lift and the lift door closed a man dressed in dark clothing emerged out of the shadows; it was the Russian man, Aivars who was doing some homework before the arrival of Ivan who would soon be joining him from Latvia. Aivars had been at the pub watching Egbert and Annie earlier that evening and he had followed Egbert from Bridgewater Place to the pub when Egbert had set off at around 17.45. When at the pub he had taken photographs of Egbert and his car and the woman and her car, he had taken photographs of them kissing. When the woman drove off from the car park he had ridden his motor bike back to Bridgewater Place as he wanted to see where Egbert would park his vehicle when he arrived back at home. Once Egbert had got into the lift Aivars took more photographs of the security inside the car park at Bridgewater Place and of the CCTV cameras on the perimeter. He didn't know at this stage where or when they would make their move, but he knew it was important to be ready.

As Aivars rode away from the car park, the SIS agent also came out of the shadows and with the photographs he had taken of Aivars he was hopeful that they would be able to identify the man and find out who he is.

SIS Update

The next day Joanne was sat at the desk in her office at SIS HQ when her email notification pinged; there was a report from the SIS agent with the pictures of Egbert and Annie and pictures of the unidentified man who was in the underground car park of Egbert's apartment. She read the short report which told her that Egbert and Annie seemed to be getting on well, this was also confirmed by the picture of them kissing in Egbert's car, she had a smile to herself and thought, *"Lucky Annie."*

She was more concerned to find out who the man was in the car park who was also taking photographs, but he had been wearing a hood and it was not easy to get a clear view of his face; perhaps the forensics team might be able to do something with the photographs, so she sent the email to the forensics lab with a request for them to try and get a match and the identity of the man. Joanne then sent a text to Egbert to let him know that she knew he had made contact with Annie and also to remind him that he had people looking out for him and that an agent had been close to him all of the previous evening. She did not mention anything about the other man in the car park at this stage, as she did not want to panic Egbert.

Joanne felt that they were in control and she was confident that they did not need to jeopardise the mission; they would remain vigilant and check out the man from the car park and then act on the information once they had it.

The Morning After

Egbert slept in for a little longer that next morning and when he woke he read the message from Joanne on his phone; he smiled to himself and thought he should have realised that they would already have known what had happened when he met Annie, but he decided that he had not done anything wrong and that he could still complete his mission without compromising anybody. Egbert started to think about Annie and he smiled at how pleasant and fun she had been; she was nothing like the girl who had jumped out of his cupboard snarling and swearing at him all those years ago. He wondered if she did actually have any way of contacting the NHBs or was it just a pipe dream of the SIS. He also thought about his own part in this and the fact that he hadn't been able to read Annie's thoughts; why was that and should he tell Joanne or Pilkington? He decided that he would try again when they meet on Saturday and if he still couldn't read her thoughts he would make the SIS aware and they could then decide what to do.

Annie was not an early riser; it was often after 11.00 before she got out of bed, but when she woke on this particular morning she started to think about the Professor who had just come into her life; she thought he was charming, handsome and very intelligent and she had enjoyed the evening very much. It was rare for Annie to meet a man such as Egbert; she didn't really go to the places that the likes of Egbert went to. Annie was more likely to meet the chancers who fancied her for her body and also wanted somewhere to put their head down for the night. Annie had tired of meeting these kind of men and she decided that she was better off just staying at home. It had made her become quite reclusive. She felt with Egbert that she had met a kindred spirit and even though she had blocked him from reading her mind and she knew that he had been sent by somebody to spy on her, she was going to enjoy a relationship of some sort with him.

Annie turned on her computer and decided that she would do some research on her Professor; she put Professor Egbert Junas into a Google search and the search engine did the rest. She found that Egbert's father (Edwin) was indeed the man who had spent many hours using hypnosis on her at the Unit and she also saw that Egbert held a medical diploma in clinical hypnosis, he had lectured at Leeds Metropolitan University and also worked at St James General Hospital in Leeds. Egbert had written books on Quantum Communications and hypnosis regression techniques as well as the mechanics of the brain and how certain parts of the brain are involved in the decisions that it makes and also the emotions that are produced by it. In 2009 Egbert was made a Professor by Leeds Metropolitan University. Egbert took a sabbatical from Leeds Metropolitan University in 2012 to take part in a tour of speaking events, covering key world venues where he spoke about Quantum Communications. There was a link which Annie clicked on and this took Annie to YouTube. Annie was able to see Egbert in action at one of the events which he was presenting at and this brought a smile to her face; she felt proud of Egbert and she was impressed by him.

Annie went to the kitchen and made herself a cup of Earl Grey Tea; she sat and sipped it as she thought of Egbert. Maybe she would let him read her mind on Saturday?

Time to Travel

Ivan had received his instructions from Hanif and it was time for him to travel to England; he was stood in the queue at the gate in the departure lounge at Riga Airport and he was waiting to board the Ryanair flight to Leeds Bradford Airport. He was dressed in black and with his shiny bald head he was an imposing figure, he was not that tall, but at around 5 feet 11 inches and with a solid muscular figure, he was not someone that you would pick an argument with.

In the same queue were a group of English lads who were returning from a long stag weekend in Riga, they reeked of alcohol and were still in high spirits, they were speaking quite loudly about their sexual conquests over the weekend and how sexy the Latvian/Russian women were. They promised each other that they would be coming back to Riga soon for some more drinking and shagging. One of the lads had a ball and they were annoyingly kicking it around whilst in the queue; Ivan tried to ignore them but the ball kept coming close to him, Ivan moved forward in the queue and the ball hit him on the top of his head and the sight of the ball hitting the bald headed man made the lads laugh. Ivan was furious and he glared at the lads, but he did not say anything and he kept his place in the queue.

One of the lads shouted; "Sorry baldy, hey do you polish your head?" He had felt brave and his friends were egging him on; Ivan turned and stared angrily at the lad but he said nothing. The lads carried on kicking the ball around and the mouthy one decided to see how close he could get the ball to Ivan's head again and he was successful— the ball hit Ivan on the head again and the lads screamed with laughter.

Ivan's face turned red with anger and he was about to walk towards the group of lads when a flight attendant came forward and told the lads to behave themselves and to show some respect to other passengers. She was an Irish girl and very attractive and the lad's attentions turned to her and away from Ivan; she had heard their comments a thousand times and knew exactly how to deal with them, which she did in a flirty manner. Fortunately by this time the flight had started to board and Ivan was moving forwards towards the plane, although he hadn't forgotten what the lads had done or what they had said to him, he was glad that he was on his way to board the plane.

The flight was around 2 hours and 45 minutes and Ivan had listened to music through his mobile phone, he watched the lads drinking the sachets of vodka that Ryanair sell and the flight attendant had to speak to them again a couple of times during the flight due to their rowdy behaviour. The flight landed at Leeds/Bradford airport and the annoying jingle that Ryanair play came over the speakers as it does whenever they land on time. Ivan was travelling light, he only had carry-on luggage and when the plane started to empty he stood up, he purposely moved out of his seat so that he was right behind the lad who had mocked him at Riga Airport. They walked down the steps at the rear of the Plane and Ivan followed the lad, just a step behind him, he thought to himself; *"I could kill this English Bastard and all of his friends and I would be doing everybody a favour, if he knew what I was capable of he would make a mess in his pants and so would his friends."* Ivan tapped the lad on his right shoulder and the lad turned round, Ivan looked him straight in the eye and said, "You should not have said to me what you did at Riga Airport."

The lad looked up at Ivan and was about to say something clever when he saw the menace in Ivan's cold dark eyes and all of a sudden the lad's bravery left him and all that he could do was stutter out the words, "I am sssorry."

Ivan looked back at him and stared into his eyes for a moment and then said, "Never do anything like that again!"

The lad sheepishly looked down and again said he was sorry, he turned away and his legs had gone like jelly, he just wanted to get down the stairs and across the tarmac to the terminal building. Ivan had decided that it would be foolish to draw any attention to himself and decided that the lads were not important enough for him to deal with. He walked across the tarmac and entered the arrivals building; when he got to Passport Control, he was asked if his visit was for business or pleasure and he smiled and said, "I am very much here for pleasure."

As Ivan entered the Arrivals Hall, Aivars approached him and shook his hand, they then hugged like long-lost brothers; in truth they hardly knew each other, apart from by reputation, but in case anybody was watching them, it looked natural. The two of them then left the terminal building and went out to where Aivars had parked his car in the car park. In the car Ivan asked Aivars if he had got the weapons which he had requested and Aivars confirmed that they were back at their base. Ivan had asked for an M4 Carbine which fires a 5.56mm round as well as a Taurus PT92 Pistol which is a semi-automatic weapon and it fires a 9mm standard round, he had also requested a Jagged edged Sheffield Steel hunting knife, as well as 6 inch Wotan Combat knife. He had said that he probably would not need them but that it was best to be prepared. Aivars passed Ivan an envelope containing photographs of Egbert and Annie and told him that these were the targets. Ivan smiled at the photographs and he said, "Good, is the transporter ready?"

Aivars replied, "Almost, I am just adding some finishing touches to it."

Ivan then asked, "When do we lift them?"

Aivars replied, "It will be this coming Saturday."

Ivan smiled and then said, "The sooner the better for me and then I can get out of this stinking country and away from its stinking people."

The Plan

The two men arrived at their base which was an old Transport Warehouse that looked to have been empty and derelict for a number of years. Aivars unlocked the door and said, "This is where we will stay, I have made a room at the back comfortable and we can sleep there, this is where the transporter is." Aivars then pointed towards a removal wagon and said, "It has furniture inside it and we are driving the furniture to the Marbella area in Spain where we are to deliver it along with our targets. There are lots of English people who move to Spain to live and transporting furniture from England to there is commonplace and it will not draw any suspicion to us."

Ivan replied, "What if the Customs people search the vehicle?"

Aivars looked at Ivan and responded, "That is unlikely, they are more interested in stopping asylum seekers coming into the UK and don't really care too much about what or who goes into France. In any case I have two wardrobes in the transporter and both have false back's behind which our targets will be; there will be an oxygen supply in there and the targets will be bound, gagged and sedated until we get into France."

Ivan then continued his questions. "Aivars, where will we be lifting them from?"

Aivars answered the question; "We will follow the Professor from his car park at his home to the woman's home; I know that they are meeting on Saturday evening and I know that he is picking her up at 19.00, we will follow him in his car, he will set off at about 18.30 to get to her home on time and once they are together we will watch for the right moment."

Ivan continued; "How can you be so sure about the times, Aivars?"

Aivars was pleased that Ivan was asking the questions, because it give him the opportunity to show how thorough he had been and he answered, "Because as well as taking the photographs I was listening to their conversations on the power microphone— I heard it all loud and clear."

Ivan followed up with another question. "What do you still need to do in the transporter?"

Aivars responded; "Ivan, I still need to fit rubber pipes and an oxygen supply, but I should have that finished by tomorrow."

Ivan was impressed by Aivars and he replied, "OK, Saturday it is then, are the British watching them?"

Aivars confirmed; "Yes, one was watching me taking photographs in the car park the other night, but I am pretty sure they don't know who I am; they didn't try and stop me. They are obviously trying to gather information about who they are up against and they know that if they had taken me in they would never have found out; for the same reason I didn't kill him, because I didn't want them getting nervous and pulling our targets out before we have the chance to get them. My guess is that they will have two teams of agents with each team watching both the Professor and the woman. There are usually 3 or 4 agents in a team, but don't worry, I have a team of my own that will help to eliminate the threat from these agents."

Ivan replied, "I thought that I would be killing the agents?"

Aivars shook his head and replied; "We cannot risk you or I getting caught or compromised, the agents will be dealt with by a team that Hanif already has in this area, these people are desperate to prove themselves to Allah and will be thorough in what they do."

Ivan nodded in agreement and said, "Ok, you seem to have everything in hand, we will do the lift on Saturday. Right now I want some good Russian Vodka and I want to fuck an English woman, tell me that you can get me both?"

Aivars had anticipated the question from Ivan and he replied; "I can Ivan; I will be back within the hour, while I am away make yourself at home."

Aivars the Gentle Russian

Aivars was another Latvian who was born of Russian parents, so again he was classed as a Russian, but Aivars had taken the Latvian citizenship exam and he was entitled to call himself a Latvian, Aivars decided that he would be Russian when it suited him, but he would also be a Latvian when that suited him, he could use either nationality if it gave him an advantage. Aivars was a single man by choice; he was 38 and he had worked in the transportation business for as long as he cared to remember, he had started driving fork lift trucks in a warehouse in Latvia and progressed to driving HGV vehicles for the supermarket chain Maxima, which has several stores in and around Latvia's capital city of Riga. He was poorly paid and he subsidised his income by repairing vehicles for friends when he had the spare time; the quality of his work spread and he was becoming busier than he wanted to be. He had to make a decision on whether to set up his own vehicle repair business and open a garage or to carry on driving for a living, it was a problem, but it was a good one to have.

One night in a bar in the centre of the Old Town in Latvia, he was approached by a man that he had known from school and the man asked him if he wanted to work for some real money, still driving, but in this case he would be driving around Europe transporting different types of cargo, and that sometimes that cargo would be women that were being supplied into different countries for the growing sex trade.

Aivars was a man of integrity, but the money that was being offered was very attractive and suited his way of life; he had decided that these beautiful Russian and Latvian women were going to be transported anyway and that at least if he did it, he would do his best to make sure that they were transported safely and with some respect.

He accepted the job and handed in his notice to Maxima. Aivars was now a self-employed contractor and he didn't realise what kind of opportunities his new work would provide him with. He didn't know it at the time but his new employers had links with the Russian Mafia and it turned out that his new employers did appreciate his caring transporting skills, the women arrived at their destinations looking fit and well and their value increased, which made his employers very happy.

Aivars installed secret compartments into his vehicles to hide the girls and he even provided them with make-up and toilet facilities and somewhere comfortable for them to rest. The frightened girls were appreciative of what Aivars did for them and often they would thank him by giving him sex; they had an ulterior motive because they always thought that because Aivars appeared to be such a nice man that if they were nice to him, that he might release them, but Aivars was nothing if not a total professional and none of the girls were ever released.

Aivars got on well with his employer and he always did his work well for them, but more and more he was being contacted by other organisations to do work for them, his reputation had grown, and he found that he could command very good money for what he did, although with more money came more danger, but he accepted that. He had been contacted by Hanif to carry out a transportation job from England to Spain and he was being paid very well to do it; he liked the fact that he was to be working with another person who would be doing any of the dirty work that might be necessary, it helped him to keep his conscience clearer.

Forensics

Joanne called forensics for an update on the photographs. "Stuart, how is it going, do we have a match yet?"

Stuart answered, "We do not have much, but we do have something, we have managed to get a clear view of his face by artificially removing his hood and we know that he is most likely to be of Eastern European descent based on his facial bone structure and colouring."

Joanne was happy that Stuart had managed to get something, but she replied, "Thanks Stuart, but we need more than that, keep working on it please." Joanne cleared down the call and then she went to Pilkington's office and politely knocked on the door and then entered.

Pilkington looked away from his computer screen and towards Joanne and said; "Ah Joanne, what do you have for me?"

Joanne stood in front of Pilkington's desk, he didn't offer her a seat and she could see that he was busy. She replied, "Well, Egbert and Annie have met and they are meeting again on Saturday, they got on well and were photographed kissing at the end of the night, so it seems that the relationship is going where we want it to. We also have photographs of a man who was taking photographs in the underground car park at Egbert's apartment, but we still don't have a match on him, forensics have enhanced the photographs and say that he is Eastern European or of Eastern European decent, but that is as much as we know at the moment, I have asked forensics to keep working on it. Do you think that we should lift Egbert and Annie and make them safe?"

Pilkington shook his head and replied; "No, not yet, but please make sure that Egbert knows that there is some urgency now to him getting some information for us; if we lift them right now she will clam up and that will be it, she might as well be dead."

Joanne felt a little anxious and asked Pilkington, "Sir, is that an option?"

It did not take Pilkington long to answer the question. "Yes, we can't let her fall into the wrong hands."

Joanne asked a follow up question. "What about Egbert?"

Again Pilkington answered coldly, "We will cross that bridge if we come to it, for now tell the agents watching both Egbert and Annie to be vigilant."

Joanne left Pilkington's office and went back to her own office and she called Egbert; "Egbert, I have just been with Mr Pilkington and he asked that you apply some urgency and that we need to get something from Annie quickly now."

Egbert was not happy with this and he replied, "Bloody hell, I was never given any timescales for this and it's waited for 30 years, why is it suddenly urgent?"

Joanne responded as professionally as she could; she did not want to give any Egbert any concerns about their safety; "Egbert, I can only pass on what Mr Pilkington has said and he must have a good reason for saying it."

Egbert realised that there was no point complaining to Joanne and he replied, "Ok, well I am seeing her on Saturday, so I will see what I can do."

Joanne was relieved at his response and she then said, "Thanks Egbert, be careful, bye for now."

Egbert thought to himself; "*Why did she say be careful and why does everything become so urgent all of a sudden?*" He then decided that due to the new urgency he had better go and test his thought reading skills and so he took the short walk to the All Bar One wine bar on Greek Street, he ordered a glass of wine and then sat down at a table, he looked around the bar and he focussed in on a middle age man in a pin stripe suit, wearing a loud yellow tie and drinking what looked to be an expensive red wine. He looked like he was not a stranger to boozy lunchtime sessions, with his red flushed face and red nose. The man was talking to a younger man who also wore a pin stripe suit, but without the loud tie, his was much more conservative. The middle age man was telling the younger man that he was training him to be his replacement and the younger man was feeling pleased about this and he was offering to buy more wine, the middle aged man though was thinking to himself; *"The young idiot, believes me, how can he think that he could ever replace me? Young man, I will take you to a hotel this afternoon and I will enjoy your sexy young buttocks and have you on the bed."*

It was at times like this that Egbert wished he didn't have his gift and he wanted to tell the younger man to get the hell out of there, but he knew he just had to let things follow their natural sequence of events without his interference. Egbert tuned in to a young lady who was sat alone, she was a pretty blonde girl and she was clearly in a world of her own, she was drinking a glass of Chardonnay and gazing upwards, Egbert read her thoughts, she was thinking about flying to Italy within the next week, with her boyfriend and already in her mind she was lying on the beach and taking in the sun, Egbert liked this they were much happier thoughts.

Egbert looked back across at the younger man of the two and he felt sorry for him, he wanted to say something to warn him, that he was not going to get the afternoon that he had been expecting if he stayed there, when all of a sudden the middle age man leaned over to the younger man and asked him if he wanted to go to a hotel room for a massage. The younger man thought about it and quite liked the idea, Egbert read the younger man's thoughts: *"Yes, you old poof, I will go to a hotel with you and I will tell the Tribunal judge that you told me if I didn't do sex with you, I would lose my job, that should be worth a few thousand pounds."*

Egbert thought to himself; *"What the hell, they are both adults, I am glad I didn't interrupt them now, they are both as bad as each other."* The good news was that

Egbert's powers were still intact and he was able to stop worrying about them not working as they had when he had been with Annie the previous evening, he put it down to being a minor glitch, which he had never experienced before, but thought that it must be just one of those things. Egbert left the bar and went back to his apartment; he was feeling much more confident.

The Russian Party

Aivars was away for about one hour before he came back to the warehouse with two English girls and a few bottles of good quality Vodka, he had given the girls £500 each and they were more than happy to accompany him back to the warehouse. One of the girls, Rachel was a typical English rose with nice dark hair and a soft complexion and the other was, Susan a blonde but she looked much more like the experienced sexual woman that Ivan was wanting; Aivars did not really know what Ivan's preference would be but wanted to keep him happy, he had picked them up from a bar that he knew near Thornton Road, Bradford which is well known as a red light district and also a student area. Although these girls that he had picked up were not like the normal street walking girls who do it up against a wall for £10, these were young students who were working to pay themselves through university; £500 each would help them a great deal and they would be very willing and grateful.

Ivan found 4 cups near the sink, he rinsed them and then he opened a bottle of Vodka and poured some into each cup which he then handed out to Aivars and the girls, the girls knew that this was going to be a hot time and thought what the hell we might as well get drunk and enjoy it. Ivan said to them; "Are you both English?" They both said yes and he said, "Very good, I always wanted to fuck an English woman and now I can fuck two. Aivars you can have some Vodka and then you must leave, if you had wanted a woman you should have brought one back for yourself." Aivars did not argue, he took one of the bottles of vodka and he went and sat in the Transporter.

The girls giggled and continued to drink the vodka after taking their jackets off, they were both wearing short skirts and low cut tops, the blonde also had stockings on. Ivan said to them both; "Bend over and show me your sexy English arses." They giggled again and bent over they were both wearing thongs, which were fitting tightly between their cheeks. Ivan roared with laughter and went up behind both girls and slapped them hard on their bare cheeks, he laughed as he saw the hand-prints which he had left on both of them. The slaps had stung the girls, but it made them laugh also. Ivan told them both to take off their clothes and to dance naked in front of him, they did as he said and Ivan looked at them both lustfully. Ivan told them to start feeling each other and kissing each other, he drank more Vodka and found that he was feeling more and more aroused. Both girls were enjoying this, it was clearly not the first time that they had enjoyed girl on girl fun, he told Rachel to perform oral sex on Susan and he told her to do it with her sexy English arse stuck in the air. The girls obliged willingly, and they managed to slurp some Vodka before getting into position, Susan lay on her back and Rachel put her face between Susan's legs, Susan was moaning with pleasure very quickly and Rachel was moving her body very erotically. Ivan could stand it no longer and he dropped his trousers and positioned himself behind Rachel, he then grabbed her hips and thrust his manhood into her, he pumped into her as if she was a rag doll it was like watching a piston engine, she screamed in pain and asked him to stop and put on a condom.

Ivan shouted, "Fuck off English bitch, no condom." He continued to pump vigorously into her without any care for her, he shouted again; "You can have my Russian son if you are lucky."

She screamed out; "No, stop!"

Ivan ignored her pleas and carried on, he told her; "Wriggle your sexy English arse, you bitch." Rachel was crying but she was pinned in position, she could not escape him, she knew she would have to let him do as he wanted and he did. As he reached his climax he slapped her hard on her behind and told her; "Here it comes you English bitch, I am filling you with a strong Russian baby." As he ejaculated he grabbed her round her throat and he squeezed, he was breathing heavily, but was pushing his manhood into her as far as it would go. Rachel was gasping for air, she thought she was going to die, but he released his grip just as she was starting to pass out, she gulped and she managed to breathe again, he withdrew himself from her and he pushed her to one side, she lay there and she was gasping for breath. Susan had not been able to move she had been trapped underneath Rachel. Ivan shouted again; "Your turn next, you blonde English bitch!" Without hesitation he positioned himself above her and he thrust himself into her, she let out a scream, but she felt as her friend had, that it was hopeless to complain, she would just lie there until it was over. He shouted at her;

"Wriggle your ass, sexy English bitch." The girl did as she was instructed and she gyrated her hips, Ivan moaned in pleasure and he was like a man possessed with lust. He asked Susan, "How do you like Russian Cock English bitch, it is good yes?"

Susan sobbed and said, "Yes."

Ivan took longer this time but with the same result as he reached his climax he dropped his head and he bit hard on Susan's right breast, she screamed out in agony, but this did not stop Ivan, he carried on biting until he had completed his climax. He had drawn blood from the girl's breast and he continued to lick this after his climax for a few more minutes, Ivan was feeling satisfied and his needs had started to be met. He then withdrew himself and told the girls to drink some more Vodka as he needed to rest, but he would be repeating this again very soon. The girls were afraid of Ivan and did what he said, they drank more Vodka if only to dull the pain from Ivan's attention.

Aivars had heard the screaming from the girls and he had gone to investigate what was happening. He saw that the two girls were in some distress and shouted to Ivan, "Ivan, it is time for them to leave, come my friend, let's drink Vodka."

Ivan shouted back angrily; "I am not your friend and I will decide if and when they will leave, now get back in the Transporter and drink your Vodka."

Aivars thought about challenging Ivan, but he knew that if their mission was to be successful he had to stay on the same side as Ivan and so he did as Ivan had said and he got back into the transporter.

Ivan had his way with the girls several more times and on one occasion he had Rachel suck on his manhood, while he held his hunting knife next to her throat; the girl was literally sucking for her life. He then had Rachel sitting on top of him so that he could bite her breasts again as he pumped up into her, although by this time it was Susan who was moving up and down on him as she realised what was good for her and she wanted to finish him quickly.

He threw Susan off of him after he climaxed and she crawled beneath an old sheet that lay on the floor where her friend was already laying, they were both bruised and had blood on them from where Ivan had bitten them, he had bitten the Susan's breasts in several places and he had bitten Rachel's behind on both cheeks. He had enjoyed his sex and just as importantly to him he had enjoyed the taste of warm blood.

Both the girls were cowering under the sheet on the floor and Ivan walked over to them and pulled it off, they thought it was going to start all over again, but instead he put cable ties over their hands and feet and then bound each of them together, facing each other naked, he told them that they could stay like that while he rested. Ivan threw his cup against the wall where it smashed and then continued to drink his Vodka from the bottle; he was tired from his exertions and his eyes became heavy and he drifted off to sleep.

The girls were huddled together under the sheet, they were both afraid and did not know what would be happening next, but they did not want to speak in case they woke Ivan up; they did not want him starting on them again. They did try to loosen the cable ties, but it was hopeless, they just lay there hoping that they would be released soon, so that they could get away from this evil, big Russian animal.

SIS Breakthrough

Joanne was sat at her desk when her phone sounded, she had got a call from Stuart in forensics. "Joanne, we have identified the man in the hood, he is Aivars Petronsi and he is a Russian, he works as a transporter for the Russian mafia as well as freelancing for others. He mainly transports women for use in the sex trade and he is good at it because nobody has even got close to catching him. We are not aware if he is dangerous or not, but we do know that he plans carefully, which could explain why he has never been caught. We have checked CCTV cameras at airports, railway stations and ferry ports and we have found some footage of him greeting another man at Leeds Bradford Airport earlier this week, I have just emailed it to you. The man that he greeted had flown in on a Ryanair flight from Riga; we do not have a clear picture of the other man. My guess would be that both men are going to be working together to try and take Egbert and Annie, but that is as much as we can assume at the moment."

Joanne was glad to hear this news; she knew that they now had some facts that they could investigate and at last she could give Pilkington some positive information. She replied to Stuart, "Thank you Stuart, send me any data that you have on these two characters and I will let Mr Pilkington know."

Joanne got the data through and then called James Pilkington; "We have a breakthrough Sir, we are pretty sure that there are two Russian men here in West Yorkshire to try and take Egbert and Annie. I think that now we should arrange to have Egbert and Annie brought in to safety."

Pilkington responded, "Hold fire Joanne, they are both perfectly safe at the moment, we still have our people close to them, and we will carry on as planned."

Joanne was concerned by Pilkington's response and she replied, "But Sir, this is serious now, one of their operatives Aivars is a known transporter, we could lose both Egbert and Annie forever, I must insist that we pull them out of there."

Pilkington was angry that Joanne was challenging his authority and he raised his voice; "NO JOANNE!! Do not forget your place and do not lose your nerve, I know what I am doing; we carry on as I have said."

Joanne was not happy, but she knew she had little choice but to follow Pilkington's instructions; "Sir at least let me double the security we have on them."

Pilkington had calmed down and he replied; "That will not be necessary Joanne, the people we have on them are good people and if we put more people on them, they might be noticed by Annie, and that could drive her into her shell and then this will have all been for nothing. Now go and find these two Russians, they are in West Yorkshire somewhere, so surely they shouldn't be too hard to find, now get them found."

Joanne was angry and she felt that Pilkington was putting Annie and Egbert in unnecessary danger, but at this moment in time she did not know what else she could do. Pilkington was well-regarded and she didn't feel that she would be listened to if she went above him; she therefore decided to concentrate her efforts on finding Aivars and his colleague. She made contact with the Chief Constable of Yorkshire and made him aware that he had two potentially dangerous people on his patch and that they needed to be found; she emphasised that once they were found that they should not be approached without first contacting SIS.

The Chief Constable agreed and started the job of getting his police force engaged in the important but delicate search; it would involve a lot of footwork and a lot of analysis of CCTV footage, but he told Joanne that they would be thorough in what they did.

Ivan Awakes

Aivars had also fallen asleep but when he woke he continued and finished his work on the transporter, he had only drunk half of his bottle of Vodka the evening before, so he was feeling alert; he went over to Ivan who was snoring and he shook him to wake him. Ivan woke, but his eyes were red and he spoke gruffly, "What are you doing waking me?"

Aivars replied, "Ivan we have a job to do and we are doing it tomorrow, I have the vehicle ready, and now we need to go over the plan again and we need to make sure that we are ready."

Ivan was angry, he did not like being woken up, or told what he had to do and said to Aivars: "You fool, I only need my knife in my hand and I am ready."

Aivars had decided that he would no longer put up with Ivan's behaviour and he replied sternly, "No Ivan, you need more than your knife, we are not on a killing fest, we are to transport two people safely to Spain and we must do our job well, if we are to get paid; now get a wash and let's get on with our work."

Ivan was angry, he did not like to be spoken to in that way, he jumped up and he shook his head, he picked up his knife and then walked over to where the two girls were sleeping under the sheet. Aivars watched him and said; "What are you doing?"

Ivan replied, "Don't worry I have done this many times, it will be quick, if it makes you feel sick in your stomach, you do not need to watch."

Aivars was shocked at Ivan's reaction and he almost pleaded with him; "Ivan, there is no need to kill them, they have been paid well and we can pay them some more if you like, they will be happy with the money and they will not tell anybody about us; they are only young and they shouldn't die for your sex needs."

Ivan was unmoved by what Aivars had said and he replied, "What if they do tell somebody about us and we are compromised, I am sure our paymasters would not be too understanding."

At that moment the Susan woke up and she could see Ivan standing over them both with his hunting knife in his hand, she screamed out loud in both shock and panic and without hesitation Ivan brought down the blade of his knife heavily and swiftly and the point of his knife went deep into Susan's skull and her noise stopped sharply. It was over so quickly and the girl was dead as soon as the blade cracked through her skull and sliced through her brain, her eyes were wide open and the blood was running out of her broken skull and pouring over Rachel's face, who was still attached to Susan by the cable ties.

Rachel was sobbing and she turned her head to look up at Ivan. "Please, please, please let me go, I will not say anything to anybody, I will not tell anybody, please don't hurt me."

Ivan turned to Aivars and laughed and said, "What do you think now, Aivars?"

Aivars knew that it was too late and that the girl would have to suffer the same fate as her friend and he turned his back on Ivan and he walked towards the Transporter. Ivan looked at the girl her eyes tearful and her cheeks wet from the tears, she looked so sad and so desperate, right now she would do anything to survive, he decided to cut her loose from her dead friend who was lying beside, he cut off all of the cable ties and then he said to the girl; "What would you do for me if I let you live?"

Rachel looked at him and in desperation she said, "I will do anything you want, you can have any type of sex with me, anything at all that you want to do, you can do, but please don't kill me, I could already have your Russian baby inside me."

Ivan started to unbuckle his trousers and he told the girl to kneel down before him. Aivars was now walking away from the Transporter and towards Ivan and the girl, he felt so sorry for her and he knew that Ivan was torturing her; Ivan was going to use her for more sex and then he would kill her. Behind Aivars' back he was holding a handgun with a silencer attached to it, he took it from behind his back and put it next to the girl's ear and fired one shot which went straight into her brain, and it ended her life instantly. Aivars knew though that she would not have known anything about it and he was glad about that.

Ivan was livid and he looked at Aivars and he shouted, "YOU BASTARD, she was going to suck my cock."

Aivars calmly looked at Ivan, still with the gun in his hand and he said, "Then you should be glad that I did not shoot her in the back of her head, because then I might have shot off your cock as well. You made sure that the girl had to die, by killing her friend, but you did not have to torture her, now we have to be together for some more days yet and we have to finish this job, but after that I hope I never have to see your evil face again."

Ivan looked back at Aivars and he burst into laughter, and then he said, "Aivars, never get in my way again, job or no job."

Aivars was chilled by what Ivan had said, but he was not afraid of the big man, he decided that from now on that he would keep his gun close to him and if he needed to he would kill Ivan. He knew, though that they both still needed each other to complete the job successfully.

The Search

The police knew vaguely what one of the men looked like, but apart from the fact that they both had come from Latvia, they didn't know much more; it would take them days if not weeks to carry out a full house-to-house search across West Yorkshire and even then they might not bring up any information. The police started to visit all of the hotels and guest houses in the area; they went to areas where they were known for having a Latvian community, they called in at the Eastern European grocery and liquor shops, but without any success. They spoke to the known petty criminals, drug pushers and prostitutes to try and come up with some clues as to the whereabouts of these two dangerous men. They visited pubs around Leeds, Castleford, Bradford, Wakefield, Halifax and Huddersfield Town and City Centres as they thought these would be the most likely places that the two men were likely to visit as opposed to an out of town or country pub.

Eventually an officer got a lead, she had called in at the pub that Aivars had been to and a girl had remembered seeing someone like him speaking to her two student friends, Rachel and Susan, but she wasn't sure that it was definitely him. She said; "He wanted sex with my two friends and he was prepared to pay £500 each to them; it is a lot of money and they snapped his hand off, I would have gone with them as well, but I was just leaving to meet my …err friend in Leeds, he was taking me shopping. I hope that you don't think badly of us, we are not prostitutes, but it is so hard being a student, if we can take a bit of money and give a bit of pleasure, then why not, everybody likes sex, don't they?"

The woman PC Grooby replied, "I don't judge people that is not my job, other people are paid to be judges; all I want to do is find your two friends, have you any idea where they are?"

The girl replied, "No I am sorry I don't, they got into his car and then he drove off."

PC Grooby asked; "Did you get the number plate or do you know the kind of car that the man was driving, or any other information?"

The girl shook her head and then she replied; "Well, I didn't get the number plate, or the kind of car, but I think it was dark coloured, it might have been black. I am sorry though, I really don't remember."

PC Grooby took down the girl's details and then asked her for the addresses of her two friends. She also asked for the 2 girls' mobile numbers which she made a note of.

The girl said; "They live together in a flat just up Manchester Road, I don't know the address, but I could take you to it."

PC Grooby said that she would call for a car to take them there. When they arrived they went in and it was no different to any other young woman's apartment, there were clothes lying about and make up bottles and perfume all over the place, but no clues to say where the girls were. The officer tried calling both girls numbers but the mobiles were switched off. She called in and spoke to her sergeant, he took down all of the details and told her to stay at the flat in case the girls came back. PC Grooby's colleague in the car was told to wait outside and be as inconspicuous as he could. The young girl was given her taxi fare and was told to let the police know if she heard anything at all from her two friends.

At the station the sergeant went to his inspector, who brought in a couple of detectives and told them to do some research and look at the most likely places within a three-mile radius of the pub; he felt that the Russian man would not have travelled far to pick up the two girls and he guessed that three-mile radius from the pub would give them a reasonable area to focus on. The detectives got to work and the Chief Constable decided to put all of his available resources into the three-mile radius to carry out the house-to-house enquiries.

The chief constable called Joanne to give her the information and Joanne in turn advised Pilkington. A three-mile radius is still a large area to search, but at least they felt like they had made some headway which encouraged everybody. Joanne contacted the agents outside Annie's home and the agents outside of Egbert's apartment to make them aware of what was happening. She felt that between her agents and the police, surely these two dangerous men would be found and stopped before they got too close to either Annie or Egbert. Perhaps James Pilkington had been right and perhaps she had panicked a little after all.

The House Call

Annie was sat on her sofa and was looking at the Internet through her TV; she had worked out how to link her TV to her PC before the big TV manufacturers had even thought about smart TVs. She went through her Facebook messages and the various forums that she was a member of; from the viewing UFO evidence which had been verified by NASA right through to the latest conspiracy theorists suggesting that Bin Laden and Barack Obama were related. She had a wide spectrum of understanding, but she was not stupid she knew what was likely to be real and what was not real, she also knew what were maybes and what were never in this world a possibility; she had immediately dismissed the Bin Laden and Obama theory.

Annie had started to think more about Egbert and even though there was a day to go, she was thinking what she might wear and what they might do; she thought she might put some nice sexy lingerie on just in case the night went really well. She wondered if Egbert might tell her why he was really seeing her. She hoped that he would because she liked him and she had already decided that she would co-operate with him. Annie had held her secrets for long enough and now she needed to share the burden. Egbert might just be the man to help her, like his father had tried to help her all of those years ago.

The buzzer went on Annie's door so she looked out of the window and it was the police; she wondered to herself what she might have done wrong now and she hesitated in opening the door, she thought that if she kept quiet that they might go away.

The agents were watching the situation from their van and they were ready to confront the officer if needed, but they were 95% certain it was part of the house to house enquiries that were being made, to be on the safe side one of the agents got out of the van and started to sweep the public area close to Annie's home, he was only about 10 feet away from the officer and could be on him in three strides if anything was wrong and if the officer was a fake. The officer pressed the buzzer again and Annie decided to answer it, she went down to the door and asked the officer what he wanted, she still had the chain holding the door; the officer asked if he could come in, but Annie asked to see his police ID first, which he showed her. Annie was satisfied and she opened the door; the Officer apologised for bothering her and then showed her the picture of the Russian man and asked her if she had seen him about.

Annie asked, "What has he done?"

The officer told her that they were just trying to locate him and that there was nothing to worry about. Annie looked at the picture and said. "I haven't seen him, is he a foreigner?"

The officer said to Annie, "If you see him would you mind letting us know?"

Annie agreed that she would. The officer apologised for disturbing Annie once again and then moved onto the next house and rang the bell. Annie went back into her lounge and she thought about the man in the picture; she guessed that he must have done something bad for the police to carry out house to house enquiries, but she decided that there was nothing for her to be concerned about. She put all thoughts about the man to the back of her mind and she continued to research the Internet and think about her date with Egbert. Annie was carrying out some research on the "All seeing Eye" which she had stumbled across, the "All Seeing Eye" which appears on the USA Dollar bill and was a symbol as far back as Egyptian times at the top of Pyramids. It was said to be a symbol for the New World Order or Illuminati which it is alleged is made up of super-rich famous and powerful families which have been that way for centuries, some of which would be recognised as household names.

She saw on the internet that the Illuminati are said to have set up many secret organisations including the Freemasons and the Knights Templar; it also said that it is not governments that set the strategy for the world, but the Illuminati with their ancient bloodlines who pull the strings of the governments around the world. The article asked, "Is Barack Obama the most powerful man in the world?" The answer was no, but that he simply follows the direction of the Illuminati and that he does not even know that he is doing so. It said that the Illuminati have total control of the planet and its governments and even anti-governments like terrorist organisations. The Illuminati bloodline would keep this control for ever. Annie continued to read and discovered that allegedly the Illuminati directly or indirectly controlled the banks, the energy and the pharmaceutical companies and the finances, profit and power involved with these companies. She thought to herself that the only powerful body of people that the Illuminati didn't seem to control was religion, but then again, she thought to herself that maybe they do? Annie was pleased with herself for discovering something new to her, but then she wondered whether the Illuminati was just another conspiracy theory gone crazy or if there was some truth to it. Annie decided that for now that she would keep an open mind on it and would look for more facts, which she would be bound to come across during all the research that she did. Annie switched her thoughts to more pleasant ones of when she would meet Egbert later that day and she decided that these powerful individuals or Illuminati could wait until another day when she would do some more research. As far as she was concerned, as long as the government continued to pay her benefits, they were the important ones, not the Illuminati. She did, however find the subject interesting and if she remembered she might talk to Egbert about it; he is a Professor and he might know some more facts about them and even if he didn't Annie knew she could just carry on doing her research, she did, after all have plenty of time.

The Day Arrives

Egbert had set his alarm; he wanted to go to the gym and have a workout. He was excited about his date with Annie and he wanted to feel the confidence of being in good shape. It wasn't that far to the gym from where Egbert lived and he decided to run there, it was a nice warm day, so why not? When Egbert got to the gym he did his usual circuit; exercise bike to warm up, running machine for 30 minutes. He did some dead weight lifts and also some additional work on the multi gym and rowing machine. He felt that he had given himself a good all-over workout and exercised most of his main muscle groups; he had done three repetitions and 30 minutes on the punch bag which were great for his lungs and his stamina, he finished with a 15 minute warm-down on the exercise bike. After the workout Egbert went and relaxed in the sauna for a while.

The new cleaner in the gym had been quite impressed while watching Egbert working out, at the same time as he mopped the floor and he thought to himself; *"Well, it's not SIS training, but the Professor keeps himself fit, hopefully he won't need to, but I bet he could look after himself if he had to."*

Egbert was laying in the sauna and he was thinking about Annie; he had decided to tell her exactly what he was doing and he was going to tell her early that evening. Egbert liked Annie even after only a short time of knowing her and he did not want to tell her lies. When Egbert thought about Annie he smiled and he knew that he and she were going to be good friends, once all of this was sorted. He was also going to make sure that she was treated properly by the authorities once she had given them what they wanted.

Egbert was enjoying his short break from the speaking events, he had been doing them solidly for about 18 months and although it paid well, it was a little like performing in a circus. Now that he had time to reflect on this, he wondered if there might be a better way of using his skills, when this was over with Annie he might speak to Pilkington about a more permanent role. Egbert spent three 15-minute spells in the Sauna and he decided that he would finish off his workout session with some lengths of the pool; he swam 20 lengths, the last five which he did at a sprint and when he reached the end of the pool after the last length, he was breathing hard and his heart was pumping hard; he knew that this feeling meant that he had worked out well and that he had pushed himself. It was a good feeling and he enjoyed it. Egbert now felt well-prepared for anything that the evening might throw at him and he jogged back to his home to have a nice, invigorating power shower.

The Telephone Call

Hanif was sat in his modest kitchen awaiting the telephone call; he knew that the person he was waiting for was powerful enough to bring down hell upon him, he sat nervously waiting until he heard the familiar ring tone that he recognised as the call he was waiting for.

The caller started the conversation; "Hanif, do you know who I am and why I am ringing?"

Hanif replied; "Yes, I know that you are acting on behalf of my Paymaster."

The caller was happy with this response and he continued; "You will refer to me as the Voice. You do not need my name, but think about your answers very carefully, you have no room for error, any failure will be dealt with swiftly, but the paymaster is very grateful to people who deliver results, do you understand, Hanif?"

Hanif was happy to refer to the caller as the Voice, because in truth he did not know whether it was a man or a woman that was speaking to him; some voice-changing application was being used to distort the sound of the caller, but then Hanif replied to the question; "Yes Voice, I do understand."

The Voice went on to say; "Hanif, are your people ready and do they understand the importance of what they are doing?"

Hanif replied quickly; "Yes, they will lift the targets tonight, they will then be secured in the back of a transporter and taken to Spain, where they will be met by Al Qaeda who will then take them out of Spain and move them into North Africa, where they will then be held safely until your scientists arrive to take them to your own facility. We also have a team in the UK that will neutralise any threat from the British agents.

The Voice replied, "Hanif, I am aware that one of your people enjoys the taste of blood, does he know that we want the targets delivered safely and that they should only be eliminated if there is absolutely no other alternative?"

Hanif responded; "Yes, he is aware of that, he is being paid well and he will do as he is told."

The Voice then said, "Hanif, is there anything further that you need?"

Hanif replied firmly, "No we are prepared and all will go to plan."

The voice finished the call by saying, "Contact me when they have been lifted, or if anything changes."

The Voice terminated the call and Hanif was left holding the phone receiver, wondering who the voice belonged to; he didn't trust people who had to hide behind a disguise and he wondered if he was dealing with a man or a woman.

The Date

It was 17.30 and the two Russians sat in their car close to Egbert's apartment building and they waited, they knew that Egbert would be followed by a security car and their plan was to sit a few cars behind the security car. Hanif's men would deal with the security teams when the time was right and then Aivars and Ivan would take the Professor and the girl, tie them up and put them in the boot of their car and then they would take them to the transporter which was still at the old warehouse. Aivars would decide when it would all happen and Hanif's men would remain a safe distance away until they were instructed to move in. One team would take out the security car and the other team would take out the observation van, which would be situated close to Annie's apartment. They knew that the two security teams would be in radio contact with each other, but there would be nothing that either could do once Hanif's teams struck and once Aivars and Ivan had their targets everything should run smoothly. They knew that the two unfortunate girls would be found under the sheet in the warehouse, but by then they would be long gone and probably in Spain.

Egbert travelled down in the lift to the Underground car park, he walked across to his car and he got in. The Jaguar purred when it was started up, and then Egbert put Annie's address into the Sat Nav which confirmed that the journey would take 25 minutes; Egbert was pleased that it wouldn't take long because he was looking forward to seeing Annie. As Egbert joined the M621 leaving Leeds and on the way to Bradford he was totally unaware of the two vehicles that were following him and that the occupants of each of the two vehicles had very different things on their minds.

Egbert pulled up outside of Annie's apartment and he could see her looking out of the window, she was smiling at him and it made him feel happy. Annie came out of the apartment and down to Egbert's car, Egbert got out and kissed her on the cheek before opening the front passenger door for her to get in. They both fastened their seatbelts, before setting off Egbert looked at Annie and said; "Annie, there is something that I need to tell you before we go anywhere, because you might change your mind about going with me."

Annie looked back at Egbert and she smiled; "Thank you Egbert, but I already know what you want to tell me; you are not the only one that is able to read a person's thoughts. I knew when we first met that you were working for the government, but to be honest with you I felt relieved, I have carried this with me for years and I have wanted to find the right person to talk to about it. Anyway, I have been looking forward to going out with you, so don't try and wriggle out of it now."

Egbert smiled at Annie and said, "Right then, where do you want to go?"

Annie did not hesitate and she said, "I would love to go to the Cow and Calf Rocks near Ilkley, do you know them?"

Egbert smiled and replied; "Of course, I lived just round the corner at The Unit, as well you know."

They both laughed and Egbert reversed his Jaguar away from Annie's apartment and then he joined the main road; little did they know how many eyes were watching them. The security team had parked their black Land Rover, complete with a running board at either side, just around the corner away from Annie's apartment. Aivars and Ivan had carried on driving around the block to spot the observation vehicle, which was a white Ford Transit van; the satellite receiver on the top of the vehicle gave it away, as there are not many contract cleaning vans that have a dish on the top. As they came round the block they watched the Land Rover set off and follow Egbert's

Jaguar, they kept a safe distance behind and Aivars then called Hanif's contact, Mohammed and told him where the observation van was and also where they were, Aivars instructed Mohammed to make sure that his team just stayed close to the observation van and that they should wait for Aivars to give his instruction; the other team should drop in behind the BMW that Aivars and Ivan were in and remain there until they also received their instructions. Mohammed understood this and told his two teams what was to happen.

Annie looked at Egbert and said, "Do you know the legend behind the Cow and Calf rocks?"

Egbert smiled and then replied, "No Annie, tell me it."

Annie went on to say, "You know how the Cow and Calf Rocks are mainly the two large rocks that sit together, they get their name because one is large, and the other is small sitting close to it, just like a cow and calf would in a field. At the back of them is a natural amphitheatre, which I always thought could be used for concerts of some type, I have stood in there loads of times and shouted, just to hear my voice echoing. According to local legend, the Calf was split from the Cow when the giant called Rombald was running from his wife who he had argued with, he stamped on the rock and split it as he leapt across the valley. His angry giant wife chased after him and during the chase she dropped some stones that she had been carrying in her skirt and they formed the skirtful of rocks that sit next to and just behind the Cow and Calf. So, Egbert do you believe in Giants?"

Egbert smiled at the story and replied; "These days I am not sure what I believe in, there are so many weird and wonderful things that happen, where there is no obvious explanation, so why the hell not." They both laughed again.

Egbert asked Annie how long she had been able to read other people's thoughts and she answered, "Egbert, I don't know how much you have been told about what happened in the past, but it is quite a long story; I assume you know that I was visited by a Light Orb?"

Egbert nodded and he replied, "Yes I do, I have a dossier which was written by my father Edwin, he was the person who used to hypnotise you each day to try and regress you so that he could understand what had happened to you and then help you get over it."

Annie smiled and said, "I liked your father, he was a nice and caring man, but there was another man that I did not like, he came to see your father sometimes and he often finished up shouting at your father, although I don't know what it was that they talked about. I just know that the other man came up from London and he talked posh, he always looked like a banker with a pin-stripe suit on. Anyway sorry, I went off at a bit of a tangent then. I have been able to read minds since shortly after I was visited by the Light Orb, but it took me a while to understand what I was hearing and then a bit longer to block out all of the people's thoughts, which I am sure you understand had to be done, because otherwise listening to all of those voices all of the time would have sent me crazy."

Egbert knew exactly what Annie was talking about and he replied, "I know all about that, my father helped me to learn to block other people's thoughts too, but before then it was like a nightmare, I remember one day just banging my head against a wall to make it stop, but I couldn't and so I finished up with a headache as well; I was so relieved when I learnt how to control it."

Annie nodded sympathetically and then she continued, "There are other things that I can do as well; I can communicate telepathically." Annie then looked at Egbert and she sent the following thoughts into his mind; *"What do you think of that Egbert, I will teach you how to do it if you like, it is not that hard if you can already read minds."*

Egbert was speechless, but thought in his own mind, *"Wow, I would very much like to do that, in fact if you know anything about me, which I am sure you do, you will know that it is part of my mission to be able to communicate telepathically."*

Annie replied without speaking; *"Well Mr Professor, it looks like you have learned how to do it much quicker than you had planned, you are doing it now, all you have to do is to imagine, concentrate and believe it and it happens."*

Egbert sent the following thoughts to Annie, *"Thank you, I think I may need lots of practice, but this is fantastic, it is amazing."*

Annie then spoke to Egbert, "Well that will do for now, I don't want you crashing the car due to being excited, so we will speak normally for a while."

Egbert nodded his agreement and then replied; "Can you do anything else?"

Annie smiled and then said; "I can do lots of things, in fact most of my senses are heightened, and I seem to be able to operate on a different spectrum of frequencies. You know how dogs can hear higher frequencies than humans, well so can I; bats can fly around caves which are pitch black without bumping in to anything by using what is described as sonar, well I can also move around in the dark and I can sense if there is an obstacle in the way, but unfortunately I can't fly yet. When cows are in a field and wet weather is on its way, they will lie closely together because they can sense it; well, I can sense the weather changing in exactly the same way. Dogs and cats are also said to be able to see if there is something ghostly or psychic in a room and I am able to do the same. Egbert, did you ever try to read animals' thoughts? I have tried, it but it is not the same as reading a human's thoughts, but I am getting so that I can make something from those thoughts and I think before long I will be able to have a conversation with an animal through its mind. That would be pretty amazing, don't you think? I would love to try and communicate with a dolphin, they are such clever animals."

Egbert was amazed by what Annie had just told him and he replied; "This is fantastic, and can you also make contact with the aliens or the non-human beings as Mr Pilkington calls them?"

Annie replied, "Egbert, I honestly can't, or should I say I haven't been able to do so yet, but sometimes when I think about them, I feel like they are there with me, I don't know why, but it does makes me feel stronger."

Egbert was interested by this and he asked Annie; "So, you can actually speak to them?"

Annie answered Egbert's question; "Well, it is never through me trying to contact them, it is only when they make contact with me and it is all done through our minds telepathically."

Egbert asked another question of Annie, "Do they know that the humans want to contact them?"

Annie replied; "The ones that I am in contact with know that, but they will not make contact yet; they do not feel yet that the humans are ready for them and they probably have good reason for thinking that. You only have to read a newspaper, or watch the news and you will see that countries are always attacking each other for some religious, or other stupid reason. We spend millions of pounds on building fancy hotels, football stadiums and shopping malls, but we can't even feed the poor in the world who are starving. We burn fossil fuels which damage our Earth's atmosphere and even though we know it is happening we still continue to do it. There are alternatives, but we choose not to use them or to develop them and we automatically assume that if we are visited from another planet, they will have an evil intent and want to take over the Earth. Would we talk to any aliens without aiming nuclear missiles at them first? I doubt it very much. So Egbert, if you were an alien would you publicly want to make yourself known to a planet that is likely to try and blast you out of the sky?"

Egbert realised that Annie had made a lot of good points and he nodded and then he replied; "When you put it like that, you make some very compelling points, but it sounds like we could benefit so much from their intervention; surely they would be able to teach us to use different technologies that are beneficial to our planet and the people that are on it."

Annie nodded and said, "Of course they could, but first they need to make sure that the people of Earth are ready for them which is why they visit and practice on people like me, they have to make sure they get it absolutely right for when they visit their main targets; if you think about it when they visited me all of those years ago, nobody would have cared or listened if anything had happened to me. My mum would have been upset, but in the whole scheme of things nobody would have done anything and I bet all of those other children who were at the Unit were just the same, nobody would have cared and any harm to them would soon be forgotten."

Egbert was absorbed with what Annie was telling him and he asked her a question: "What do you mean, who do they intend to visit next?"

Annie looked at Egbert and replied, "Egbert, when they are ready they will visit our world leaders and they want to visit them in a similar way to how they visited me, but they have practiced because they cannot afford to have any casualties, which did happen with other people that were visited like me. Some of the people they visited ended up like cabbages, I know because I saw them at the Unit. Can you imagine what would happen if that happened to Putin or Obama. I was lucky, they visited me many times and they carried out their tests on me; they enhanced my senses as I have shown you already today, but first of all they made sure that I would not abuse anything that they gave me by carrying out their full body scans on my body and my mind. You can understand why they would need to be careful when dealing with a world leader and there is no way that they could keep coming back to scan their minds and their bodies, they have practiced and practiced so that they will be able to do it in one visit."

Egbert was hungry for more of what Annie could tell him and he asked, "How do you know all of this?"

Annie sighed, almost impatiently and then she replied, "Because they told me Egbert; they want contact with the humans on Earth as well, but they want to do it in a peaceful and harmonious way, without any risk of conflict. There is so much that they can teach us, like how to make transport that runs on water or air and not oil, how to eliminate contagious diseases, how to put enough food on the planet and in the right places, how to neutralise weapons or physical threats of violence. I know that they can teach us so many things for a fact because I have seen them, I have been to their world as their guest, not in the sense that I have visited them physically, but they took my consciousness and I have witnessed how they live in harmony with each other and the fantastic technologies that they use. So I am so glad that the British government has finally sent somebody that I feel I can trust that will help me to help the NHBs, as you call them, to make contact. Egbert, your father knew all of this thirty years ago and he said that he was going to stay in contact with me and help me when the time was right, but he never contacted me so I kept the information to myself, just as he told me to; it wasn't hard because the Light Orb's showed me how to lock my mind, which is why you couldn't read it when we first met. I don't open my mind on a first date ha, ha ha."

Egbert smiled at Annie, he liked her humour as well as what she was telling him, but then he replied; "I am sure that my father would have stayed in contact, but sadly he died in a car crash, a short time after you left the Unit."

Annie looked sad and she responded, "Oh Egbert, I am so sorry to hear that, but maybe it was meant to be that you would come to help me, to continue your father's work."

Egbert nodded and said; "Thanks Annie and I hope that I can help to carry on his good work and fortunately I have a contact working for the British government who knows how to open all the doors that we need to open."

The Ambush

Aivars called the number which Hanif had given him to contact Mohammed who was in charge of a West Yorkshire terrorist cell. He used the loudspeaker in the car; "Mohammed, this is Aivars, I want you to get in front of the security vehicle, the black Land Rover and then slow it down so that we can get in front of you. Then I want you to take it out; I know you boys have staged many crashes to raise funds from fraudulent insurance claims, I read about it all the time in Latvia; England is known as the whiplash capital of the World. The agents in the vehicle need to suffer more than whiplash, I am sure that you know what I am saying?"

Mohammed was very aware of what was required and he simply replied, "Yes, we know how to do that."

Aivars went on; "Once you have taken out the Land Rover tell your other team to take out the observation van at the woman's apartment, if not, as soon as they lose contact with the Land Rover, they will start pressing all kind of alarms."

Mohammed replied; "Do not worry, we are ready and God will protect us."

Aivars responded to what Mohammed had said. "As long as your God makes sure you get the job done, all will be good."

Mohammed was not happy that Aivars was speaking about his God in that way, but he did not respond and the call ended. Aivars turned to Ivan and said, "They are ready, we will make the lift soon, "

Ivan looked back at Aivars and said, "These boys of Hanif better get it right or they will need more than their God to protect them if anything goes wrong."

The convoy of vehicles were travelling along Manningham Lane and away from Bradford and towards

Shipley, the road was wide enough for Mohammed to get in front of the Land Rover, and then for Aivars to get in front of their vehicle; it would make the occupants of the Land Rover anxious about the distance between them and Egbert's Jaguar, but not enough for them to do anything rash. It would then be just a matter of watching the route they were taking to time the ambush. Mohammed saw a clear piece of road and he made his move he signalled right to overtake the Land Rover and then pulled in front of it whilst slowly decreasing his speed to allow Aivars to get in front of his own vehicle. Aivars managed quickly to get in front of Mohammed and Mohammed then increased his speed to keep the Land Rover driven by the security team behind his own vehicle. The security team still had a good view of Egbert's Jaguar and they were happy to continue like that for the time being; they would look for an opportunity to get in front of the Range Rover that had pulled in front of them the first chance they got. Richard, the driver of the Land Rover knew that if needed to he could always switch on his siren and flashing lights and get close to Egbert's Jaguar very quickly.

They travelled through Shipley and then turned left to go towards Baildon; they went over the cattle grid and across the Moor road and there was no possibility of overtaking on this stretch of road. The moor road was narrow and was barely wide enough for one car, let alone two cars. As they came off the moor, the moorland was replaced by five feet high dry stone walls with grass fields on the other side of the walls. Only a couple of months earlier this road and the fields would have been covered in snow and would have been barely passable. As Mohammed reached the bottom of the twisting desolate road he applied his brakes hard and he heard the familiar skidding noise coming up behind him and he and his fellow occupants braced themselves for the inevitable bang at the back of their vehicle, which always followed.

They had orchestrated this type of incident many times before and had scammed insurance companies out of their money by claiming whiplash injuries, which are so difficult to detect by doctors. It is a good form of income and it helped to keep funds coming into their terrorist cell for when they would be called upon to do their God's work.

After the crash, first Mohammed the driver got out holding his neck and he was shouting at the car behind him, then one by one each passenger got out of the Range Rover; they were also holding their necks and their backs and they were claiming that they were in pain, moments later out came their mobiles to take photographs of both vehicles, which is a typical technique that is used when carrying out an insurance scam. Photographic evidence usually ensures that the insurance company does not defend the claim.

Richard, the driver of the security vehicle was concerned and he wasn't sure if the vehicle in front was part of an insurance scam or whether they were being ambushed, but he knew that they had to get past the vehicle that they had just collided with and there was no room to drive round it. He told his colleagues to ready their weapons but to remain where they were and that he would try to sort it out. Richard got out of the Land Rover and said; "Look it was my fault, I was too close to you, here are our details, all your costs will be covered now let us get past, we are in a rush."

Mohammed walked towards Richard to take the paper he was offering, but when he was only two paces away from him, Mohammed dropped to his knee and pulled out his hand gun and fired at Richard; before Richard realised what was happening, he had a black hole between his eyes and he was dropping to the ground dead or dying. Mohammed's colleagues then took out their weapons and started to fire at the two men who had been left inside the security vehicle, but by this time the two men had taken up a defensive position and they were firing back. There were five Asians and only two of the security team left, and the security team knew that they had to finish the Asians off quickly so that they could get in pursuit of Egbert's Jaguar. Two of the Asians got reckless and did not give themselves enough protection and they were both dealt with quickly by the two experienced security agents who knew exactly where to aim for maximum effect. However, the two agents were pinned down and at the moment they would not be going anywhere. Mohammed moved to relative safety at the front of the Range Rover and he took out his mobile to call the other team near the observation van, he gave his command; "Take out the observation van now!"

His colleague replied; "Yes Mohammed, I am throwing the switch now." Within the van the agents did not know what had hit them; first they could not breathe and then they felt their bodies turning as if to ice, they were paralysed and they were powerless and then they were dead. "It is done Mohammed, they are all dead, I turned on the nerve gas that we had piped into their air vents, it worked instantaneously; first it paralysed them and then it killed them."

Mohammed ended the call and put his mobile back into his pocket and then he continued to fire at the two agents in their Land Rover. It was a deadlock situation, neither side was gaining any advantage which was not a bad thing for the Asians because the agents were not in a position to protect the Professor and the woman; however Mohammed wanted to get it over with. He decided that the best way would be to make sure that the black Land Rover could not be driven and then he would move their own vehicle far away from the scene so that the British agents had no possibility of transport. He fired his gun at the two front tyres of the black Land Rover and then he fired again through the radiator, the tyres flattened and the radiator immediately started gushing water, it was at that point Mohammed knew that the vehicle would not be going much further. Mohammed then managed to get back inside his Range Rover and he shouted for Hassan, who was in a good position behind the dry stone wall to stay behind and continue the fight. Hassan was able to keep the agents pinned down which would mean that Mohammed and Ahmed could go and help Aivars and Ivan to capture the Professor and the woman. Ahmed was stood on the front bumper of the Range Rover has it drove away from the battle scene, just until they managed to get out of shooting range from the security agents, he then got inside the Range Rover and sat in the front passenger seat next to Mohammed. Mohammed sped down the road to catch up with Aivars and Ivan and has he approached he saw their black BMW parked up in a hotel car park close to the Jaguar of Egbert. It was in the car park of the Cow and Calf Hotel, looking over the rocks of the same name.

Mohammed thought to himself; *"Damn! The Professor and the woman must have decided to stop for some refreshments; that is inconvenient and must have given Aivars and Ivan a surprise, they will not be happy."* Faint gunfire could be heard in the background, but it was an isolated area and anybody would most likely have thought that it was just somebody firing off guns on their land to perhaps keep the rabbit population down.

Mohammed pulled into the car park and he walked over to Aivars and asked, "What happens now?"

Aivars replied; "Why is there still gunfire and why did you not finish the job?"

Mohammed was not happy with Aivars' question, he felt that he had adopted exactly the right tactics for the situation, but he replied; "There are two of them left and one of my men has them both pinned down, they cannot follow us because I made sure that their car cannot be driven."

Ivan turned and looked at Mohammed and exploded, "YOU FUCKED UP, YOU ARE A FUCKING AMATEUR, you left to save yourself!"

Mohammed looked angrily back at the big man, and he reached for his gun, he is a proud man and he was not prepared to have his bravery challenged in this way, just in time Aivars got between the two men and he calmed the situation down. "Don't be stupid you two, we should not be killing each other. Mohammed put away your gun, we can fix the situation." Ivan wanted to cut Mohammed's throat there and then, but Aivars was right and Ivan then looked at Aivars and said; "I am going back to finish it, or they might just find another form of transport and still get here and stop us doing what we came to do."

Aivars looked back at Ivan and said, "I don't like it, I need you here, but you are right and I would guess we have 30 minutes at least, before they come out of the hotel."

Ivan turned and said to Mohammed, "You are coming with me, the other one can stay here with Aivars, tell me that the observation vehicle at least is taken out."

Mohammed hated the big Russian by now, but he replied, "Yes they are all dead."

Ivan got his M4 Carbine and his Taurus Pistol out of the back of their BMW and marched towards the Range Rover, he got into the passenger seat and he told Mohammed to drive, they drove back to where the Land Rover was and they saw one agent lying dead on the ground and Hassan was draped over the wall with blood pouring from a head wound. There was another agent who looked to be dead in the Land Rover. The other two of Mohammed's team who had been shot earlier were dead where they lay. Ivan looked at Mohammed and said; "There were three agents, one of them is missing, where is he?"

Mohammed looked back at Ivan and said; "He can't have got far, Hassan was a great warrior; the agent will at least be wounded."

Ivan said, "Your Hassan is dead and there is a British agent somewhere who is not, you have caused this by driving away and not staying to finish your job. We need to tidy up this mess and get out of here, get these bodies into the Land Rover quickly and we will push it through this gate and into the field and then into the lake, the sign says deep water, so the vehicle should sink quickly."

Whilst Mohammed was pushing the bodies into the Land Rover, Ivan was looking around with his Taurus Pistol in one hand and his hunting knife in the other, he could see nothing that would say where the other agent was, but he also couldn't be sure that he wasn't being lined up as a target by the agent; he decided it was better if he left the scene quickly and got back to Aivars, the agent, if he was alive, was on foot and it would take him some time to catch up with he and Aivars. "Mohammed, let's get the vehicle into the lake, you sit in the driver seat and drive it to the lake, I will stand on the running board, keep the window open so I can hold on." Mohammed did as he was told it was only about 20 metres and it didn't matter about the engine overheating. Mohammed reached the edge of the lake when he felt cold steel with a sharp point on the nape of his neck, he did not have time to wonder what it was as Ivan applied pressure to it and pushed the blade through the back of his neck to the front of his throat and then twisted the knife to ensure that the Jugular vein would be severed. He pulled out his knife and felt Mohammed's warm blood on his hand, he had missed this taste it had been a few days since his last kill, he smiled and said to Mohammed, "Now you will know never to take out your gun and point it at Ivan, you fucked up and this is your reward, you can go and see your God now."

The man was gasping and dying, his body was almost lifeless, apart from a few twitches, as the blood drained from him he could not say or do anything.

Ivan opened the door, reached over and selected drive on the gear stick and then he took off the handbrake. The vehicle moved forward and entered the lake and within only a few minutes all trace of the vehicle had disappeared into the depth of the lake apart from the bubbles which rose to the surface of the water, but soon the bubbles stopped too. Before he got back into the Range Rover he looked around again for any trace of the agent, but he was nowhere to be seen, Ivan did not have time to look for him so he got back into the Range Rover and he sped back to Aivars.

Aivars and Ahmed were sat in the front of the BMW when Ivan pulled into the car park, he walked over to them and he asked if anything had happened, Aivars replied; "No, they are still inside; where is Mohammed and did you finish the agents?"

Ivan replied "Mohammed has gone to his God to apologise for his mistakes and I don't know where one of the agents is, but he has no transport and he is alone and maybe even wounded."

Aivars said; "They will send others to find us; if the SIS have lost contact with both their teams they will check the tracking information on the Professor's Jaguar and with the Internet and GPS they will be able to pinpoint exactly where we are."

Suddenly Aivars had a thought and he excitedly said; "Wait, I know what to do, I will remove the Tracking device from the Professor's car and attach it to the Range Rover, it will only take a few minutes. Ahmed, when we have the tracker attached you will drive the Range Rover far away from where we are and you must keep driving for as long as you can, if you can get to a motorway do so and travel at speed, but within the British speed limit. If you get caught use your gun, you must attract all the attention away from what we are doing here and you must buy us some time to make up for Mohammed's mistake. If you do this you will be serving your God well."

Ahmed nodded and said he would do whatever was necessary.

Aivars checked and there was no sign of the Professor or the woman and he went to work on removing the tracking device from the Jaguar; Aivars opened the driver's door without any problem, in all of his years in his profession he had never come across a make or a model that he couldn't break into. He soon located the tracker which was located just at the back of the steering wheel and he quickly detached it. He then went to work on fitting it to the Range Rover and although he would not have got 10 out of 10 for the aesthetic look of the finished article, he had the tracker fitted and functional within minutes. Fortunately it had its own standby battery so it had continued transmitting. Aivars looked at Ahmed and said, "Right Ahmed, on your way and make sure that you don't fail this time."

Ahmed drove off in the same direction that they had come from, but then he turned left down Station Road towards Burley-In-Wharfedale, as coincidence would have it this route took him right past where the Unit had been.

Agent Whitham

Charlie Whitham had been with the SIS now for 4 years and he was coming to the end of his term with them; although he was half-looking forward to retiring he was still as professional as ever, because he knew that one lapse of concentration could cost him his life. During the shootout, he and his colleague were pinned down by the Asian who had a dry stone wall between him and them and there was nowhere that they could escape to, which was not acceptable as they had to find a way to get to the Professor and the woman. Charlie managed to get out of the back window of the Land Rover and he planned to get into the field and behind the Asian so that he could take him out. Once through the window Charlie got close to the ground and he edged his way along his side of the wall away and he was moving away from the gunfight, he was hoping to find a gap or a broken part of the wall that he could get through; he knew that if he tried to climb over that the Asian would probably be able to shoot him. His luck was in as he came across a damaged part of the wall with just enough room for him to get through. Charlie's colleague and the Asian were still exchanging gunfire and then all of a sudden it stopped and there was a magical silence. Charlie held his breath and listened for movement, but could hear nothing. After around 1 minute, Charlie looked over the top of the stone wall and saw the Asian with arms extended in front of him holding his handgun and pointing it towards Charlie. Charlie in a flash extended his own arms and took aim at the Asian, but before he could pull the trigger the Asian had let off a couple of round towards him. The first one missed, but the second one stung his shoulder and made him wince with pain; Charlie felt the burning sensation on his shoulder, he was shot but he couldn't think about that now or he would end up dead. In pain and in controlled anger Charlie stood up and fired back at the Asian and although he missed with his first shot, the second and third shot hit the Asian in the head and his face quickly became unrecognisable; the Asian slumped over the top of the dry stone wall and he did not move again. Charlie instinctively knew that the Asian was dead, he had hit him exactly where he had intended to, just like he had been taught during his extensive training.

Charlie needed to check to see how his colleague was, but he feared the worst, he went back to the Land Rover, but he was too late, his colleague was already dead. Charlie tried the radio to make contact with the observation van, but there was no response from it at all. He checked his own wound and he realised that he had been lucky and it was just a graze. He knew that his next job was to get to wherever the Professor and Annie were. He took the mobile phone out of his pocket to call for help, but as is often the case in the countryside he had no coverage and for now he was totally alone. Then all of a sudden he felt that his luck was changing he could hear a vehicle's engine in the distance and it was coming towards him and was coming quite fast, he was about to wave to it until he realised that it was the Range Rover; they were coming back to finish off the job. Charlie went to the back of the Land Rover and he used it as cover so that the occupants of the Range Rover could not see him, he started to run and then he climbed over the stone wall just as the Range Rover came to a stop. Charlie was about 100 metres away; he had thought about staying to fight with the enemy and then take their car, but he only had a few rounds of ammunition left and he didn't know how many of them there were.

He saw a bear of a man that he had not seen before and he was obviously looking around for Charlie and then he saw the Asian lifting the bodies into the Land Rover, Charlie decided to stay motionless so as not to give away his hiding place. He saw the Asian get into the driver's seat of the Land Rover, while the big man hung on the side of it, he then saw them take it to the lake and then drive it into the lake, but he did not see the Asian man get out of the Land Rover, although he did see the big man looking around again before getting back into the Range Rover and driving off. Charlie did not know what had happened to the Asian, but he stayed quiet and still for a few minutes longer, just to make sure that the Asian hadn't somehow got out of the Land Rover and had stayed behind to find him and then to finish him off. Charlie picked up a loose stone and he threw it across the road so that it hit the wall. It made a crashing sound which was loud enough to attract attention, Charlie then watched and listened for any movement, with his gun in his hand and at the ready. There was no noise or movement, so he did the same again, but as before there was no response; Charlie figured out that the Asian man must have gone down in the lake with the Land Rover and he guessed that big man must have killed him for whatever reason, but at least this meant that Charlie was now free to try and get to the Professor and Annie, although at the moment he was not sure how he was going to do that. Charlie racked his brains to try and remember when the last time was that they had passed any houses but, try as he might he couldn't remember. Charlie had to make a choice which was either to walk back from where they had come from, which meant that he would be going away from the Professor and Annie, or he could walk in the direction that the Range Rover had travelled and hope to find somewhere on the way, where he could find help.

Charlie's shoulder was sore, but he knew that the bullet had only burnt the skin, when he got the chance he would apply some antiseptic and a dressing, but until then he was fully functional. He set off walking in the direction that the Range Rover had driven off and he hoped beyond hope that something or somebody would turn up to help him.

Communications Down

Joanne picked up her phone to call Pilkington; "Sir we have a problem, we have lost contact with both of our security teams, we are still trying to get to the bottom of what has happened."

Pilkington then said sternly, "Can we still track Egbert's vehicle?"

Joanne replied; "Yes Sir, it is moving at 30 MPH towards Leeds at the moment, it looks like it is heading towards the M621."

Pilkington responded; "Ok, as long as it is moving I am not too concerned, there must just be a problem with the two teams' communication equipment."

Joanne was very concerned, but Pilkington didn't seem too bothered and she said, "But Sir, we can't contact them on their mobile phones either."

Pilkington felt Joanne's concern and he responded to it; "Where are our nearest Units to them?"

Joanne finally thought that Pilkington was realising things were serious and she replied, "We have a team in Sheffield and one in Manchester doing some routine surveillance work."

Pilkington then said; "Ok Joanne, give them the passwords to access the tracker on Egbert's car and mobilise them, tell them not to intercept the vehicle, but just report back once they have a visual on it, it will take them both around 30 to 40 minutes to get to Leeds in any case."

Joanne was still concerned that enough was not being done and she said, "Sir, I think that I should get the police involved, Egbert and Annie might be in danger."

At this point Pilkington lost patience with Joanne and replied angrily, "Out of the question, I am not having PC Plod trampling all over this, they would put Egbert and

Annie in even worse danger, it is an SIS assignment and we will deal with it."

Joanne was concerned that Pilkington was not making the correct decisions, but she was also feeling frustrated because she felt out of her depth, she was not sure who she should go to, to voice her concern. She didn't feel that she could tell Pilkington and she was still new to the department; she guessed that it was how everybody must feel on their first real assignment, especially when where there was so much at risk. Joanne took out the mobile phone from her handbag and she went through her contacts until she came to Egbert. She hesitated, but then she pressed the call button. It rang several times but with no reply and there was no voicemail facility activated; Joanne pressed the call button again and the same happened. Joanne decided that because he was driving that Egbert had not taken the call, so she decided to leave it for now, she looked at the PC screen and the tracker showed that he was on the M621, heading towards the M62 or M1; she would keep watching until the vehicle stopped and then call again.

Joanne started to question whether she was being irrational; there was nothing suggesting that Egbert and Annie were in danger that evening, it appeared that Egbert was still driving, the communication loss could just be a technical problem and maybe the mobile coverage where the teams were was just poor. On a positive note, they had two other teams heading towards Egbert's car which they were still tracking. Maybe this was all normal, maybe she should just accept that Pilkington was right, so far he had been with everything else? It was Joanne's first major assignment; she had been requested by Pilkington because she had shown promise in her administrative role since joining SIS, she had studied psychology at University and she had excelled in certain projects like the understanding and use of body language, thinking from another person's perspective, and how people react differently to stress. Right now she was reacting to stress and she realised that she needed to get a grip of herself. She thought about Pilkington and she realised that he had seen something in her and now she felt bad about doubting him; she decided to relax and to trust in his judgement more than she had been doing.

Sensing Danger

Egbert and Annie were sat next to the Log Fire, they were soaking up the atmosphere and enjoying each other's company whilst having a drink. They had a lot to talk about and Egbert was amazed at some of the things Annie had already told him. Suddenly Annie turned to Egbert and said, "Egbert we need to go, we are in danger, I can feel it."

Egbert looked surprised and asked, "What do you mean?"

Annie was looking anxious and replied, "I told you before that I can sense things before they happen, well right now I am sensing danger for us both and it is close by."

Egbert shared Annie's concern and he asked her, "What kind of danger?"

Annie impatiently responded, "Bloody hell, this is not the time to be asking all of your questions! Tune in to my mind now."

Egbert looked at Annie concentrated and tuned into her mind, but it was not her thoughts that he was reading, it was a man's thoughts that he didn't know, a man that was close by and one that was thinking; *"When they come out, they will both get a crack on the skull and they will both go in the boot of the car, as far as I am concerned we will deliver them alive, but they may have one or two minor injuries, I am sure that the people who want them will soon make them feel better and I will get my money. If they don't come out soon though I am going in for them, there are not many people in there and it will not take long to silence them all and we can be on our way."*

Annie looked at Egbert and asked, "Did you get that?"

Egbert nodded and said, "Yes I did, bloody amazing, how did you do that?"

Annie sighed and then said; "There will be time to discuss it later, but for now we need to get out of here, have you got any ideas?"

Egbert thought for a moment and then he replied; "Well, they will be watching my car and if we sneak off, based on what he was thinking, he will come in here and some of these people will be hurt, if not killed. We need to cause a distraction, I will set off the fire alarm and people will go out into the main car park where my car is; we could then slip out of the kitchen back door go down through the side car park and over the wall at the back of the bottom car park, are you up for it?"

Annie nodded and said, "It is as good a plan as any that I have, let's do it."

They stood up and walked away from the cosy fire and towards the kitchen door; next to the kitchen door was a small break the glass fire alarm and Egbert took hold of the little hammer and he hit the glass and broke it, the button inside was released and the fire alarm started to sound. Both Egbert and Annie started to shout, "Fire, fire, get out into the car park, quick, quick!" Egbert and Annie then walked through the kitchen door and into the kitchen and headed towards the back door which led to the side car park. One of the staff looked at them, but didn't have time to say anything before they were out into the side car park. They continued down to the bottom car park when Annie said, "Quick, follow me." Annie climbed over the low wall at the left hand side of the bottom car park and Egbert followed her, she said; "We need to keep low for about 100 metres and then we can get across the road and up into the Cow and Calf Rocks, they will be looking for us and it is only just getting dark, so we will have to be careful."

Egbert thought to himself and then replied, "If they see us, run as fast as you can and I will try and hold them up, there are SIS Agents who are watching after us they will protect us, I just don't know where they are right now."

They gradually made their way over the moorland; which was a mix of heather and bracken and they got to a place about five metres from the edge of the road, but they dare not make a dash for it as it was still too light. They decided to lie on the ground where at least there was some cover and they wouldn't be seen easily. Egbert then said, "We will have to stay here until it gets darker, either that or we will have to crawl a lot further down until after the bend in the road and then crawl back up on the other side of the road, until we can make a dash for the Rocks; if we do that I think that there is more chance that we will be seen. At the moment my guess is that they will be waiting near my car for us to come out of the hotel, but there were not that many people in the hotel and there is no real fire, so it will not take them long to realise that we have done a runner and they will start to look for us."

Annie replied, "Let us stay here, I think it should get dark soon and anyway it is bloody hard work crawling through this undergrowth."

Egbert looked at Annie and he could see that she was tired and that she had cuts on her bare legs. He asked her, "Are you OK, this is not the first date that I intended for us?"

Annie smiled and replied; "Don't worry, it is just a different kind of date, and you sure know how to treat your ladies."

They both smiled and lay still waiting for it to get darker, but then they heard footsteps coming towards them from further up the road; the person was about 50 or 60 metres away and Annie could just about make his face out, it was the man that the police had shown her a picture of earlier that day and at the rate he was walking he would be on them within a few minutes. They could not crawl fast enough without drawing attention to themselves and if they started to run, they would be seen by the man and more than likely would be caught. Egbert thought about confronting the man, but didn't know how many of them there were and he decided that it was too big a risk. He signalled to Annie to stay still and quiet. Annie sent a message back to him telepathically; *"Of course I am not going to move Professor, I have seen this man before, he is wanted by the Police, they showed me his picture earlier today, but did not say why he was wanted. He is Eastern European I believe."*

Egbert thought to himself; *"I don't know why Eastern Europeans would want us, unless there is a price on our heads because of what Annie knows, bloody hell I never signed up for that."*

Annie replied to Egbert's thought; *" I never signed up for this either, but I guess they would have come for me at some stage whether you were involved or not, so let's just get away from the bastards."*

Egbert sent his thoughts back; *"I agree, if this guy gets much closer I am going to have a go at him, when I do that, run down the road as fast as you can."*

Annie read his thought but she did not reply, she realised that Egbert had her best interests at heart and she appreciated it, but she knew that she was not going to be able to run very far either in her shoes or in her bare feet. The man who Annie had recognised was Aivars and he was now only about 20 metres away from them. Egbert was concerned because he didn't believe that they were hidden well enough. It was getting darker, but he thought that as the man got closer he would be bound to see them. Egbert looked around for anything that he might be able to use as a weapon, but there was nothing apart from a small lump of wood, which Egbert decided would have to do, he reached out and he held the wood in his right hand. Egbert was ready to jump up if the man got much closer. They both lay there silent and motionless when all of a sudden the sky started to darken and then there was a loud crack of thunder; there were no street lights in the area and the only light was coming from the windows of the hotel, it was still light enough for them to be seen, but the crack of thunder had made the man stop in his tracks. It was as if somebody had thrown a switch and turned the moon and all of the stars off, apart from one star which had remained and which was shining brightly, but then surprisingly that lone star moved so fast across the sky and simply vanished. Egbert was amazed by what had happened, but he knew that the sky in that area was well known for doing strange things and that over the years there had been many reports of strange sightings. Egbert assumed that he had seen a shooting star for the first time in his life and he was pleased to have seen it, but he was even more pleased that it was now pitch black. Annie simply looked up at the sky and smiled appreciatively. Egbert looked back towards the man and was hoping that he would turn around and go back up the road towards the hotel; Egbert's hopes were answered when there was another loud crack of thunder and a flash of lightning, followed by a sudden downpour of torrential rain. The man turned round and he started running back up the road. Egbert guessed that the man couldn't see anything and that he was going back to his car to get a torch. There was another flash of lightning and all of the lights at the hotel went off, it must have been hit by a fork of the lightning. In the darkness Egbert sensed that they now had an opportunity to run for it, he could not see Annie it was so dark, but he sent her a message to her mind; "Let's go Annie." He heard her moving and he knew she had got his message, he felt out and he took her hand as they ran across Hanging Stones Lane and through the gravel of the visitor car park and then up and into the famous rocks. It was so dark and they couldn't even see where they were putting their feet, but now it was Annie who was leading Egbert by the hand, she seemed to know exactly where they were going and she confidently avoided every obstacle and guided Egbert around the same obstacles with ease. She transferred a thought to Egbert, *"I know this area very well, it is one of my favourite places, I used to hide here all day when I was at the Unit and they would look for me, but they could never find me. When I went back to the Unit at the end of the day they used to tell me off, but I didn't care. I come back here sometimes and I sit in the cave that I used to go to, that is where we are going now, we will be safe there."*

Egbert smiled to himself; he was confident in Annie. It was still pitch black, but Annie knew exactly where the cave was, she pushed aside a big bush at the front of the cave and then pushed aside some smaller dead bracken and sticks which had been fastened together to make a cover for the entrance and then they went inside. Egbert thought to himself; *"How the hell did she do all that in the dark?"*

Annie thought back; *"I told you that I had senses like a Bat."*

Once inside the cave which was also pitch black they felt much safer and as they listened to the heavy rain falling outside, Egbert reached out and pulled the cover over the door and the bush, which had already sprung back made the entrance to the cave almost impossible to see for anybody looking from the outside. The rain continued to fall but the sky started to lighten and the world was no longer quite as dark or as scary. Annie moved towards the back of the cave and Egbert moved the cave entrance cover slightly so that he could just see out, he looked up to the hotel car park and he saw that the lights had come back on, the car park had emptied apart from two cars; his own car and another dark-coloured car, which looked to have two people sat inside it, he couldn't see the men, but he could see what appeared to be lit cigarettes that shone more brightly as they were sucked. He also looked up towards the sky and he could see that the moon and the stars had reappeared; it was just as if somebody had switched them back on. He watched for a while longer and saw two fire engines arrive at the front of the hotel, they had obviously been alerted by the alarm that Egbert had set off, and they were only there for a few minutes the manager must have explained that the alarm had gone off by accident and that they were not needed. As the fire engines left, the two people in the dark car also left the car park and drove down Hanging Stones Lane to the car park belonging to the rocks. They were now parked less than 100 metres away from their cave. Egbert knew that these people were his enemy and he did not like them being so close, but he felt that for now they were in a good place and that they would not be easy to find. Egbert securely put the cover over the cave opening and he went towards the back of the cave, Annie was at the back of the cave which was a good 20 metres from front to back, it bent around to the left and at the back of the cave there was good standing room with it being about two metres high, better than at the front of the cave where it was only about one metre high and about the same width. The cave opening was smaller, but it had still been big enough for them both to crawl through. At the back of the cave Annie had lit a candle which looked to have been there for some time, it was in fact almost 30 years old; Annie had taken a few boxes from the Unit and left them there when she had found the cave all those years ago. She had also taken boxes of matches, string, paper and pencils, knives and forks and spoons from the kitchen and a few plates and cups, she had made it a home from home. Not everything though was 30 years old; Annie had obviously been back a few times over the years and taken blankets and cushions, as well as some tins of food and bottled water, she had made this place her own little hideaway. Egbert looked at Annie: she was small and slim and physically she didn't look very strong, but he admired her spirit. He guessed she hadn't changed that much in all of these years and even though they were still in serious danger, he was glad that he was with her. He allowed himself a smile and then thought to himself that he might feel a bit safer if they also had his cousin John sharing the cave, John had been a good Rugby League player and knew how to look after himself, he could do with his cousin John right now. Annie was looking tired and it was no wonder, crawling through the undergrowth and then running in the dark for 150 metres would tire anybody out. Egbert suggested to Annie that she should lie down and get some sleep and that he would keep watching from the front of the cave. He said that he would wake her if anything happened. Annie smiled and she gladly agreed, she lay down on a blanket over a flat rock and rested her head on a cushion, Egbert then covered her with a couple of blankets; he couldn't resist it and he leaned over and kissed her forehead, she looked up at him and smiled and said, "Thank you for caring and for looking after me, I am not used to it."

Egbert smiled back and Annie soon closed her eyes and went to sleep. Egbert had lots of thoughts about the day most of which he couldn't answer. *"What had happened to the SIS, where were they? Who was it that was trying to take them? Who was behind them being taken? How much did his father know about Annie, it seemed that there might be more than he had been previously aware of? How lucky they were that the storm came when it did and how the hell are we going to get out of this mess?"* Egbert for once was alone with his thoughts as he sat and kept a watch out of the covered cave entrance.

Annie only slept for a couple of hours and then she woke up and went to the front of the cave where Egbert was, she asked Egbert if he wanted to try and sleep for a while, but Egbert said; "I am ok, I think my adrenalin is on overdrive, those people are still in the car in the car park below, and I guess that they are sat planning what they will do next."

Annie looked at Egbert and she said, "What are we going to do?"

Egbert could tell that Annie was worried and he replied, "We can't stay here for ever, I need to make contact with the SIS to let them know where we are, the trouble is I left my mobile phone in the Jag up at the hotel, I need to try and get it."

Although Annie was worried, she didn't want Egbert taking any risks and she responded, "That is risky, how will you get out of the cave without them seeing you, and it is a long way up to the hotel car park?"

Egbert smiled and then replied; "Well, it is still dark so that will give me some cover, does the cave go any further back Annie, maybe there is another opening?"

Annie replied; "It does, but it gets very small, maybe I could squeeze through and see how far it goes."

Egbert knew that Annie was trying to help, but he replied, "This one is my job; I want you to stay safe in here."

Annie reluctantly agreed and Egbert pushed the cover to one side and he crawled out of the cave and continued to take the long crawl up towards his car, Annie pulled the cover back and watched Egbert slowly crawling through the undergrowth of Ilkley Moor, towards where his car was parked. She knew it would take him a while and she just hoped that he would not take any risks.

A Call for Back Up

Egbert and Aivars sat in their car smoking their cheap Latvian cigarettes and they were wondering what they would do next. Ivan asked Aivars, "Did you see anything before you came back to the car?"

Aivars replied, "No, but they can't have got far, they would have been close to the ground and moving slowly I guess; they wouldn't have risked standing in case they were seen. The only time they would have stood up was when it went dark, if I was them I would have made my way up into the rocks and found somewhere to hide, everywhere else is too open. They are probably within spitting distance of where we are right now."

Ivan thought for a few moments and then he replied, "You should call Hanif and tell him we need some more of his boys to help us search this area, we need to find them soon before the British work out what is happening, once they catch up with Ahmed they will start to back-track on the tracking signal and they will be on their way to us."

Aivars nodded and took out his mobile phone and made the call. Hanif looked at his mobile and saw it was Aivars and pressed to accept the call. "Aivars, I trust that you are calling to tell me that the mission has been successful."

Aivars answered, "Not yet, we have dealt with the British government security, but the Professor and the woman have escaped, we are sure that they are close by and that they are hiding."

Hanif was not happy with Aivars response and he replied, "You fool, let me speak with Mohammed."

Aivars replied; "I can't Hanif, unfortunately he was killed by the British."

There was a short silence and Hanif said, "Are there any of my men still alive?"

Aivars then explained, "Yes Ahmed is driving away with the tracker device so that the British think that he is the Professor and the woman. The team that dealt with the observation vehicle are all ok as far as we know."

Hanif thought for a moment and then replied, "Ok, leave it with me I will get back to you soon."

Hanif ended the call and then knew that he had to call his contact acting on behalf of his paymaster. He called the number and it was answered in the disguised voice, he couldn't tell whether he was speaking to a woman or a man and the voice said, "Has everything gone to plan?"

Hanif responded, "No, we have lost some good men and we haven't caught the professor and the woman yet."

The voice then said slowly, "Then what you are telling me is that you have failed?"

Hanif started to feel nervous, but replied; "We believe that we are close, we have eliminated the British agents and the Professor and the woman are hiding close to where my men are, we just haven't found them yet, but we will and then everything will be back on track."

The voice answered; "Then you are in luck, because I happen to know within a few feet exactly where they are. When the woman was in hospital, a small microchip was placed at the back of her ear, a very small chip, smaller than those which are used on pets, her movements can be tracked, give me one moment."

The voice looked at the PC screen and then entered the appropriate code and the chip transmitter came up on the screen, Annie was in the middle of the rocks at the Cow and Calf, on Ilkley Moor the voice then said, "Tell your men that they will find them in the rocks, where they are hiding, the chip is accurate to within around 10 feet, so they will need to search a 20 feet radius, do you think they can manage that?"

Hanif confirmed, "Yes, we will get on it."

The voice then replied, "I will text you the co-ordinates, now find them and get this job finished."

Hanif received the co-ordinates and looked at them on Google Earth, he then called Aivars and explained to him roughly where the Professor and Annie were hiding. He asked, "Now Aivars, do you think you can find them without me sending any more of my men to get killed?"

Aivars replied, "Yes, we will find them."

Aivars turned to Ivan and told him what had been said and then they got out of their car, Aivars was carrying his handgun and Ivan had his handgun in his waistband and his hunting knife in his right hand. They started to walk up through the car park and towards the centre of the rocks, exactly in a line to where the cave was located.

Transport

Charlie walked into the driveway of the farmhouse and hoped that he wouldn't be heard by dogs or set off any security alarms or lighting; he did not have time to be subtle, he just needed transport and he needed it quickly. He walked over to the silver Shogun parked outside of the house and he tried the driver's door which opened. He looked to see if the keys were in the ignition, but although the people round here were trusting, they were not that trusting. Charlie got into the driver's seat and he loosened the starter wires under the dashboard and then he joined them together to complete a circuit and the car noisily came to life, he selected first gear and took off the handbrake and he was on the move, he checked his rear mirror and there were no lights that came on in the house and he felt relieved, he was on his way and hopefully would soon catch up with the Professor and Annie. Charlie drove along until he came to a crossroad, left, right or straightforward, which way should he go? He decided that if somebody was taking a direct route to somewhere the guess for going straightforward had to be the favourite one, so he went straight across the junction and on the way towards Ilkley. He checked his mobile phone and he had a signal, he pressed the call button and Joanne answered.

Charlie then said; "Joanne, it has been a fuck up, I am the only one left and so far I have not been able to make any contact with the observation vehicle."

Joanne asked; "What happened, Charlie?"

Charlie replied; "We were compromised Joanne, a vehicle full of Asians got between us and the Professor's car and then stopped suddenly our vehicle shunted into them, we couldn't get past because the road was to narrow; Richard got out to talk to them, they were all suffering from whiplash, holding their necks in agony and it looked like a typical insurance fraud set up. Poor Richard didn't have a chance they took him down and then all hell broke loose, we took a few of them out, but then one of their guys put a shot through our radiator and shredded our tyres with his automatic. He and his mate then drove off leaving one of their guys behind, but we couldn't go anywhere as he had a good position and he had us pinned down; our vehicle was fucked and we just had to take his fire until he ran out, but it didn't look like that would happen anytime soon. I tried to get behind him while Bill covered me, but he got Bill and then I just had to wait for my chance and hope that he didn't get me before I got him. He give me my chance, he put his head a bit too high above the wall he was hiding behind and he got me in my shoulder, but I pinned him in his head and that was it game over. After I got him, I went back to our car and tried the radio, but then the other Asian came back with a big guy; he wasn't Asian he looked to be Eastern European, but I didn't get a close look at him, they loaded our car up with the bodies then and pushed it into the lake, I didn't see the Asian again, but the big guy got back into their car and then he drove off, the same way that he had come from. There was nothing I could do Joanne, I was short on ammo, but I have managed to get some wheels and I am on my way to try and find them."

Joanne had listened and taken some notes and then she replied; "Charlie, it's ok you did what you could and we are pretty certain that the Professor and Annie are safe, in fact we are tracking them along the M62 towards Hull as we speak."

Charlie was puzzled by Joanne's comment and he said, "That can't be right, why would they go towards Ilkley and then towards Hull, they could have picked up the M62 much easier from where Annie lives?"

Joanne replied; "I don't know Charlie, but we have a couple of teams not far away from the car now, so we will soon have a better idea."

Charlie thought about what Joanne was telling him and then he replied, "I am going to continue on this road for a bit to see if I can see anything, they had a big Range Rover so I will look out for that, I will call in if there is anything to report."

Joanne replied; "Ok Charlie, have a look round and then report back in an hour."

Charlie replied, "Will do, Joanne."

The call ended and Charlie reached into the glove compartment. He found a first aid kit and applied some antiseptic over his shoulder wound, which stung like hell, but he knew it was worth the pain. Charlie continued to drive along the country lane towards Ilkley.

Ahmed was driving along the M62 and heading East towards Hull and he was thinking about what he had been told to do by the Russian, which was to use his gun, but he was thinking that the main point of the plan was to confuse anybody tracking him for as long as possible and that for him to die in a gun battle to do this seemed to be a waste and he was sure that it was not what God would want. God would want his death to be for a more glorious cause. Ahmed decided that this was not his day to die; he had watched Aivars connect the tracking device on his vehicle and he heard Aivars say that it had battery back-up. Ahmed decided that somebody else could take the tracker to its final destination and he pulled off the Motorway into a Service Area at Ferrybridge; he looked around and he saw exactly what he was looking for, it was a HGV with Dutch licence plates, it was probably on its way to Hull for the ferry across to Holland. Ahmed parked next to it and within a few minutes the driver came out of the services carrying a large coffee, Ahmed was stood against his Range Rover having a cigarette and as the driver got into his cab and started the engine, Ahmed walked to the back of the vehicle and as calm as you like tied the tracker to the door handles. The HGV drove off and Ahmed smiled as it disappeared into the distance, he got back into the Range Rover and was happy that quite soon he would be at home with his lovely wife and their children, when he had set off the previous day he did not know whether he would ever see them again, he joined the M62 and went in the opposite direction to the HGV and the tracker.

Annie in Hiding

Annie was still looking out of the cave entrance, she could no longer see Egbert but she hoped that he was safe and that he was close to his car by now, but then suddenly she did see something, she saw two men from the car that was parked in the Rocks car park walking towards her, she initially felt like screaming, but she gathered herself and she watched them as they walked; they were not looking straight at her, their eyes were scanning the area, they were not sure where she was and they were looking for her. They were 15 to 20 metres away and they startled circling the area as if they knew she was somewhere close by, but how could they know that, had they caught Egbert and had he told them? She tuned into their minds; first the one from the photograph of, he was concentrating and shining his torch, all she picked up from him was; *"They would be hiding in something big enough to conceal them, so it would be a tree or a cave or behind the stones or they would be lying flat to the ground and trying to cover themselves with the vegetation, come on Aivars, think and see them."*

He was completely focussed but Annie noticed that he did think "they" as opposed to "her." Which meant he thought that she and Egbert were still together and that meant that Egbert was safe and that this may work in their favour, because it could give Egbert time to get some help. Annie then tuned into the other man's mind; this was the man she had tuned into before, when she had first sensed trouble and then let Egbert listen in through her mind. *"Where are they, I have a good mind to kill them anyway for causing me this trouble, but they are wanted alive, so I will keep them alive for now, how would I hunt them if they were wild boar back in the forests in Latvia? They would be hiding and then they would come out into the open and try to drive their tusk into my leg, I should hunt these people like I hunt the wild boar. Get down on the ground look for clues, any footmarks in the wet ground, these would be recent since the rain, is there any smell of perfume from the woman or aftershave from the man?"*

As Annie watched Ivan crouched down and he was shining his torch and then he shouted to Aivars; "They came this way, there is a print from the woman's shoe and one close to it from the man, they were both running so they hit the ground heavier and it is sunken into the ground more. We are close to them; I will smell them soon, just like I do with the wild boar."

Ivan knew that they were close so decided to speak loudly to try get some reaction from the quarry he was hunting, much as he would do to bring a wild boar out into the open. He spoke loudly; "Professor and Annie, come out now and you will not be harmed, we have people that want you, but they want you safe, so you can trust us. I have to tell you though that I am not a patient man and I will be paid as long as you are alive, so do not make me angry, because I will not kill you, but I will give you much pain."

Annie was listening and was wishing right now that Egbert was with her.

Ivan continued; "When I am at home in Latvia, I go hunting in the forests for wild boar, they are ferocious animals and they are frightened of nothing, I hunt the boar with a knife just like this." Ivan held the knife up and Annie saw its jagged blade glinting in the moonlight.

"When I am in the forest I get on my knees and I watch for the boar and I wait for it to charge me, they only have small legs carrying their big bodies and heavy skulls, but they are soft where their throat is. As the boar comes towards me with its small legs carrying it as fast as it can, it will keep lifting its head up as it moves its head from side to side, practicing for when it gets to me and it can slice its tusk into me and hurt me badly and if it does that the tables will be turned and it will have the advantage. So

I do not let that happen, I kneel and my knife handle rests on the ground as the boar comes towards me my timing has to be perfect, I watch for the boar to start to lift its head and with my two hands I swing the blade of my knife under its chin and slice through its throat and my long blade plunges into the boar's brain, one last twist and the animal falls to its side, dead and I will be eating wild boar for my evening meal, ha ha ha ha! I hope that I do not frighten you both, but you can see I know how to hunt and kill well and I will hunt and find you, it will be much better for you if I am not angry when I find you."

Annie thought about making a break out of the cave and running; it was not light yet and she might be able to get away and hide somewhere else, at least she might be able to buy Egbert some time so that he could get help, but then she thought that if she stayed there she would be safe and if she was quiet enough they still might not find her. The two men moved ever closer to the entrance of the cave and she heard Ivan say to Aivars.

"I can smell a candle burning, they are hiding in a cave and they have lit a candle."

Annie immediately went to the back of the cave and she covered the candle to extinguish the flame, she kept the candle covered to stop it giving off fumes, but had she done it quick enough before the two men could find her?

Ivan laughed and then said; "They are very close, because they heard me talking to you and they have put out the candle, I can't smell it any more, soon I will be able to hear them breathing or maybe the woman will cry and I will hear that, but we are very close, maybe within 2 metres."

Annie thought to herself; *"Fuck you, you big bastard you won't hear me crying and if you stick your head through this cave entrance you will get a rock smashed in your face."* Annie peeped through the opening and she could see the two men, who were only about two paces away; even if she wanted to run now she would have no chance. She thought about sending a telepathic message to

Egbert to tell him to come back, but she knew that it would only put Egbert in danger and she decided against it. Should she stay where she was, or surrender?

In the Car Park

Egbert had reached the roadside on the opposite side to the hotel car park and he could see his car parked where he had left it, he looked around but he could not see anybody around it, he looked down the road and up the road and again there was nobody in sight, should he keep low and crawl across the road or should he make a dash for it and get to his car. How should he play this, should he call Joanne or should he just go into the hotel and call the police, maybe he could drive down and ram into the car that was parked with the two men in it and he could get them to chase him to give Annie time to get away. Egbert decided that he wasn't trained for any of this and maybe the best thing to do would be to call Joanne and ask her. It was starting to get light if he didn't go soon he would have no protection from the darkness, so he stood up and he ran across the road, he was glad he had reversed into the parking space, at least the driver's door was away from the view of the two men. He took his keys from his pocket, but when he looked at the lock, he could see that they were not necessary, his car was already unlocked, he opened the door and the interior light went on, Egbert cursed himself; he shut the door and the light went off, but would the men have seen it in those few seconds whilst it was lit? It was too late now to worry about it, Egbert opened the glove compartment and he picked up his mobile phone and he checked it, it was still charged, but it said there were two missed calls, he checked and he saw that they were both from Joanne. Egbert was about to call Joanne when a vehicle pulled into the car park and was coming straight towards him, he couldn't tell what kind of car it was because it had its full beam pointing straight at him and it was blinding him. Egbert thought to himself, *"Shit, what do I do now, they have me?"* There was no point him trying to move his car because the vehicle was blocking his way. The next thing he knew his door opened and there was a man stood there pointing a gun at him.

The man said; "Come with me quickly."

Egbert didn't recognise the man, but he knew that he wasn't one of the two Eastern Europeans looking for him, he sounded to be English.

The man repeated; "Quickly Professor Egbert, into my car, now!"

Egbert did as he was told and the man drove out of the car park and along the road away from the rocks.

The man looked at Ebert and said; "I am Charlie Whitham; I am SIS and I am here to look after you."

Egbert read into the man's mind and he could tell he was telling the truth, he then said; "Thank Christ Charlie, but we need to go back for Annie, she is hiding in a cave, and there are two men in the Stones car park who are looking for us."

Charlie replied; "Don't worry we will go back for her, I want to see if the men follow us, were there just two of them?"

Egbert answered; "Yes, they both look to be Eastern European."

Charlie nodded and then said; "Ok, I am going to turn the car around now and head back towards Annie if those two bastards are following us I am going to ram them off the road." Charlie turned the car around and headed back down the road.

Egbert then asked, "Charlie how did you know it was me?"

Charlie smiled and then answered; "I didn't Professor, but I recognised your car, I have followed it enough times and it was either you or one of the bastards that is trying to take you, so I was either going to rescue you or blow his fucking head off."

It was Egbert's turn to smile and then he said, "In that case Charlie, I am glad you recognised me."

Annie Captured

The two Russians outside of the cave saw the car interior light momentarily go on in the car park of the hotel and they knew it was Egbert's car, but Ivan also knew that either the professor or Annie was close by as he had smelled the candle and noticed that the smell had gone when it was put out. He turned to Aivars and said; "We must find them now, or we must start firing bullets and try to kill them, but we need to get out of here soon." They then saw the headlights of another vehicle in the car park and saw the vehicle head off in the opposite direction. Ivan took out his gun and he fired off two shots into the stones and he shouted "COME OUT NOW OR YOU DIE."

The bullets were so close to the cave entrance Annie was sure that they knew where she was and she decided to move to the back of the cave, it was then that Ivan heard the faint sound of a footstep, he followed the sound and he found the cave entrance, he shouted into the cave; "COME OUT NOW, IF I HAVE TO COME IN THERE, YOU WILL BE SORRY."

Aivars told Ivan to step aside and he spoke in a quieter voice; "Miss Brown, come out now and we will not kill the Professor, we know that he has gone to his car, he cannot go anywhere because we have cut the tyres, he will be coming back to you, he may even be almost here by now and if he is we will kill him. If you come out now we will simply take you to our car and we will drive off leaving the Professor safe." Aivars had quickly worked out in his mind that the Professor was the most likely one to go for help and it was he who had switched on the car light; he didn't at this stage know who the other car belonged to, but he wanted to get away quickly in case it contained British agents. Aivars continued; "Miss Brown we know that you are in there and we will come in and when we do it will not be pleasant, my friend Ivan is not a gentleman like the Professor."

Annie read the mind of the bigger man and she knew that he certainly wanted to kill somebody, which was all he could think about; she could almost get high on his adrenalin. She read the mind of the other man and he did seem a lot calmer and he was thinking to himself; *"Please come out, there is no need to get hurt and I don't want to let this bastard loose on you, he is crazy and I am not sure I can control him."*

Aivars then said; "Miss Brown, you have 10 seconds and then Ivan is coming for you, one, two, three, four, five, six, seven, eight."

On eight Annie moved the heather to one side and stuck out her head she looked at the two men and half-spoke and half-sang, "Morning." It was Annie's way of dealing with the situation, she was never going to stop being Annie, even when she was in danger.

Ivan moved towards her and slapped her hard across her face and said; "You bitch, you have caused me a lot of trouble and I do not like your English humour, now get out here."

Annie was angry and her face stung from where Ivan had hit her, but she came out of the cave, glaring at him all the time as she came out through the entrance. She was well aware though that it was not a good idea to anger him more, she read his mind and it was filled with aggression and hatred.

Aivars turned on Ivan and said, "That is enough, she is not to be hurt, let's get her in the car and let's get out of here."

Ivan turned and growled, "The bitch deserved it, what about the Professor?"

Aivars replied; "Do you see him standing here, Ivan? No, and neither do I, we will take this woman now and if we get the chance we will take the Professor later, no doubt the gallant English gentleman will come to rescue her."

Ivan replied; "I am going to check inside the cave, just to make sure that he is not hiding like a coward inside it, hold the woman." With that Ivan shone his torch and went inside the cave, he looked around and was satisfied that the professor was not in there. Ivan turned around and emerged from the cave and said; "He is not there, I will take the woman to the car." Ivan took hold of Annie's hand and he part dragged her down the hill away from the stones and towards their car, he opened the boot and threw her into it, he fastened her hands and her feet and he also put the tape over her mouth. He then said, "Now bitch, you are not so funny now are you?"

Annie tried to kick out at the big Russian and she managed to catch him a glancing blow on the chest, but with her feet taped together she could not kick him with any force. Ivan was angry that this woman had dared to kick him and he clenched his fist and aimed a blow to her face, Annie saw the big man's right fist coming towards her and she instinctively turned her head away from it, she felt the blow on her right temple and she felt the immediate pain, but that was quickly followed by everything going dark as she became unconscious from the weight of the blow.

Aivars shouted at Ivan and said; "We are not supposed to hurt her, you idiot."

Ivan turned angrily towards to Aivars and replied; "No woman hits me and gets away with it; she will sleep for a while, but she will be ok, NOW DRIVE!"

Annie lay still in the boot of the car, for now she was blissfully unaware of anything that was happening.

The Drive to Bradford

They drove down Hanging Stones Lane towards Ilkley and Aivars turned to Ivan and said, "We will drive slowly and carefully back to the warehouse; I don't want to be stopped by any British police or because of any British agents that you failed to kill."

As they drove around the corner to where the Cow and Calf hotel was, Egbert noticed that the car was no longer in the Stones car park and he said; "Maybe they drove off when they saw your lights."

Charlie replied; "I doubt it, they have probably got Annie with them, but let's check the cave just in case."

The two men parked in the Stones car park and Egbert led the way to the cave, he was excited and hoped beyond hope that he was going to see Annie's smiling face, when they got there he could see that the door covering had been moved to one side and he knew immediately that they had taken her. He called out her name and he went inside the cave and called out again several times, but as he expected there was no reply he turned to Charlie and said; "You were right, she has gone, they didn't come towards us so they must be headed away from us and towards Ilkley, let's go."

They ran down the slope towards the car and quickly got back into it. Charlie started up and set off at speed, their tyres spinning on the surface of the car park, very quickly they were driving down Hanging Stones Lane on their way towards Ilkley. Charlie turned to Egbert and asked if he had his mobile phone and Egbert confirmed that he had, Charlie then asked Egbert to call Joanne and give her an update. Egbert took out his mobile and pressed the call button and then put the mobile phone on to loudspeaker. The phone at the other end rang twice and was then answered by Joanne who had recognised the number; "Egbert, are you alright?"

Charlie responded; "Joanne, I am fine, I am with Charlie, one of your agents; we are going after Annie, two men have got her."

Joanne asked, "Whereabouts are you Egbert?"

Egbert answered; "We are driving from the Cow and Calf Rocks towards Ilkley, it is the only way that they could have gone, we can't be too far behind them. They are in a black BMW saloon car Joanne, I am sorry I don't know the registration, I never got close enough to the car. Joanne, you are on loudspeaker; is there anything that you need to tell Charlie?"

Joanne replied, "Charlie, you need to call in once you have a visual on the BMW, do not get too close to it, but let me know where it is and I will get the local police to give you some back up."

Charlie nodded and then replied, "It is daylight now, so we should be able to see them fairly well from a distance, my guess is that they will either head towards Leeds or Bradford when they leaves Ilkley, but I am not sure about the police support, we don't want to spook them, we already know they are dangerous. Leave it with me Joanne, put the police on standby and I will let you know if and when we need them to get involved, do we have any more agents in this area?"

Joanne answered, "Not at the moment Charlie, we have two teams chasing the tracker which was on Egbert's car, but obviously I know now that it is a decoy. I will divert one of the teams to come and support you and the other car team can check out who is driving the vehicle with the tracker on it."

Charlie then said, "Ok Joanne, but remember it is Sunday morning and there will not be much traffic about yet, if all of a sudden there is a lot of activity, the bad guys will know we are on to them and they might panic. Joanne, one last thing, you could speak to the police and make sure they don't pull me in for borrowing this car, it would be the last thing we need."

Joanne then replied, "I will sort it, get Egbert to text me the vehicle details. I will let Mr Pilkington know what is happening and you take care, let me know as soon as you might need some assistance."

The call ended and Joanne then called one of the security team following the tracker to divert them back towards Charlie and Egbert and then she called James Pilkington.

Pilkington answered the call. "Joanne, what is happening?"

"Sir, Egbert is ok, he is with Charlie Whitham and they are trying to find the car that is carrying Annie, she has been taken by the Russians. I want to get the police involved, Sir."

Pilkington replied sternly to Joanne; "No, I have told you that I do not want them any more involved than they are already, we can handle this. Have the Police had any success on their house-to-house activity in finding where the two men are basing themselves?"

Joanne knew it was pointless arguing her point with Pilkington and she replied, "No Sir, but to be fair to them, it is like looking for a needle in a haystack."

Pilkington was not in the mood for excuses and he responded, "Don't stick up for them, they have failed and I can't afford for them to mess this up."

Joanne then told Pilkington, "I have diverted one of the teams following the tracker back towards Bradford, it is obvious now that the tracker is a decoy."

Pilkington seemed to calm down and said, "That should be enough, get me a helicopter fuelled and a pilot to take me up North, I need to make sure that this is handled properly, I will leave now for the aerodrome and it should be ready for when I get there. It will only take me 15 to 20 minutes and then the flight north should be less than one hour, meet me at the aerodrome and bring your weapon, you might need it.

The call ended and Joanne immediately arranged for the helicopter, she then went to her safe and took out the pistol that she had so far only used at the shooting range. She got into her car and travelled the short journey to meet up with Pilkington at the aerodrome.

Pilkington started to get himself ready and he took out his shoulder holster and strapped it in place, he then placed his pistol in the holder, he had not used a weapon in quite a while, but he was ready for whatever the day might bring.

In Pursuit

Charlie sped down Hanging Stones Lane towards Ilkley, the Shogun vibrated as the tyres went over the cattle grid as they left the moor. As they entered the town they saw the railway station on their right and a number of retail stores as well as the customary charity shops in front of them. Charlie turned right after the station towards the traffic lights where he knew he would be turning right towards Leeds and Bradford.

Egbert asked him, "How do you know we are going the right way?"

Charlie replied; "I don't, but on the basis that we came from the Bradford direction yesterday, I think this is the way they would go. I am just hoping that we get a visual on them soon. If I were them I would be driving steady, so as not to draw any attention to myself; the last thing they need is to be pulled over by the police for speeding."

Egbert concentrated and he tried to communicate with Annie: *"Come on Annie, are you ok?"*

"Come on, think back to me, Annie give me a clue where you are?"

Despite Egbert's efforts there was no answer and their only option was to continue driving along the route towards Bradford. Charlie was driving faster than the speed limit, but he knew that he had to try and make up ground on the black BMW, he was only hoping that they were being sensible and also that there weren't any over-zealous police officers about, he knew that he could show them his ID card and they would let him proceed, but that would still delay them. Charlie was beginning to have doubts that they were on the right road, but was not sure what his other options were, he could turn around or head towards Leeds but he couldn't be sure if it was the right choice or not, he decided to give it another 5 minutes and then he would call Joanne to get some police assistance.

Annie started to come round and her head was throbbing; she remembered being manhandled into the boot of the car and also the big Russian hitting her, she was feeling angry but also she was feeling fairly helpless with her feet and hands fastened. Annie tuned in to the two men in the front of the vehicle and firstly she read Aivars' thoughts; *"This man is an animal, he would have killed her back there, I thought he was a professional; but I think he has lost control, the first chance I get I will speak to Hanif and ask if I can finish this job alone and then I can put a bullet in his head."*

She then listened into the thoughts of Ivan; *"If not for me this job would fail, Aivars is not tough enough. I will get the woman and the Professor to where they need to be and if I need to teach them lessons along the way then I will, the woman is just a woman and I will fuck her and tame her before we get to where we are going and the Professor will not be so smart, when he feels the power of a proper man. I know that he will come for her, but when I finish with him, he will be like a lamb and then Hanif or whoever he is working for can do what they want with him and the woman."*

Annie already knew that the big man was an animal and reading his thoughts had not changed her mind; she now knew that the other man would also kill, but she decided that she would rather he was around than the big man. Annie started to concentrate to try and send a message to Egbert, she hoped that he was not too far away; *"Egbert, I am here, can you sense me."*

Immediately the thoughts came into Egbert's mind and he thought back; *"I have you Annie, are you alright?"*

Annie replied with her thoughts, but it was probably not what Egbert was expecting; *"Egbert, I am fucking angry, a week ago you were not in my life and now all of this has happened, the big bastard hit me hard enough to put me to sleep and I am hurting, I am all trussed up like a*

Christmas Turkey, what the fuck is going on? Who the fuck are these people and where are these fucking secret agents that are supposed to be looking after us, what do I pay my taxes for?"

Although the situation was serious, Egbert had to smile, this was the first time that he had been told off telepathically, he then replied, *"Annie, I am so sorry, but everything I have told you is true, I am with an agent now and we are coming after you. You have to believe me, we are going to get you out of this, but we need your help."*

Annie felt calmer and she responded; *"I believe you, but what the fuck. Sorry Egbert, I know you are trying to help me, what do you want me to do?"*

Egbert thought back and he answered Annie's question; *"Can you use your sonar skills and tell me where you are?"*

Annie thought a reply, *"I wish that I could, but I am inside this boot and I can't sense anything through it, neither could a bat, if it was trapped inside here."*

Egbert was desperate to get some helpful knowledge and he thought of another question for Annie; *"Have you any idea at all where you are headed."*

The BMW started to slow down and Annie could feel it as it made her body roll towards the front of the vehicle, she sent back a thought to Egbert; *"Just a minute, we are slowing down."* The car slowed down and then stopped at traffic lights; Annie tuned into Aivars' mind, he was looking at a sign and he was thinking, Annie read Aivars' thoughts; *"Left for Leeds, right for Bradford, right it is."*

Annie immediately sent Egbert a message: *"I don't know where we are, but it must have been a junction with a choice for Leeds or Bradford, we are going to Bradford."*

Egbert looked at Charlie and told him, "I am in contact with Annie, we are on the right road, they are going to Bradford."

Charlie looked back and said, "How the bloody hell do you do that?"

Egbert smiled and replied, "It is a long story, I will tell you when we get out of all this. Annie is tied up in the boot of the car."

Charlie then asked, "What else can she tell us?"

Egbert once again sent a message to Annie; *"Do you have any other of your extra senses that will help us to find you Annie?"*

Annie sent a thought response; *"Wait, let me concentrate, they are listening to some Eastern European rubbish on their music system, it probably won the Eurovision Song Contest at some time, I need to push it out of my mind. I am not getting anything different, the driver is concentrating on driving and the other one is humming the song in his mind. Wait, there are a lot of people nearby, I can hear their thoughts, there are too many to focus on, but now I can hear engines and I can smell rubber, it could be an airport, yes, I can smell rubber a plane has just landed. Egbert, I am near an airport."*

Egbert sent a thought back, "Well done, I know exactly where you are Annie, don't worry we are not far behind you, it is Leeds Bradford airport."

Egbert told Charlie what had been communicated and they both felt some relief, Charlie told Egbert to call Joanne again and put the call on loudspeaker. Egbert called Joanne and when the call was answered Charlie said; "Joanne, it's Charlie, they are on their way to Bradford, but I don't know exactly where to, do you have any ideas?"

Joanne replied; "Based on the house-to-house search I suspect that it is close to the centre, but I don't know exactly where."

Charlie then continued; "Ok, Egbert is in contact with Annie via some mind thing that they have going on, so all being well we should know soon. How far away is the other security team?"

Joanne answered; "They are not far away at all, they are parked up just off the M62 at Chain Bar, so that they can go to either Bradford or Leeds; I will tell them to head for Bradford Centre. Myself and Mr Pilkington are on our way to you too, we are in a helicopter heading north, we should be there in around 30 to 40 minutes, as soon as you have a destination let us know and don't go in before you advise us, we need to keep both the Professor and the woman safe."

Pilkington looked at Joanne and said; "Joanne, I am taking over the operation now, you have done well, but it is ultimately my neck on the line, we will leave the security car where it is parked near the M62 for now, I don't want too many people involved it will increase the danger for Egbert and Annie."

Joanne was concerned by Pilkington's response and she said, "But Sir, that means that there is just Charlie, you and I, surely we need some back-up?"

Pilkington was not happy that his authority was being questioned yet again, but he replied, "Charlie is a good agent, he will locate where they are going and once we know that we can decide if we need back-up or not, they won't be expecting us and we will have the element of surprise."

Joanne was still concerned and she asked, "But Sir, are you sure?"

Pilkington had had enough of Joanne questioning him and he firmly replied, "You insult me, I was doing this type of work while you were still feeding from your mother's breast, the three of us can easily take care of these two Russians; perhaps you are doubting yourself Joanne, perhaps this is all too much for you?"

Joanne was the one who now felt angry and she turned to Pilkington and said, "No Sir, I am not, but I want to put on record that I think you are making mistakes on this job, we should have back-up close by, that's all I am saying."

Pilkington dismissively replied, "Joanne, your point is noted, now just do as you are told and sit back and enjoy the ride, is this your first ride in a helicopter?"

Joanne, didn't even look at Pilkington, she was seething, he was deliberately trying to undermine her and make her feel like a child; she was aware of this technique from her psychology studies and she felt that something was not right, but she did not know what it was.

In View

It was only moments earlier that Egbert had been swapping thoughts with Annie and now he could see the airport on his left-hand side, Charlie accelerated and as the way was clear. He went through the traffic lights just as they were changing to red. They were driving down the hill from the traffic lights when they saw a black BMW turn right; they were not close enough to tell if it was the right BMW, but they were close enough to take a chance on it. They followed the car and then Charlie eased off the accelerator, he didn't want to get too close to the BMW, he wanted to get to wherever they were going without any conflict. Charlie was concerned that they only had one gun between them and that even then they were low on ammunition and his problem was that he did not know what kind of firepower the two men had.

Egbert sent Annie a message, *"Annie, we are right behind you don't worry, I can see your black BMW in front of us, just stay calm."*

Annie replied, *"Don't worry, I am calm, but watch these two, they have no fear of killing, especially the big one."*

Charlie eased off the accelerator even more and then dropped back further so that they could only just see the BMW. Aivars looked in his rear view mirror and saw the vehicle behind them, but it was too far away to be of any threat, Aivars was confident that they were not being followed and even if they were it was just one car and it probably contained the Professor, which meant that they would get a chance to capture him.

Egbert asked Charlie, "What is the plan, why are we dropping back, we are so close; can't we try and rescue Annie now?"

Charlie could understand Egbert's concern and he replied, "It is too risky, I don't have enough ammunition and I don't know what weapons they have got, if it is anything like the Asians that stopped us they will be well-armed, this way we can follow them to their base and then we can call for help and that way there is more chance of us getting Annie back safely."

Egbert was happy to go along with Charlie, he seemed to know what he was doing. "Ok, you're the boss, where do you think they are going?"

Charlie responded to Egbert's question. "We think that they have a base near the centre of Bradford, probably somewhere that is quiet so that their comings and goings won't have been noticed. There are plenty of buildings like that near the centre of Bradford, there are plenty of businesses that suffered through the recession and plenty of empty buildings, we will know soon, we only have a few miles to go, before we get to the centre."

Egbert then asked, "What do we do once we get there, Charlie?"

Charlie answered, "We observe and then we report back to Joanne and Pilkington and then we wait for the cavalry to arrive. I have been involved in lots of situations like this, don't worry, all will be good."

The rest of the journey went smoothly, Charlie stayed well back and Aivars did not alter his driving pattern, he remained confident that he was in control. Eventually they arrived in Thornton Road, Bradford and it was about half a mile from the centre. The BMW signalled left to turn into an old transport depot. Following the turn Aivars drove up to the large door of the warehouse where he stopped and then he turned to Ivan and said, "Go and check it out Ivan and make sure that we have not had any uninvited guests, I will keep the engine running just in case."

Ivan went inside with his knife in one hand and his gun in the other, he looked around and saw that nothing had been touched, the only difference from when they had last been there was the rancid smell from the decaying bodies of the two young girls hidden under the sheet towards the back of the warehouse. Ivan went back to the large warehouse doors and opened them so that Aivars could drive inside; he then closed the doors once the car was inside. Ivan went to the back of the BMW and he roughly grabbed hold of Annie and he pulled her out of the boot, he tore off the tape from her mouth and freed her legs, but for now he left her hands fastened behind her. Ivan pointed to the sheets and he laughed; "If you want, English bitch you can go and lie with those other two English bitches under that sheet, or you can do as you are told." Ivan sat her in the chair next to the desk and fastened her hands to the desk securely.

The rancid smell filled Annie's nostrils and she felt sick, but she knew that there was nothing she could do for the time being. Annie sat there watching the two men who were busy loading some boxes at the back of a removal wagon, she decided it was a good time to send Egbert a message; *"Egbert, I am inside an old warehouse, are you nearby?"*

Egbert sent his thoughts back to Annie; *"Yes Annie, we are parked at the entrance to the depot, what have they done and are there just the two of them?"*

Annie responded; *"My hands are still tied Egbert, but my legs and my mouth are free, there are just the two of them, they are loading some boxes into the back of an old removal wagon, they both look to have a pistol and the big man has a long knife in his belt. Egbert, they have already killed some girls in here and their bodies are under a sheet, there is blood on the floor and it stinks."*

Egbert was concerned to hear that the two Russians had already killed but he responded; *"Ok, just do as they tell you for now and don't take any risks."*

Egbert turned to Charlie and told him what Annie had communicated to him. Charlie said that he would update Joanne. Charlie took out his mobile and called her, "Joanne, we are at an old transport depot on Thornton Road, Bradford, it is only about half of a mile from the centre just on the left, there is an old sign saying Baldwin and sons Transport Ltd. We are parked at the entrance. There is a large warehouse in the yard and they have driven their BMW into it and then closed the doors behind them, Annie is safe, but has her hands fastened her. There are only the two men, but it looks like they have already killed two girls in the warehouse. Annie says she can smell the decaying flesh. The fact that they have killed makes them more dangerous, because they have little to lose."

Joanne passed the information to Pilkington and then she asked, "Charlie, do we know what weapons they have?"

Charlie answered; "It sounds like they both have a pistol and the big man has a knife, can you send the other car over and we can go in and finish this?"

Joanne then looked at Pilkington and asked; "Sir, Charlie has the situation under control, he is asking for the other car to join him so that they can go in."

Pilkington responded; "Not yet; is there anywhere that we can land the helicopter near the warehouse?"

Joanne asked Charlie the question and he confirmed that they would be able to land in the transport yard right outside the building.

Pilkington nodded and then said, "Ok, call the other car and get it to the entrance of the depot, they must make sure that the entrance is blocked, and then tell them to standby until I give them orders. Tell Charlie to go to the warehouse and see what he can see, but not to go in until we get there, we are going to land in the yard. Tell him to leave Egbert in the car, we need him safe."

Joanne told Charlie what had been said.

Charlie asked, "Joanne, why don't we get the other car inside as well, we will easily overpower them?"

Joanne replied to the question, "Mr Pilkington thinks that it will cause too much of a risk for Annie, he says that we have to do it his way."

Charlie had been around long enough to know not to argue with a senior officer's instructions and he responded; "Ok Joanne, I understand".

Joanne was not happy, she could tell that Charlie thought that the other team should be brought in, but for now she had no choice but to follow Pilkington's orders.

Whilst at the back of the removal wagon Aivars turned to Ivan and he said, "We need to be quick, there was a car behind us for some of the way and we may have been followed, it could be the agent who you did not kill and maybe the Professor, let us move quickly and get away from here."

Ivan looked angrily at Aivars and replied, "I did not fail to kill anybody, it was Mohammed who failed and he has paid the price. I am ready for anybody who comes, don't you worry about that."

The Rescue Attempt

Charlie turned to Egbert and told him to stay where he was, but Egbert refused and said that he was going with him. Charlie said, "Egbert, you don't even have a weapon, you will be a danger to both me, you and probably Annie."

Egbert looked at Charlie and he replied, "Don't forget, I can communicate with Annie and that could give us an edge, I will keep out of the way."

Charlie thought for a moment; he did not want to go against Pilkington's orders, but Egbert had made a good point. Charlie replied; "Ok, make sure that you do, but you must do whatever I tell you, or you might get us all killed."

The two of them got out of the parked car and walked up the driveway into the transport yard, where they could easily see the warehouse building, they hid behind a skip while Charlie worked out a strategy for the rescue. Charlie asked, "Egbert, can you check with Annie what is happening inside?"

Egbert sent out a thought to Annie; *"Annie, has anything changed?"*

Annie thought back, *"No Egbert they are still at the back of the removal wagon, wait a minute, Egbert the big one is coming towards me, keep concentrating Egbert, keep tuned into my thoughts, you will hear what is said."*

Ivan was walking over to get her the loading of the truck was finished apart from Annie, he walked towards her with a sneering smile and said, "Now, English bitch we are about to leave, with or without your Professor. Maybe he has followed you, maybe he is a coward, because he has changed his mind and he is hiding, no matter, we have a little time and I think me and you can have some fun in the back of the wagon. Did you have sex yet with your Professor, he will be all gentle and kind like a woman, you should have sex with me, you can feel a real man inside you. It doesn't matter anyway bitch, because I am going to use you for my enjoyment; I only have to get you there alive, nobody said I can't fuck you. You can scream bitch, because nobody can hear you."

Annie said nothing; she just continued to concentrate so that Egbert could hear the conversation via her mind, all the time though she looked at Ivan angrily. Ivan cut her hands free from the desk and then pulled her up from the chair and he spun her around, he held his left arm around her throat and with his right hand he took his knife from his belt and he cut through the tape holding her hands fastened. He tried to lift up her skirt with his knife blade, but Annie decided that enough was enough and she stamped down hard on his foot; Ivan released his grip around her throat, just enough for Annie to wriggle free.

Egbert felt all of this through tuning in to Annie and he turned to Charlie and said; "Charlie, I am going in, the bastard is going to rape her."

Charlie urgently replied; "Wait, Pilkington and Joanne will be here soon, I can see the lights of their helicopter up above."

Egbert had though made up his mind and he then said; "There is no time Charlie, I have to go now, you wait if you want to." Egbert ran towards the warehouse door, he slowed before he got there to pick up an iron crowbar that lay on the ground. He knew that he needed some help against this big angry man. Egbert ran and as he did he thought to himself; *"I wish my cousin John was with me, he would know exactly what to do with this crowbar, he has always been able to look after himself, I wish he was in my corner right now."* Egbert reached the large door with the small door within it and he rushed in. He looked at Ivan and he said, "Did you wonder where I was you big bastard."

Ivan turned and saw Egbert stood there with the iron bar in his right hand. Ivan shouted to Aivars, "Come and get the woman Aivars, I am going to have some fun."

Aivars shouted back, "Ivan remember that they are both wanted safe and sound when they reach their final destination and the Professor will not be here alone."

Ivan shouted back to Aivars, "I am simply going to remove that iron bar from his hand, I will leave enough of him alive to keep our paymaster happy, you get the woman and watch out for anybody else that might come in."

Aivars was well-aware that there would be other help coming for the Professor and he shouted, "Be quick you fool he is not alone, I can hear a helicopter landing, we need to get out of here." Aivars grabbed hold of Annie and dragged her towards the removal wagon, he had his right hand around her throat, and he clumsily threw her into the back of the lorry and closed the door from the outside. He then aimed his pistol towards the door in readiness, for what he was sure would follow.

Ivan walked towards Egbert, he did not even bother to take his knife out of his belt, as he got closer Egbert raised the metal bar with his left arm so it was above his head. The Russian watched the iron bar and he waited for it to come towards him; at that stage he would grab it and take it from Egbert and then he would give Egbert a taste of the crowbar. Instead Egbert swung his other arm with all his might and he felt his right fist connect with the big man's jaw; the force of the blow made the Russian stagger backwards. Egbert then transferred the iron bar to his right hand and he brought it down towards the Russian's head, but just in time the Russian moved his head to the right and the metal bar hit him on his left shoulder. The Russian grimaced with the pain but he still moved and danced towards Egbert, he was angry and he was going to make Egbert pay for putting the pain into his shoulder. All of a sudden a shot rang out, it was Charlie who had come in from the side of the warehouse through a broken window, his shot just missed Ivan, but it alerted Aivars to the fact that there was somebody else in the warehouse. Aivars turned quickly towards Charlie and he fired, but Charlie was too quick for him and dived to the ground for cover.

Charlie returned fire, but this time it was Aivars that was too quick; Charlie knew that he had little ammunition left and that he was now at the other man's mercy, he needed to quickly find something which he could use as a weapon. Charlie stayed hidden behind some empty wooden crates, but Aivars also remained hidden from Charlie. Aivars was hiding because he didn't know how much ammunition the British agent had and Charlie was hiding because he had only a few rounds to fight back with.

Meanwhile Egbert backed away from Ivan, he was trying to line up one blow with the crowbar to take the Russian out, as Egbert wheeled around to his right the Russian circled towards him.

Behind the boxes Charlie looked urgently for any other weapon that he could use, now that he was low on ammunition and he saw a hammer, which he pulled close to him with his right leg. Aivars saw the right leg stretch out and he fired a bullet into it. Charlie groaned with pain as he felt the hot bullet enter his right leg. It was agony and he already knew that the bullet had shattered his bone. All that he could do now was to wait for the other man to approach him and do whatever he could with the hammer; the fight had suddenly become very one-sided. Aivars waited and waited for Charlie to show himself, but without any success, so he slowly edged towards the injured man.

The fight between Egbert and Ivan continued, but Egbert had not been able to land the killer blow. The Russian took the knife from his belt and moved now confidently towards Egbert. Egbert swung the crowbar towards Ivan's knife to try and dislodge it from his hand but all that happened was a ringing noise caused by the two pieces of metal clashing together. When Egbert had swung the crowbar, he was then off-balance and the Russian saw his opportunity which he took; he lunged his knife at Egbert, but Egbert saw it coming and just in time he moved to the side to avoid it. As he moved to the side he brought the crowbar crashing down on Ivan's head, it caught him heavy and the big Russian fell to the floor.

Egbert aimed a kick at the Russians head to make sure that he was out and he connected hard; the Russian did not move. Egbert was riding high now on adrenalin, but then he heard another shot and felt the heat of a bullet close to his right cheek, it had missed him by no more than an inch. Aivars had seen what had happened to Ivan and he knew that he had to take control of the situation, if that meant killing the Professor, then so be it. Egbert did not need to feel a second shot come close to him, he dived behind the desk where Annie had been sat, before he had arrived, he needed time to think out what he could do. Egbert thought about moving to pick up Ivan's gun, but each time he moved Aivars fired and pinned him down. Egbert decided to stay where he was until help arrived.

Aivars had not received any fire from Charlie for a few minutes now and he confidently moved out from his hiding place and walked towards the agent who was lying behind the boxes; the agent was a sitting duck and he knew that his enemy knew it. Charlie had managed to get himself up into a seated position and he held the hammer in his right hand in readiness and his almost-empty gun in his left hand. Aivars stood with the boxes between him and the agent and he peered around the corner whilst giving the agent the smallest possible target, he saw that the agent still had his gun in his hand. Aivars looked behind him and although he could not see the Professor he fired a shot towards the desk just in case. The shot was just above the desk, but it was enough to make Egbert keep his head down. It was time for the agent to die and Aivars moved around the boxes with his pistol pointing at Charlie. He said to Charlie, "You are a brave man and you are injured in your leg but you do not need to die, put down your weapons, you cannot have many bullets left and you cannot throw the hammer fast enough to hit me before I have fired at least two bullets into you. Why do you not have more people here, you are foolish if you thought you could beat us with just two men."

Charlie lifted and pointed his gun at Aivars when he heard a shot, at first he thought Aivars had fired at him, but then he realised that he had not been hit, Charlie fired and he hit Aivars in the chest. The Russian dropped to his knees in front of Charlie and then Charlie saw a large black hole with blood seeping out in the back of the Russian's skull as the Russian lay face down. He looked to the door and he saw the silhouette of a person, stood with their legs about the same width apart as their shoulders, he then realised that the person had the shape of a woman and her arms were outstretched in front of her in the classic pose of somebody firing a handgun at the shooting range. It was Joanne: she had just killed the man that was going to kill him, and the young rookie had saved Charlie's life.

Egbert came out from behind the desk and shouted to Joanne, "I am going to get Annie." Egbert ran over to the back of the removal wagon and he opened the doors and Annie was stood there, Egbert helped her down and then she said, "You took your time didn't you?" Then she put her arms around him and hugged him close.

Whilst they were hugging they heard the noise of somebody dropping to the ground and they both looked up, it was Joanne who lay on the ground, the big Russian had regained his consciousness and come up behind her and hit her with his large fist at the back of her head; she had immediately dropped to the ground unconscious.

Ivan saw the dead body of Aivars on the ground and the injured agent who was unable to move and he then looked at Egbert and Annie and he said, "So it is just you two and me now, and we are getting out of here before any more of your friends turn up."

Egbert looked back and said; "You are too late you bastard, my friends are already here, there is a helicopter outside and a car at the gate, you cannot get away."

Ivan had a confident smile on his face and he said; "You are wrong English, I can do anything if I have you two, they will not risk you coming to any harm."

Egbert let go of Annie and he turned his body full on towards Ivan and he said, "Well Russian bastard, come on then!" With that Egbert ran towards the big Russian and hit him with his shoulder right in the centre of the man's chest; this was one trick he had remembered from watching his cousin John. He took the wind out of the big man and the force of the charge even caused Ivan to drop his knife which had been in his right hand, Egbert did not want the knife anywhere near the big man so he kicked it away and towards Annie, who picked it up and held it in her two small hands. While Egbert was kicking the knife away it gave the Russian his chance— the Russian brought his big right hand down on Egbert's left cheek and Egbert stumbled, but remained on his feet. Egbert threw back a right fist of his own and hit the Russian on the side of his face, but this time the Russian did not even flinch. Egbert threw his head in the direction of the Russian and the head butt landed full on the Russians nose and Egbert felt the nose break under his forehead; this was another trick that his cousin John had taught him. The Russian swayed backwards, but brought his right boot into Egbert's groin area and Egbert collapsed to the ground in agony; this was the Russian's chance and he strode over to where Annie was kneeling, she looked to be kneeling half in prayer and half in meditation with her eyes closed.

The Russian mocked her. "Ah, ah, ah, bitch, you think if you close your eyes I will disappear, unfortunately for you it is not true, now give me the knife, I have decided that I don't need the Professor, he is too much trouble, but I still need you so hand it over." Ivan walked towards Annie and she never moved an inch, she did not reply, she just knelt there with the knife loosely in her hands, almost as if she did not have the strength to lift it.

The Russian was smirking and reached down to take it from her, when suddenly Annie's eyes opened wide and she held the knife in both hands with the blade pointing upwards, she threw the blade up with all her might and it struck the Russian under his throat, she carried on the action and pushed harder and then she turned the blade to the right. Annie shouted to the Russian, "Is this how you kill wild boar, you big Russian bastard? Annie moved to her side to avoid the Russian falling on her, but the Russian never answered, he was dead as soon as the blade sliced through his throat and went into his brain.

Egbert saw it happen from where he was laying on the floor and he could not believe that Annie would have had the strength to do it. He was amazed, but Annie had done it and surely now they were all safe.

Annie looked up to the corner of the warehouse as if she was looking to the heavens in thanks, but she saw what nobody else had noticed, a small bright light which almost immediately went out.

The Clean Up

Pilkington had been stood outside of the warehouse door with his pistol in his hand and at the ready to shoot any of the enemy who might emerge from the warehouse. He could hear that the sound of the battle inside the warehouse had stopped, but he was not sure what he would find inside, or in fact who would be left standing. As far as Pilkington was concerned he had followed the correct protocol and he had maintained a second wave of attack or defence, depending on which way the battle had gone. Pilkington called for the security car at the entrance of the drive to come into the yard and adopt a defensive position and he then moved forwards towards the big warehouse door; he slowly opened the small door within it and took a breath before he walked in. Pilkington had his pistol pointing in front of him and he was ready to fire, if he needed to. On entering the warehouse he saw Joanne lying on the floor, Egbert was slowly getting to his feet, Annie was stood next to the big Russian who was lying next to her feet. He looked over and saw the other Russian lying at the end of some boxes, but he could not see Charlie. Pilkington checked Joanne's pulse and he was happy that she was ok, he asked Egbert how he was and he said that he was fine; Annie also said that she was fine and Pilkington continued to walk over to where the dead body of Aivars was lying. Pilkington moved to where the boxes were and then he saw Charlie who was sitting upright, with his back to the wall; he could not move as his leg was shattered. Pilkington looked around the rest of the warehouse and he saw the sheet on the floor, he went over to it and he lifted it, he felt sickened when he saw the two naked girls lying underneath it. He covered them over and turned around. Pilkington went back to the door and he called for the agents from outside to come into the warehouse. All was ok, but there was some cleaning up to do.

Egbert had got to his feet and he had gone over to Annie, he asked,

"Are you ok Annie?"

She replied, "I am fine Egbert, in fact it was quite therapeutic when you consider that big bastard hit me twice and then tried to fuck me."

Egbert smiled and then replied, "Good girl, I hope I never get on the wrong side of you."

Pilkington was kneeling next to Joanne as she came round, he said to her; "You did well Joanne, how do you feel?"

Annie was still dazed, but she replied, "I am ok Sir, how are Egbert and Annie?"

Pilkington helped her to her feet and he responded; "They are both fine and the Russians are both dead, so it all went pretty much to plan. Are you fit to fly, or do you need any hospital attention?"

Joanne smiled and said, "No Sir, I am ok, He just stunned me, that's all."

Pilkington then put his hand on Joanne's shoulder and he said, "Right, I want Egbert and Annie out of here, before the local police turn up, that will just complicate things, do you think you can manage it."

Joanne answered; "Yes Sir, do you want me to take them to HQ?"

Pilkington shook his head and replied; "No Joanne, I want them out of the UK until this settles down. The helicopter can take you to Leeds, Bradford Airport, call this number and there is a airplane there that will take you to Spain, they tell me Marbella is good at this time of the year and I think those two deserve a bit of time to recharge their batteries, plus it won't do you any harm to have a bit of a rest."

Joanne as professional as ever replied, "Sir, protocol says that we should have a debrief at HQ."

Pilkington looked at Joanne and he smiled, he then replied, "Joanne, do as you are told, you won't get many orders telling you to have a rest in this job, so enjoy it while you can."

Joanne then said, "What about passports, Sir?"

Pilkington answered impatiently; "Joanne, if you keep asking questions, I am going to put you in a bloody ambulance myself and somebody else can take them. The pilot Phillip Joseph will have all of that sorted out for you by the time that you land. I will come out in a couple of days and we can take care of the debrief then."

Joanne went over to Egbert and Annie and ushered them to the helicopter. As they left the warehouse, Egbert nodded to Pilkington, but Annie just stared at him; she was sure that she recognised him from somewhere, but she could not remember where it was from. They boarded the helicopter and as they started to hover above the ground the police cars and two Ambulances were turning into the entrance of the driveway, it was of no concern to them, because in a few hours all of this would be behind them and they would be sunbathing in the Costa del Sol.

Back in the warehouse, Pilkington was checking on Charlie and he said; "You have done well Charlie, there will be a commendation in this for you."

Charlie was in pain and he felt tired, he answered Pilkington; "Sir, that won't bring my mates back and I guess it is going to be some time before this busted leg is fixed, you would be better giving a commendation to Joanne, because she really saved my bacon there."

Pilkington nodded and then said; "Well Charlie, don't you worry, you will be looked after and so will Joanne."

The police officer in charge approached Pilkington and asked for a statement of what had happened. Pilkington said, "Get this man to hospital and then remove all of these stinking bodies and I will give you what information you need for your report, I will remind you that this is SIS business and you must record what I say exactly."

Bound for Spain

The three of them sat behind the helicopter pilot and were silent, partly because of tiredness and partly because of what had happened in the warehouse. They were all lost in their own thoughts; Egbert was amazed that little Annie had managed to kill the big Russian in the way that she did, Annie was impressed at how Egbert had won his battle with the Russian and Joanne couldn't help thinking that it was wrong that they were flying off to Spain, but she did concede that Pilkington had been right in his dealing with the rescue, so maybe she should stop questioning his decisions.

Joanne called the number for Phillip Joseph, the pilot of the airplane and he told them where to meet him at the airport. They didn't go to the normal departures gates, they met him at the northwest side of the airport, away from all of the commercial flights. When they got to his office they made their ways to the washrooms and cleaned up as Phillip was finalising getting the aircraft ready for take-off; within 40 minutes they were up in the sky and heading south towards Spain.

Phillip was a tall, good-looking black man who liked the ladies and he flirted outrageously for all of the flight with Joanne and Annie, but he was also likeable and Egbert spent some time chatting with him as well, "So Phillip, how did you get into do this for a living?"

Phillip replied, "Well man, I used to fly charters for passengers between the islands in the Caribbean, but the work dried up and I decided that I could either stay in Jamaica to drink the rum all day like my brothers, or I could come to England and I could get myself another job. So when I was 20 I came to England and I got myself a job as a welder; the pay was good and I had done lots of welding in Jamaica on the aircraft, so I knew what I was doing. As time passed by I was missing flying amongst the clouds so I passed my UK flying licence and I rented myself this Cessna, man. First of all I did a lot of private charters, which paid good money, but then I did a rush job for Mr Pilkington and I have never looked back since. Now I do loads of work for the British Government, so I think I am doing pretty well, man. I am saving up to buy my own Lear jet. I don't ask any questions and I keep my head down and I get paid well and the Government makes sure that I don't get any problems with passports or customs, so it all works well man. I flew the big boss Cameron to Spain a few weeks ago and I have taken Prince Harry to Scotland a couple of times; he is a brother. I like him man, he makes me laugh, and he has a heart of gold, if you was blind you would think he was a black man."

Egbert laughed at this and continued laughing as he went back to his seat and then Phillip turned and said to all of his passengers; "Ok, sisters and brother, enjoy the flight, there is no on-board entertainment other than what you make for yourselves, but there is a fridge at the back with a variety of drinks, including Jamaican rum and champagne stocked within it. The flight will take roughly 3 to 4 hours and should be pretty smooth, if anybody wants to come up and see the view from the flight deck, you are more than welcome, but only one at a time please. We will land at Malaga airport and then I will take you the rest of the way by helicopter while they refuel my plane."

Once the airplane was levelled off up in the clouds Annie went to the flight deck and sat down next to Phillip, she asked him to talk her through the control panel and the procedures that he had to take when taking off and landing, Annie had always been interested in the workings of machinery and technology.

Annie then turned towards Phillip and said, "Did you ever see any UFOs when you were up here?"

Phillip smiled and looked back at Annie; "I am not sure sister, but I think I have, I have seen things move across the sky at phenomenal speeds, far too fast for them to be airplanes; do you believe in UFOs and things?"

Annie smiled and then said, "Yes Phillip, I do, but it is a long story, maybe I will tell you it sometime, but not today, one thing though if you look to the East right now, can you see anything?"

Phillip looked to the East and he saw what looked like a light in the sky, which seemed to be moving at the same speed as them.

He took a double-take and then said, "Wow sister, is that what I think it is?"

"It might be," said Annie as she got out of the co-pilot's seat and returned to her own seat.

Phillip was smiling from ear to ear, he believed that he had finally seen a UFO, he would enjoy telling that story over a few rums, but only when he had stopped working for the government, because for now the reason he got the work was that he knew how to keep quiet.

The flight continued to run smoothly and Egbert and Annie both enjoyed the Champagne although Joanne stuck to the soft drinks; as far as she was concerned she was still on duty. Joanne, still being professional went to the flight deck and she asked Phillip exactly where they were going.

Phillip replied, "We are going to an hacienda in the Spanish mountains, it used to be a race horse stable, but since the racing stopped at Mijas, the trainer moved out and the British government bought it and use it as and when they need to, it is somewhere away from the masses, it is a nice place with a swimming pool and fitness centre and I am sure it will be very relaxing. They have a chef there who specialises in Mediterranean Cuisine. I will land you right in front of the door in the helicopter."

Joanne liked the sound of it, it sounded safe and peaceful, she then said, "Where can we get some new clothes, Annie has blood on her dress and we could all do with a change of clothing?"

Phillip replied, "Don't worry Joanne, they have somebody at the hacienda that will go and get you new clothes, you just have to tell them what style you want and the size, you won't even need your credit card, it will all be taken care of."

For the rest of the flight the passengers relaxed and Annie even fell asleep. Egbert looked at her and he thought to himself, *"She could sleep on a washing line, that one."* It made him smile.

As they started to fly over the Andalucía region of Spain, Phillip made an announcement; "Sisters and brother, we are flying over the Costa del Sol and I will be taking the plane down very shortly into Malaga airport, then we will transfer to my helicopter and then up into the mountains, please fasten your seatbelts and put your seats in the upright position, I hope you have had a pleasant flight."

Within less than thirty minutes Phillip was landing the helicopter on the large open area at the front of the hacienda. The three of them left the helicopter and thanked Phillip as they were leaving. Phillip turned off the engine and he also got out and he went over to a man who had come to meet them, the man shook Phillip's hand and they swapped a few words. Phillip then got back into the helicopter and very quickly he was back into the sky and on his way back to Malaga Airport to pick up his Cessna, which he would then fly back to England.

The man turned to the three of them and welcomed them to the hacienda and then he led them inside the main house; the outside had looked beautiful, but inside it almost looked like a palace with its marble floor and wall tiles and the rare antique pieces of Spanish furniture. The man turned to them and introduced himself as Williams. He was a small, wiry muscular man and he had character; he had not always been a House Manager, in fact before the British government rewarded him with his name Desmond Williams and a place to live high in the mountains of Spain, he had worked for them and he had helped them to bust a major drug dealing gang in the Midlands. He was safe where he was, but back in the UK there were a few people that would skin him alive. Williams said to the three of them, "If you need anything whilst you are here please let me know, I know that you want some clothing and there is a catalogue over there belonging to a fashion outlet down in Marbella, just pick what you want and let me know the size and I will send somebody to buy them for you. I will now show you to your rooms and please feel free to explore this fine hacienda and treat it as your home; there is a pool at the back, which has been bathed in sunshine all morning, I am sure that you will want to enjoy it for the rest of the afternoon, the waiter by the pool will serve you refreshments as you require them. You will find an assortment of swimming attire inside your wardrobes, I am sure they will be fine until your new clothes arrive. Now please follow me to your rooms."

All three rooms were spacious and had pretty much identical furniture in them, they were situated two next to each other and another one opposite the two along the same corridor, the two next to each other had a view out over the back of the hacienda where the pool was and the third looked out over the front of the hacienda and up to the gallops and the stables.

Annie felt like she had won the lottery, she went into her room and straight to the wardrobe where she found herself a bikini and a robe to wear, she undressed, but before putting the bikini on she got into her shower to remove any remaining blood that she had on her from the big Russian. Egbert did the same, he was glad that they were there all three of them together and he felt safe. He had witnessed Joanne in action and he knew that she would keep a look out for them. Joanne walked into her room and she sat on her bed for a while and then she started to weep, she had never killed a man before and she felt sadness, but she knew that if she hadn't killed him, he would have killed Charlie and maybe even the rest of them; she didn't know why she was weeping, but she put it down to the whole emotions of what had happened over the last few days. She knew that now she had killed she was a live operative for SIS and she would no longer be working in an administration role. She went and showered and found a bikini that fitted her and then she went outside to the pool at the back of the hacienda, Egbert and Annie had already found the sunbeds and were relaxing at the side of the pool. Egbert was drinking a gin and tonic and Annie a white rum with lemonade. Joanne ordered a fresh orange juice and picked out a sunbed near to the other two; she checked her handbag to make sure that her pistol and some spare ammunition were inside it and then she put her handbag under the sunbed. Joanne had already spotted that there was a security team positioned discreetly around the hacienda, but she felt safer with her gun close to her, especially after what had happened in the warehouse.

Writing the Report

It was Sunday early evening and Pilkington was back at his home writing up the report of what had happened regarding Annie and Egbert; he wanted to make sure that he sent the report off to the Foreign Secretary before the day was over, even though he had already given him a briefing over the phone, which the Foreign Secretary had insisted upon. In fact, he and the Foreign Secretary had regular conversations about the case, because the Foreign Secretary had stressed that he must be kept up to date at all times. Pilkington knew that he had plenty of other things to do on Monday morning and he didn't want to spend it writing a report. The Foreign Secretary would be happy, he would be able to report back to the USA, Russia and the other interested countries that Egbert and Annie were safe and that they were under British government supervision. It was now clear that Annie was happy to provide whatever information was needed and that she felt comfortable with Egbert; the case was going to have a happy ending and the world was going to be a much safer place because of it. At 21.00 Pilkington felt that he deserved to open a bottle of vintage Rioja and enjoy it with some cheese and crackers. It was a simple pleasure but one that he enjoyed immensely, he just had a couple of things to do first before he could sit down and fully relax.

Hanif had been waiting for an update from his people and he was fearing the worst because it was now late in the evening in Chechnya and he had not received it, but then he got a call that he didn't want but that he had to take from the all-too-familiar number, after he answered it he heard the disguised voice. "Hanif, your men have failed, what do you have to say for yourself?"

Hanif hesitated, but then he replied, "I don't know what happened."

The voice continued; "I know you don't Hanif, the two Russians were killed by British security and Annie who was one of the targets, and she wasn't even trained in combat. There is nobody now to transport them to meet with your friends in Spain."

Hanif was worried, but he replied, "What do you want me to do?"

The voice replied; "It is already done, they are being transported to a British government safe house in Spain, I should have arranged it all in the first place, but because of you my cover is now at risk, you are a complete failure, if I didn't need you to liaise with Al Qaeda you would already be dead and when I consider this further you might still die."

Hanif nervously replied to the voice, "I have good relations with Al Qaeda and I can assure you that I alone can arrange for them to do as you require, I am still a valuable asset to you."

The disguised voice was silent for a moment or two and then it continued, "Hanif, I will fly out to Spain on Tuesday, arrange for one of your friends to meet with me at Sinatra's Bar, it is in Puerto Banus on Tuesday at 16.00, I will give him the location of the Professor and the woman, there is a security team at the hacienda that will need to be dealt with and there is a woman British agent there, she can also be eliminated. Please make sure that your people deal with it properly this time. Do you understand, there can be no more mistakes?"

Hanif responded, "Yes I understand, there will be no more mistakes."

The voice continued to say,; "Tell your contact that I will be wearing a grey pin stripe suit, I doubt that anybody else will be wearing a pin stripe suit in Sinatra's Bar at four o'clock in the afternoon and tell them to come up to me and say; Is that an English paper, do you mind if I have a quick look at it? I will reply and I will say; Of course, would you like a drink to go with it? They will reply and say; Yes, I would like a Bombay Sapphire and tonic with lime, please. Both parties will then know that it is safe to proceed, can you be trusted to do what I ask?"

Hanif replied, "Yes, absolutely!" The call ended.

The voice then switched off the voice-changing application on his mobile phone and then he made another call; the call was answered with a simple Yes. This time the roles were reversed and the person being called was using an application to change their voice. The caller then went on to say, "Everything is good, Al Qaeda will have the Professor and the woman on Wednesday, the Illuminati will very soon have everything that they need to make contact with alien life which will give you the extra control of the planet that you need, and after Wednesday there is nothing more that I can do."

The voice at the other end of the line replied; "You have done well, the Illuminati are grateful to you, although I don't think the British government or the other governments will be too pleased at what you have done, after Wednesday you need to disappear and you will never surface again, you must understand that. When Al Qaeda hand over the Professor and the woman to my people there will be £30 million placed in a Swiss account for you; you will pay Al Qaeda and whatever is left you may keep, you will never be seen again and likewise if you fail you will never be seen again, do you understand?"

The caller then said, "Yes I do, nothing will fail, with my money I will disappear off of the map; there will never be anything linking Al Qaeda and the Illuminati, certainly not from me."

The reply then came; "Have you ever mentioned the Illuminati in your discussions with your contact?"

The caller then responded; "No. They only know us as the Paymaster."

The disguised voice then said; "Ok, go and succeed in your mission, and when you do you will have done the Illuminati a great service, the world will be free of interfering governments and we will have total control. One final point: I want you to be there when Al Qaeda have the Woman and the Professor, you must witness it and call me when it is done." The call ended.

The man who had made the call was pleased with himself, after Wednesday he would be very rich and he would live the life that he felt he had always deserved; he had kept his identity safe from Hanif of Chechnya and nobody in the British government would suspect him, he would simply disappear and be presumed dead. He would leave enough clues that he was dead so that nobody would even bother looking for his missing body, his disappearance would just be a terrible incident that had happened when he committed suicide in the Mediterranean Ocean after the pressures of his work had finally caught up with him. He would read his obituary in the Times and with his newfound wealth he would change his appearance, adopt a new identity and then live in luxury on some tropical island with young women pleasing him forever and obeying his every need; who said that money cannot buy love?

The Foreign Secretary

It was late Sunday evening and the Foreign Secretary, Justin Madeley was in his office in central London along with his personal assistant. They were preparing for an interview that he was to take part in the following morning for BBC breakfast television; relations between the UK and Spain were not good and he felt that he should tell the British public what was being done about it.

Like most politicians, he had been educated at Oxford and not unlike David Cameron he was a wealthy man in his own right, through his inheritance but also the successful family business which he owned. Justin had moved into politics when he was in his forties and he was still only fifty; it was felt that had it not been for the coalition government and the fact that Nick Clegg was Deputy Prime Minister that Justin would have been a safe bet to be Cameron's deputy. As it was Justin had arguably the most important job in British politics after the Prime Minister, he travelled the world and was a very influential person, especially with some of the emerging countries, and of course some of the established leading countries.

Along with his many other roles Justin had been given the responsibility for overseeing the project to gain the co-operation of Annie Brown to find a way to contact NHBs, and because of this James Pilkington was working as a direct report to Justin who demanded frequent updates on the project from Pilkington, which Pilkington thought was unnecessary, but had no choice but to comply with his orders.

Justin had gone into his office to make a private call and he had closed the door, which was unusual; Jane his personal assistant took the opportunity to go and make some fresh coffee while he was on the call. When Jane came back with the coffee Justin had finished the call and he then said to her, "Jane, I need you to arrange a flight for me to go to Spain on Tuesday morning, I need to fly into Malaga and I will return on Thursday from Madrid late afternoon. There is no need to arrange any accommodation for me, but I will need a car and a driver. I will not need you on this trip, so you can have a quiet couple of days without me." Jane put the coffee down on the table and made a note of Justin's requirements and said that she would sort it first thing on Monday morning.

Justin then went on to say, "If anybody asks, it is Gibraltar business."

The Hacienda

Egbert and Annie had enjoyed a good time by the side of the pool and even Joanne forgot that she was on duty for a while as she enjoyed a swim in the crystal, clear water. Both Annie and Egbert had read Joanne's thoughts and it was clear that she was feeling stressed and worried about their safety, but they believed that she was just feeling the pressure of being young and as she saw it, in charge. Egbert and Annie had been flirting with each other through their telepathy and they were certainly feeling comfortable in each other's company; they had decided after the last day or so which they had endured that they would enjoy themselves at the hacienda for as long as they were there. The Mediterranean sun had started to lose some of its heat and the three of them went to their rooms to get ready for dinner which was to be served in the main banqueting hall at 19.30 with drinks at 19.00. It all seemed very formal, but with the formality came the feeling of comfort and safety. Laid out on each of their beds were the clothes that they had selected and each of them chose what they would wear that evening, although there was some formality to the dinner, the dress code was smart but casual. They all carried some bumps and bruises from the last few days, but they each were letting them drift away either in the shower or in the bath whilst they relaxed.

Annie thought about the moment that she had killed the big Russian and she wondered why it was that she was not feeling bad about it; she had decided that he had got what was coming to him for what he had done to her and probably what he had done to many others. Her only hope was that they were not having wild boar for dinner. Joanne had reconciled in her mind the killing of the other Russian, and she knew that she had done her job and she had done it well, so she now felt proud and she guessed it would be something that she would just get used to; after all, this was now her job. Egbert showered and as he washed himself he felt good about the way he had fought the big Russian and beaten him to the ground, he felt happy that both Annie and Joanne were safe and he was looking forward to spending some relaxed time with them at dinner.

The time for drinks soon came around and they assembled in the banqueting room, there was a bar with a waiter and they were looked after royally, the décor in the banqueting room looked to be a blend of Spanish antique and Scottish tradition. There were bagpipes on the wall along with the heads of stags, wolves and wild boar, Annie thought to herself; *"There is no bloody escape from the wild boar."* But then she smiled; *"At least we are all here safe, there was no guessing what would have happened if the Russians had got their way."*

The starter was a choice of Spanish tapas followed by fresh sea bass and a dessert of strawberries and cream, washed down with a white Rioja. During dinner Egbert asked Joanne about the Russians. "Joanne, what do you think the Russians would have done with Annie and me? Would we have been safe?"

Joanne looked back at Egbert and she answered, "I don't know Egbert, you saw what they were like, but they were acting on behalf of somebody else and I really don't know who that was."

Egbert then went on to say; "When will we meet the scientists and specialists who want to meet with Annie and I, and what do they expect?"

Joanne again answered Egbert, "Mr Pilkington is the one who should be answering these questions, but it is simple really. I guess they just want to see how much Annie can tell them about communicating with the Non-Human Beings and ultimately they want to try and make contact with them; your job is to help the process through your mind-reading skills."

Joanne then looked at Annie and she asked, "Are you ok with that Annie?"

Annie smiled and replied, "Yes, I am ready, I can't guarantee anything though, I will tell them what I know, but it is down to the Non-Human Beings as you call them, whether they will accept contact, I believe that they are specific now in who they want to have contact with."

Joanne was intrigued by Annie's response and she followed up with a question, "Who would that be, Annie?"

Annie replied, "World leaders; Obama, Putin and all of the rest, I don't know them all so I am not even going to attempt to guess at them."

Joanne nodded and then said, "That's fair enough, Egbert will be there to help you and if I can ever help you I will."

The rest of the evening was filled with relaxed conversation and each of the three of them felt comfortable with the other two. Egbert and Annie enjoyed having a few drinks and Joanne continued sipping her fruit juice but she continued to keep her handbag close to her side, when it was time for bed they all went to their rooms at the same time and to their own beds, it had been a long few days and any romance that there might have been could wait for now. However, it didn't stop Egbert and Annie continuing to flirt telepathically from their rooms, but that was as far as it went and it wasn't long before tiredness got the better of them and they were asleep.

Recreation at the Hacienda

Egbert woke early and decided to have a run around the estate of the hacienda; he put on the running clothes and shoes that he had requested from Williams and he looked forward to breathing the fresh mountain air and feeling the warm sun start to get warmer on his skin, but with the knowledge that he would be finished before it got too warm. As he got to the front door there was a man with a gun in a holster on his waistband, Egbert nodded to him, but the site of the gun reminded him of the dangers that they had faced during the previous few days and although it brought back some bad memories, he did feel happier that there were people there to protect them. He ran out of the front door of the hacienda and across to the Gallops where the racehorses would have trained. He decided to see how fast he could run along the Gallops, but within 100 metres he was glad that he was not a racehorse; the surface of the Gallops was not grass as it is in the United Kingdom, it was more sandy, bolstered by man-made fibre, just as it is at the race tracks of Spain. His feet sunk into it and his legs weighed heavy. He decided that he would stick to running on the grass in future. His lungs were starting to burn as he pushed himself hard, but he was enjoying the feeling of the honest pain that he was enduring, he knew that waiting for him was the cooling pool at the back of the hacienda. Egbert got to the far end of the Gallops when he saw the stables which had at one time contained 20 racehorses and he decided to have a look inside, he had never been to a stables before and it was too good an opportunity to miss. The inside of the stables were fresh and clean and they looked as if they had been made ready for some new arrivals. He saw the tack hanging on the wall, he saw horseshoes which were in a basket, just waiting for a blacksmith to attach them to the hooves of the horses. He looked around and saw the hay bales, fresh and ready to be fed to the horses and he noticed the pitchforks lined up against a wall; it was clear that horses could be kept here again very quickly. Money had been spent on the stables to ensure that they were maintained in good order. Egbert looked around and he cast his mind back to being in the transport warehouse where he had been only the day before and he reflected on how run-down it looked and how it had not been maintained at all, he let his imagination wander and he thought to himself; *"Would I have tackled the Russian any different if I had fought him in here, yes I would have stuck the big bastard with one of those pitchforks and then Annie might not have had to deal with him."* He wondered if his cousin John would have dealt with the Russian any differently to how he had and he decided that he probably wouldn't and that made him feel good. He looked around the stables one last time before he continued his run. He left the stables and looked up at the mountain peaks that surrounded the hacienda and he thought to himself, "It is so good to be alive, this is perfect and I could certainly get used to this." Egbert continued his run and took in the scenery and the beauty all around him; he could even see the Mediterranean Sea in the distance, and it looked blue and welcoming, with a few boats dotted amongst the waves. He couldn't help but notice the security men around the perimeter of the grounds, he saw at least half a dozen and he also noticed CCTV cameras at frequent intervals, so he guessed that there would be others inside the hacienda in a control room somewhere and they were probably watching his every move. When Egbert got back to the hacienda it was still only 08.30 and he noticed Joanne was having breakfast but there was no sign of Annie. He went over to Joanne and said that he would have a quick shower and that he would come back and join her, if that was ok, she smiled at him and said that she would wait.

Only 15 minutes later Egbert was sat at the table with Joanne and he was enjoying a cup of coffee and some fruit. He asked, "Have you recovered from yesterday yet?"

Joanne looked up and smiled and said, "Yes, I am fine, it was quite a day though."

Egbert nodded and said, "It certainly was, you did well, and you saved Charlie's life for sure, that Russian was about to kill him."

Joanne was pleased that Egbert had said that and she smiled and replied, "Thanks, I guess I just did what I had to do."

Egbert then went on to say, "Well I bet Charlie and his family are very glad that you did."

Joanne smiled and then changed the subject, "Where did you run to?"

Egbert pointed over to the window near the entrance of the hacienda and said, "I went over to the Gallops and up to the stables, they are in good condition, they have been well maintained; how long is it since horses were kept there?"

Joanne answered, "I am not sure, Egbert, I think the Mijas Racecourse closed about 2 years ago. I understand that the trainer decided to go back to England, the only other main racecourse in Spain is at Madrid and it was too far away for him to travel."

Egbert replied, "Well, he must really love his racing, because this place takes some beating."

Joanne nodded and said, "I know what you mean, it is beautiful."

Egbert then went on to say, "I also noticed that there is plenty of security here, is that normal or is it because we are here?"

Joanne answered; "It is normal, the British government use the hacienda for many things, so it is important to make sure that it is secure at all times, you shouldn't worry about it, in fact just the opposite, and it should make you feel more safe and relaxed."

Egbert smiled. Joanne had reassured him and he decided that he would follow her advice and relax. He then said, "When do you think we might leave here, Joanne and what is waiting for Annie?"

Joanne took a drink of her coffee and then answered, "I think Mr Pilkington is due to arrive tomorrow, he told me that the Foreign Secretary might also be dropping in to thank both you and Annie, but I think we will go back to the UK before the end of the week. Annie will be interviewed by government specialists to see what she can tell them about her experiences with the NHBs and then they will try to determine if there is any way that they can make contact with the NHBs."

Egbert nodded and then he said, "I can help with that, Annie will need to be regressed, it all happened a long time ago and she was only a child at the time; she trusts me now and she knows I would never hurt her. I will gradually ease her back in time and capture her experiences with her."

Joanne smiled and then replied, "That's good, it seems that Mr Pilkington was right about everything, I feel bad that I doubted him."

Egbert shrugged his shoulders and he smiled he then said, "I suppose that goes with the territory, he will have been pleased deep down that you questioned him, it shows that you have a brain and that will have reinforced to him— he also knows now that you have plenty of courage and that he was right to give you the job."

This made Joanne feel good and she smiled and answered, "Yes, thanks, you are right, it has been good to talk with you, I have been beating myself up over it, all is good now, and we should enjoy the next few days rest before we have to go back to England."

They both smiled and were finishing what was left of their coffee when they heard somebody coming into the room and in a half-singing, half-speaking voice they heard the word, "Morning, what's for breakfast, I am starving? I need some energy, it is hard work lying by the pool all day."

They both looked at Annie and laughed, she could lighten anybody's mood with her cheerfulness. Egbert then said, "Come on Annie, sit down, get your breakfast and let's get out to the pool, let's enjoy the glorious sun, I have just got back from my run and it is going to be a hot one."

Life seemed so normal, they could have been three friends who had come to the Costa del Sol for a holiday, the adventures of the previous few days were fading into the past. Egbert summed up the mood whilst lying by the pool, "How good does life get, I am lying next to a beautiful, blue shimmering pool, underneath a glorious blue sky and a hot sun, and I have two beautiful, sexy women just hanging on my every word."

Annie threw some ice out of the ice bucket at him and both women laughed. "That should cool you down, hanging on your every word indeed, you nutter!"

The day continued in the same vein, with plenty of banter and a feeling of closeness which had been built between the three of them and Egbert continued his flirting with the two women who both enjoyed it; in fact, they felt so relaxed that Annie and Egbert did not even use their mind reading and telepathic skills. They stayed by the pool all day and Egbert even drifted off to sleep on his sun bed and Joanne had a few glasses of the chilled champagne that the waiter had brought to her.

Annie and Joanne were getting on well and Joanne asked Annie what it had been like to have contact with the NHBs and Annie was happy to answer the question. "At first it was very scary, imagine being a young child, who only knew the comfort of her mum and her sisters and brothers and then all of a sudden in the safety of your own home whilst in bed at night, you see a light the size of a pea get bigger and bigger, and as you watch its very presence paralyses you and enters your body. I was unable to move and this thing entered me and made me feel like I was being squashed by a ton of weight; I felt that I stopped breathing as it searched all over my inner body like it was scanning me, it frightened me, Joanne and I was powerless to do anything about it. I tried to shout but nothing would come out of my mouth, my sister and brother were in the same room and this was happening as they slept, it seemed to last for hours but then it left me and I just lay there really weak and shattered. It came again and again over many nights and I couldn't explain it, not even to my mum, but each time it came I felt that I grew stronger inside and the thing seemed to be less evil, although at first I don't think it cared whether it left me for dead or not. As time passed by I saw a softer, gentler side to it and it communicated with me, it wanted to take me to where it came from, but I refused to go, although eventually I agreed and it took me, not my body but my consciousness and it showed me its world. It was so peaceful and so loving, I met its family and I saw how they all loved each other; it showed me a brand new world, where there was no disease, no wars, no hatred, but where there was total acceptance. I felt love and I felt like I was adopted and that I was part of its family. I was taken there many times and each time I saw something new; they have so many things that they could teach us on this planet and they did tell me that I would be a very important part of the development of Planet Earth, but that it would happen over a long time and that it would not happen quickly. They taught me to appreciate everything and I looked at colours and saw them differently. I looked at animals and saw them as people just like you or me, albeit they are in a different kind of body; I could sense when the weather was about to change, but it didn't matter because I learned to appreciate rain and wind and I knew that theirs is a much better way than we have on our Earth. There was a downside, though, because when I woke up in my bed the next morning and had to face a normal day of going to school, I was shattered and I couldn't go. In any case, I knew that school teachers couldn't teach me anything that I didn't already know after what I had seen and in fact I could teach them so many things that they didn't know. That was why they took me to the Unit and I believe it was not for my development, but that it was for their development; they knew I had experienced things and they wanted to know more about what those things were. Egbert's father used to hypnotise me and he encouraged me, he was a nice man. I loved it at the Unit and I didn't really want to go back home, but of course I did have to. But do you know, Joanne the light orbs have stayed with me and when I need them they always protect me, that's why I was never really afraid of the Russians; I killed that horrible man, but it was the light that gave me the strength to do it."

Joanne looked at Annie and then replied; "That is so amazing, can you contact them whenever you want to?"

Annie shook her head and then replied, "No Joanne, I can't, but that's the amazing thing, I don't need to, they are always there when I need them. Don't forget they heightened my senses so that I can read thoughts and send messages telepathically; I think my mind is like a radio transmitter and they are picking up my frequencies all of the time."

Joanne was engrossed by what Annie was telling her and then she asked, "Why then did they let you get kidnapped by the Russians, why didn't they rescue you straight away?"

"Joanne, that's easy, just like a child it can only develops as it experiences things and they have to let me to experience those things, so that I get the buzz of dealing with them and with it the full awareness of what is happening. If a child reads a book or watches a film, they are relying on a reflected experience, it can never be their own, but once you have your own experience you just know that it is unique and you totally get it. I have learned that you should never regret your experiences, even if they were bad ones; they made you what you are today. The trick is to learn from the experiences, when you shot that man yesterday, the important thing is to learn from it, but never regret it; his actions put him in that position, not yours and you did what you had to do. I am not sure how I came through what I came through, but it was amazing and I am glad that I did."

Joanne was amazed by the conversation that had just taken place and she looked at Annie and smiled and then she said, "You are amazing and do you know, I think those light orbs were right, you will help to change this world."

The two of them put their arms around each other and embraced each other like they were long-lost sisters, each of them proud and pleased that they knew the other one. Egbert let out a loud snore and he woke himself up, which made the two women burst into laughter; it wasn't so much the snoring noise, but the look of shock on his face as he awoke. The day passed well and all three of them had enjoyed a relaxing day which had put them all in a good mood as they went to their rooms to get ready for dinner.

Egbert was the first to arrive in the banqueting hall and he noticed Williams sat at a table in the corner so he went over to chat with him. Williams saw him coming and turned towards him and said, "Have you had a good day Professor?"

Egbert smiled and nodded and then said, "Yes, it was very good, but please call me Egbert."

Williams smiled. "Can I get you anything Professor?"

Egbert took this response to mean that Williams did not want to get too close, but Egbert accepted that it was Williams being professional and that he had to keep his guests at a professional distance; after all if one of the Royal Princes were there he couldn't really go around calling them Harry or William. Egbert replied to Williams, "A gin and tonic would be great, thanks."

Williams went over to the bar and ordered the drink and then left the room. The waiter took Egbert his drink and Egbert sat waiting for the girls to join him. He wondered where the Control Room would be, but then he decided that he didn't really need to know, he picked up a newspaper from the table it was an English paper and it was that day's edition. He looked at the front page and there was a photograph of the warehouse in Bradford where they had been on Sunday, he read the headline to himself; *"Russian Mafia Drug Bust in Bradford Warehouse. Yesterday a British security team raided a disused warehouse in Bradford and closed down a Drug Farm operated by Russians which were believed to have connections to the Russian Mafia, two unnamed Russian men were killed during the raid and two young women were found dead hidden under some sheeting. It is thought that these women were to be transported as part of an illegal sex trafficking business in a specially adapted Removal Wagon which was also seized during the raid, it is not known why the women died. A spokesman for National Security said; "At this stage we can give no further details due to ongoing but important investigations, but our Security Services have struck an important blow against the war against criminals who try to undermine our UK security."*

Egbert thought to himself, *"Well I guess that ties up any loose ends, I wonder what would have been said if I or Annie had been killed, and what about those two poor women?"* Egbert decided not to dwell on it and thought to himself, *"If the information that Annie holds is as important as they say it is, then I guess some collateral damage has to be acceptable."*

Annie and Joanne came into the room and ordered some drinks from the bar, the mood was good and Egbert decided that he wasn't going to spoil it. They all had a couple of drinks and then they sat down for dinner. Egbert asked Joanne if she had heard anything from Pilkington and she confirmed that he would be arriving the following evening and that the plans would then be made for them all to be transferred to a secure centre in the UK, where work would begin with Annie. Joanne confirmed that she had received an email from Pilkington earlier in the day; it did not confirm one way or another if the Foreign Secretary would be dropping by, even though he apparently was due to be in Spain on some official business.

Egbert replied; "That's good, I guess we can get back to some kind of normality and that we will be no longer at risk."

Joanne looked at Egbert and said, "Egbert, after the last few days and with a view to what might happen from their work with Annie, I am not sure life will ever be normal again."

Egbert thought on Joanne's reply and then he laughed and said, "Ok, all the more reason to enjoy ourselves whilst we can." With that Egbert topped up the wine glasses.

The mood was still good and it was a flirty evening, it felt almost like the end of term when they were at school, or the last day at work before a holiday begins. Midnight soon arrived and the three of them set off for their rooms. Joanne went into her room and as Egbert went to open his door Annie said to him, "Egbert, why don't you come to my room for a nightcap?"

Egbert looked at Annie and replied; "Well Annie, I guess one more drink won't do any harm and it's not like we have to go to work or anything in the morning."

Egbert followed Annie into her room and then Annie turned towards him and said, "So you think I have a sexy ass, do you, you naughty professor, I have been reading your mind all the way down the corridor."

Egbert couldn't help but smile and then he cheekily said, "Annie, how do you know it wasn't Joanne's ass that I was looking at?"

Annie smiled and said, "I know whose ass you are fancying, so stop thinking about it and do something about it, but I must warn you it has been a while for me and you might get more than you bargained for."

With that Egbert took Annie in his arms and they kissed, slow and sexy, it was the kiss that had been waiting for the right moment and this was the right moment. Annie moved backwards towards the bed and then she stopped and pulled off her dress to reveal some sexy lingerie that she had chosen from the shop in Marbella. She asked, "Do you like these?"

Egbert's eyes were almost popping and he replied, "Oh yes, very much."

Annie undid her bra and let it fall to the ground, she pushed out her breasts. "And do you like these?"

Egbert felt like a schoolboy who had seen his first naked breasts and he replied, "Oh yes."

Egbert started to move towards Annie, when she said; "Stop right there Egbert, just watch for now, I will tell you when I am ready." Annie took hold of the waist of her panties and she eased them down so they dropped to her ankles. Egbert looked intently, he liked how he was feeling. Annie had a lovely shapely body and she looked so sexy.

Annie teased Egbert and said; "Egbert do you know that ass you have been fancying, would you like to see it?" Egbert did not need to answer and Annie did not need to read his mind to know what he was thinking, she turned around and she wiggled her sexy ass very erotically.

Egbert was mesmerised and simply said; "Wow!"

Annie knew exactly the impact she was having on Egbert and then she said, "Now, you can come over here, my body is yours to enjoy, but make sure that I enjoy too, because then I might allow you to stay the night."

Egbert did not need a second invitation, he walked over to Annie and he gently felt her skin from her shoulders down to her waist, he felt the curves of her sexy ass and the firmness of her breasts. Annie undid Egbert's belt on his trousers and unfastened the button above his zip and then lowered the zip on his fly, his trousers dropped to his ankles. Annie undid each button on his shirt and enjoyed the look of his manly chest as she did so. Within seconds they were both stood there naked and their hands were wandering all over each other with their mouths feverishly kissing. Annie sent a message into Egbert's mind; *"Egbert, when I orgasm, as I surely will, tune into my mind and you will experience what I am enjoying, I think you will enjoy it."*

This made Egbert even more excited and he thought he would burst. Several times that evening they made love and each other's orgasm was made more powerful by knowing that the other was experiencing it at the same time. Annie was more than satisfied and Egbert had never enjoyed sex like it. As Annie lay in bed cuddled up to Egbert, Egbert asked her; "Did the NHBs teach you how to do that?"

Annie simply replied, "No, that was just a gorgeous side-effect. Now let's sleep and if you are a good boy, we can enjoy it all again before breakfast, or maybe instead of breakfast."

Egbert cuddled up to Annie and then said, "What about Joanne?"

With a devilish humour Annie responded; "Well Egbert, I hadn't planned on it, but she is a good looking girl, feel free to invite her to join us."

Egbert tried to correct what he had said, "I meant for breakfast!"

Annie was still in her mischievous mood. "That's ok we can all have each other for breakfast, I am sure it would be very enjoyable."

Egbert was speechless but he was very happy, this was a nice way to go to sleep.

At around 08.30 Egbert awoke and Annie was stood naked looking out of the window of the room, the sensuous curves of her body were silhouetted by the light from the window. Egbert looked at her for a few moments and then said, "What a gorgeous view that is to wake up to."

Annie laughed and told him he should have gone to Specsavers. Egbert jumped out of bed and went over to Annie and he held her tight as they kissed once more and then he said, "Annie, believe me you are gorgeous, I don't need to wear glasses to see that."

Annie's Lights/Pitts

Annie was pleasantly flattered and replied, "If you say so then, you kind and sexy Professor. Now do you want to call Joanne to come and join us or shall we go and get some breakfast?"

Egbert couldn't tell if Annie was serious or not and he replied, "I wouldn't know what to say to her, I am quite shy you know."

Annie laughed and then said; "Come on then, get dressed, let's go and have some breakfast, I might mention it to her later."

Egbert liked the idea of it, but didn't know if he could go through with it, but he thought to himself; *"What the hell, why not, it's all about pushing boundaries and being outside of your comfort zone."*

Annie looked at Egbert and said; "Exactly!"

Egbert looked back at Annie with a furrowed brow and said, "Annie, will you stop reading my bloody mind."

They both laughed and left the room, Annie went to the dining room and Egbert got himself a quick change on the way.

Sinatra's Bar

The man with the grey pinstripe suit wearing designer sunglasses had taken a scheduled flight from Heathrow to Malaga where his driver had met him and then taken him to Puerto Banus; he had given himself time to walk around the pretty harbour before his meeting and he looked at the expensive luxury yachts which were moored up. He decided that he would buy one with the money that he would make and that he would indeed live the life of luxury for the rest of his life. At 15.45 he went into Sinatra's Bar and sat at a table with his back to the wall; he knew that what he was doing was risky and he wanted to make sure that he could see any threat that might come towards him, with his back to the wall he only needed to worry about what he could see. The waiter came to the table and the man ordered a Bombay Sapphire with tonic and slices of lime, he then sat with his newspaper in his hand waiting for the man from Al Qaeda. The waiter brought the drink over and at exactly 16.00 three people entered the bar, and sat at a table, The man looked them up and down and after a short while he decided that they were not there to meet him. The man had already decided that he would stay until he had finished his drink, but after that he would leave in case he had been compromised, he certainly did not intend staying any longer than 10 minutes. At 16.04 a tall, elegant, and beautiful olive-skinned lady entered the bar and walked towards him and said; "Is that an English paper, do you mind if I have a quick look at it?"

He was surprised to see a woman, but he replied, "Of course, would you like a drink to go with it?"

The woman replied; "Yes I would like a Bombay Sapphire and tonic with lime, please."

The young lady took a seat next to him and he handed over the paper. He waved the waiter over and he ordered the drink. She was a beautiful girl, the man estimated that she would be in her late 20's and he was pleased that she was wearing a tight-fitting short black dress with not very much underneath it, he could see that she was certainly not wearing any concealed wires or a microphone, they would easily be spotted when she was dressed like that. He asked her if she would open her handbag and put her packet of cigarettes onto the table, but at the same time open the bag so that he could see inside it. There was nothing to indicate any recording device, but there was a small handgun, which he guessed the girl would not be frightened of using if she had to. The girl looked at the man and said, "You must be warm, why don't you remove your jacket?" He knew that she was also checking him out for any wires or recording device and he was happy to oblige. The girl leaned across and she smiled at him she ran her hands over his chest and then kissed him on his cheek as she then ran her hands up and down his back to feel for any wires that might be under his shirt.

The man looked at the girl and said, "You do know, that anybody looking at you will think that you are a professional girl doing a trick for me an older man?"

She replied, "I do not care what people think, I do care about the money which we will be paid for doing this. Since the British and Americans have damaged our trade in drugs from Afghanistan and other of our key locations we have had to find income from other sources, we are simply diversifying our business to create new revenue streams. When will we be paid our fee?"

The man smiled and answered; "When you hand over the package to the Paymaster's people, they will contact me and I will then transfer the money as agreed to the account which Hanif has already given me the details of.

The woman looked coldly into the man's eyes and said, "We want £15M."

The man stayed calm, but looked back equally as coldly into the woman's eyes and said, "That is not what we agreed my dear, we agreed £10M."

She responded, "I am not your dear, but we still want £15M."

He looked at her and asked; "What is your name, my dear?"

"I am Ayesha, which you do not need to know, but you do need to know that we want £15M and that if we do not receive it there is no place on earth that you or your family will be safe. I do not need your name, but I would like to know it as I have given you mine."

The man looked at Ayesha and then removed his sun glasses and said, "My name is James Pilkington, I am the head of SIS and your friend Hanif nearly screwed this whole operation up, it was me who made sure that we got the package into Spain so that you could earn any money at all."

Ayesha remained cool and replied, "If Hanif screwed up as you say, he will be dealt with, but we still want £15M to do this job, I will be risking many good men."

The waiter brought back the drink for the girl and Pilkington thanked him, but then he looked away and weighed up his options; if he walked away now, he would have failed the Illuminati and would be killed, if he agreed to the offer, he would be reducing his own amount of payment, which was not part of his plan. What should he do? Pilkington looked back at the girl and said, "Ok I agree to £15m, but the job needs to be done tonight."

The woman nodded and said, "That is no problem, my team is ready, tell me where it is to take place."

Pilkington looked towards the newspaper he had given her and he said, "If you open the newspaper at the middle page you will see a map with the co-ordinates on it, it is a hacienda in the mountains above Mijas, there is only the mountain road that leads to it, but there is enough area at the front of the building to land a helicopter. There is also a plan in the newspaper showing the hacienda and its grounds."

The girl did not open the newspaper, but replied, "Tell me about the security that will be there?"

Pilkington kept looking intently at the woman and responded to her question. "There will be eight people armed who guard the perimeter and the house itself, there are two people in the control room watching the CCTV, who are also armed and there is a female agent who is with the two targets. It does not matter if she lives or dies, but if you want your money the two targets must be taken safely."

The woman was a professional and she was clearly very experienced, she then said, "I understand that, do you have photographs of the two that we are taking?"

Pilkington looked at the newspaper again and said, "Yes, at the centre of the newspaper as well as a photograph of me, your people need to make sure that I am not harmed or again you will not be paid as there will be nobody to transfer your funds."

The woman answered, "I understand, what kind of weapons have the security team?"

Pilkington replied, "They all carry hand guns including the female agent."

Again Ayesha asked a question. "Where will the security team be positioned?"

Pilkington continued to answer them, these were all sensible questions and all questions that he would have been asking, if he were in the same position. "Through the day, they patrol the perimeter and then they take it in turns at manning the gate. Once it becomes dark the security team lock the gate and stay inside the hacienda, they stay in the rest room unless they are instructed by the control room to attend any part of the hacienda or the grounds. Through the night, they work a shift pattern which includes covering the control room while half of them sleep. The teams work seven days on and seven days off normally starting on a Saturday. The CCTV cameras are infra-red and covers all of the public rooms in the hacienda, it covers the perimeter, and it looks both up and down the mountain road and covers the front, rear and sides of the hacienda. There are separate cameras at the stables and at other key points around the estate, all of the cameras can be operated by remote control and so the views can be changed."

Ayesha then made the point, "We need to get somebody inside to take out the control room, can you help with that?"

Pilkington looked at her appreciatively and he was impressed by her, until recently they would have been enemies, but now they were on the same side. He then replied, "Well, the timing will have to be perfect, but I can take out the control room, how will you get to and into the hacienda?"

Ayesha was equally impressed by Pilkington and she answered, "My team will arrive in two electric vehicles which are almost silent in operation, we will get an helicopter as close as we can within a couple of kilometres to the hacienda and once we have secured the hacienda and have the two targets, the helicopter will come in to do the pick-up. We will then fly direct to our base in North Africa where arrangements will be made for the two targets to be handed over; you will come with us."

Pilkington looked surprised at the woman and replied; "That is not part of the deal, my plan is to get as far away as I possibly can, the British and probably the Americans will be looking for me."

The woman looked at Pilkington and stared coldly at him and said, "Then you will be safe with us until you pay us and then you will be free to go wherever you want to go."

Pilkington was not happy that he had to go with them, but he did understand why they would want him to be there. He asked, "How do I know you won't do me some harm once you have the money?"

She looked back at him angrily and said, "If we want you dead, you will be dead, but assuming that your Paymaster is as powerful as we think he is, he may need us again and you may be more use to us alive than dead. Do you agree with me Mr Pilkington?"

That was the first time she had used his name during the whole conversation and the way she said it sent a shiver down his spine; he believed that he didn't have very much choice in the matter, he returned the cold stare and then said, "I agree to your terms." Pilkington knew that he had an ace up his sleeve, which he did not want to reveal at this stage, but he knew that the Foreign Secretary was in Spain for the next two days and that he knew all about his security arrangements and if need be he could trade his own life for that of the Foreign Secretary. He knew that Al Qaeda would gladly make that deal, he also thought that he might be able to negotiate some of his money back into the bargain.

Pilkington asked, "What time will you arrive at the hacienda?"

Ayesha answered, "We will arrive at the hacienda at precisely 02.00am; you will deal with the control room 3 minutes before that, which will give us chance to get right up to the gates in our vehicles without being seen. Is there anything else that we should know?"

Pilkington shook his head and said, "No, I think you have pretty much covered it, I will call you with any information that I think you will find useful, if any comes to light."

Ayesha put her cigarettes back into her handbag and picked up the newspaper and then she said, "Good, now Mr Pilkington, I have a lot to do and I must leave to prepare my team."

Pilkington stood up in a gentlemanly manner and said, "Before you go, give me a number that I can reach you on, in case anything changes that you need to know about."

The woman also stood up and passed Pilkington her number, he kissed her on both cheeks and then she walked away carrying the newspaper, she had not touched her drink, and Pilkington watched her walk away and thought to himself, *"You certainly are one evil, cold bitch!"* He was impressed, though by her thoroughness and he was comfortable with what was about to happen in the early hours of the following morning. Pilkington finished his own drink and then he also finished the drink that Ayesha had not touched, he left Sinatra's and walked the short distance to the underground car park where his driver was waiting; they then set off for the hacienda.

The Final Night at the Hacienda

Like the other days, the three of them had spent a relaxing time around the pool, apart from in the afternoon when they went to the fitness centre for an hour or so. Joanne hadn't really wanted to go to the fitness centre, but she liked to keep both Annie and Egbert in her sights and she thought that she should join them. Egbert worked out on the lifting equipment and Joanne went on the running machine next to him; Annie had decided that she had enjoyed enough exercise in bed with Egbert the previous evening and that she would just relax in the Jacuzzi. There was little talking while the two of them exercised, but Annie couldn't resist flirting with Egbert's mind while he was lifting the weights. Egbert replied to her flirty telepathic thoughts; *"Behave yourself woman, I could do myself an injury here with these weights and then I won't be able to do any of the things that you keep putting in my mind."*

Annie couldn't help herself, she enjoyed the whole mischief of it. *"Egbert can you see Joanne's ass from where you are, she does look so sexy, I could fancy her myself?"*

Egbert raised a smile and said, *"Give up Annie, these bloody weights are heavy."*

Egbert did though have a sideways glance and he couldn't help agreeing with what Annie was thinking. He thought to himself; *"What is this woman doing to me, I am a well-respected Professor of Quantum Communications and she is making me think about things which I would never have imagined, I like it but it's not me."*

Egbert was grinning from ear to ear as he lifted the weights and he looked over at Annie in the Jacuzzi and she was giggling away. Joanne got off the running machine and said that she was going to get into the Jacuzzi with

Annie. Egbert said he just had a few more repetitions to do and that he would join them. Egbert was enjoying the attention of the two women, but he didn't feel comfortable about it; deep down he was a shy man, even though he had stood up in front of hundreds of people and given talks, he had always thought sex to be a personal thing between two people and he knew that he would not be able to go ahead with anything more adventurous than that. He couldn't decide if Annie was being serious or not and she was very good at locking her mind, he was not always able to read it. What he didn't realise was Annie knew this and she was simply titillating and teasing him, she had no intention of sharing him with another woman, whether she liked that woman or not; meanwhile the two women were laughing and he wondered what it was they were laughing about.

Egbert finished his weights and went and got into the Jacuzzi, sitting opposite the two women, but they both moved and sat at either side of him, their flesh touching his, he was feeling a little hot under the collar and he was sure that Annie must have told Joanne her intentions, and he was just about to say something when the two women started to laugh again.

Annie through her laughter said, "You daft sod, we are just winding you up."

Joanne chipped in as well. "Egbert you are a very attractive man, but I am on duty....maybe when I am off duty it will be a different matter."

The two women laughed again and Egbert also saw the funny side of it and he started to laugh also. The three of them had become good friends in the short time of being together; it had diverted their attention away from how serious the situation had been for the last few days. They spent another 30 minutes in the Jacuzzi chatting away to each other and then they got out to go back to their rooms so that they could get changed for dinner.

When Joanne entered the main building Williams was waiting and he told her that Pilkington, who had called ahead, was expected in around 20 minutes; she told

Williams that she would go and change and then she would come back to reception to wait for him. Joanne went to her room and got changed; she was back in the reception area about 5 minutes before Pilkington walked in. Williams always made a fuss of Pilkington, because it was he that had arranged for Williams to have the job at the hacienda. Williams smiled and said, "Ah, Mr Pilkington, how nice to see you again, can I get you your usual drink, I hope you have had a good journey."

Pilkington smiled warmly back and replied, "Nice to see you to Desmond, and yes the journey was fine. In my gin and tonic I will have lime instead of lemon for a change, I seem to have developed a taste for it."

Williams nodded and replied, "Yes Sir, I won't be a moment."

Pilkington looked at Joanne and ushered her to a table and they sat down, he then said, "Now Joanne, come and tell me what has been happening, I trust that everything has gone according to my plans, as they normally do."

Joanne nodded and then replied, "Yes, Mr Pilkington everything has been fine, I also wanted to apologise for some of the things I said to you when we were on our way to the warehouse, you did know what you were doing, and I should not have doubted you."

Pilkington smiled and nodded like an elder statesman and said, "Don't worry about it Joanne, it was your first assignment, I was right but you do still have a lot to learn. Having said that, it all worked out well and you performed admirably when you were needed. I wouldn't be surprised if you received a commendation for what you did in the warehouse."

Joanne liked this acknowledgement, it made her feel proud and she said, "Thank you Sir, but I was only doing my job."

Pilkington smiled again and said; "That's the spirit, well done girl. Now tell me how are Egbert and Annie get along?"

Joanne replied; "Well Mr Pilkington, I would say, very well, they spent the night together last night and they have certainly bonded well over these last few days."

Pilkington was genuinely pleased to hear this; he knew that for his plan to work, it was important that both Annie and Egbert got on well. He replied; "That's good, it should make it easier to extract the desired information from her, if she is feeling relaxed in Egbert's company. What time are you eating tonight, Joanne?"

Joanne confidently responded; "We normally eat at 19.30. Will you be joining us Sir?"

Pilkington shook his head and replied, "I am afraid not Joanne, I have some things to do, but we will be going back to England tomorrow, so enjoy your last night and please make sure that everybody gets to bed just after 24.00, I want an early start in the morning and I have arranged for Phillip Joseph to be here at 09.00. Incidentally I have taken care of the report, so there will be no need for a debrief meeting."

Joanne was surprised that there would be no debrief meeting, but she thought better of challenging Pilkington again and she accepted what he had said and then replied, "Yes Sir, I will make sure that everybody is in bed in good time."

Pilkington said cheekily, "From what you have told me, it sounds like Egbert and Annie won't need too much encouragement." He laughed at what he had just said and Joanne also smiled. Pilkington went on to say, "Now, I am going to my room and do not want to be disturbed, please pass my regards onto Egbert and Annie?" With that Pilkington stood up and left the bar area.

As he walked away Joanne said, "Yes Sir, we will see you in the morning."

Pilkington wandered over to Williams and pointed at the gin bottle, "The same again Desmond, please."

Williams reached for the bottle and said; "Yes Sir, coming right up."

Williams passed the drink to Pilkington and Pilkington then asked him, "Desmond, Joanne told me the room numbers that everybody was in, but I must have a memory like a sieve, what are they again, I will write them down, I might just give them a personal wake-up call in the morning, just to ensure that there are no delays." Williams wrote their room numbers against their names onto a piece of paper and passed the note to Pilkington, who then left the bar area and went to his room.

Pilkington had decided that he did not want to be in either the company of Egbert or Annie that evening; he did not want them reading his mind, as he was afraid he might give the game away. Joanne went back to her room to finish getting ready for their last evening together; she wasn't sure what would happen once they got back to England, she didn't know whether or not she would still be assigned to Egbert and Annie or whether she would be put onto a new assignment, but either way what would be, would be.

At just after 19.00 the three of them congregated in the bar area and Joanne told Egbert and Annie what was happening and that they had to be in bed early. The two of them smiled and Annie said, "No problem, we are happy to comply with your wishes." They had their dinner and drank some wine and the conversation was as friendly as it had been since they had arrived, although Joanne was not as flirty and Egbert couldn't work out whether it was due to the fact that he and Annie had slept together or whether it was because Pilkington had arrived. In any case he decided that it was ok and he felt more normal about the situation. When midnight arrived the three of them went off to their rooms, there was no hesitation by Egbert or Annie and they did not even try and hide the fact that they would be spending the night together as they went into Annie's room. Joanne went to her own room and she was quickly asleep, she knew that the next day was going to be an important one. They had been in bed for less than an hour, Annie was laying in Egbert's arms when she suddenly spoke out, "Egbert, something is wrong, something is going to happen, I can feel it."

Egbert had just been dozing, but woke quickly and said, "What do you mean Annie, what do you feel?"

"I am not sure, but whenever I feel like this something happens. Can you go and get Joanne, I would feel safer if there was somebody in here with a weapon?"

Egbert was genuinely concerned, he had learned to trust Annie's senses completely, he said, "I will Annie, but maybe I should tell the security team as well?"

Annie shook her head and said, "There is no point, what would you say to them and what could they do, I don't even know myself what it is, I have no idea what to tell them, about what might happen."

Egbert quickly got dressed and he went and knocked on Joanne's door, he knocked a couple of times more until she heard him and then she came wearily to the door and looked through the small viewer and saw it was Egbert, she opened the door and said, "What is it Egbert, why are you dressed?"

Egbert looked worried and said, "It's Annie, she says that something is going to happen, can you get dressed and come to her room, she doesn't know what it is, but she would like you there.?"

Joanne quickly woke up and was turning back into her room when she said, "Of course, I will be just a few minutes."

Egbert asked; "Do you have another weapon, maybe it would make sense if I was armed?"

"No sorry, I just have my own handgun."

Egbert accepted what Joanne had said and then he turned and he went back to Annie's room. Only a few minutes later Joanne knocked on Annie's door, which had been left unlocked and she entered and spoke to Annie, "Can you tell me what is going to happen?"

Annie looked worried and she shook her head and said, "No, I don't know, I just know that we are all safer if we are together in this room." The three of them discussed whether they should let Pilkington and the security team know what Annie was feeling, but they decided that they would wait for a while before doing that, until they had something to tell them that made sense.

Meanwhile Pilkington was sat on his sofa and he looked at his watch and saw that it was now 01.18, he knew that he should make his move to the control room in about 30 minutes' time. He called Ayesha, the woman that he had met at Sinatra's Bar and she answered. Pilkington said; "It is Pilkington. I wanted to let you know that my woman agent is in room 12 and the Professor and the woman will most likely be together in room 15. While they were at dinner I have drawn an X on the outer wall of room 12, just to the right of the patio door frame. Your people should recognise it easily."

Ayesha replied, "Fine, she will be one of the first to die, what about the control room, are you ready?"

Pilkington answered confidently, "Yes I will enter at 01.55 and close it down at 01.57; from that point the security team will not be aware of any activity outside of the hacienda. You will be able to drive right up to the gates and will not be seen."

Ayesha was pleased that Pilkington seemed to be in control and then said, "Then all is set, there will be eight of my people in the two cars and I will be in the helicopter which will land once the hacienda is in our control. Everybody knows who you are, so you will be safe; if you have to fire at my men, fire well over their heads?" Pilkington acknowledged what Ayesha had said and the call was ended

Pilkington sat on the sofa watching the timer on his pocket watch, it seemed to take an age, but gradually the minute hand settled on 01.50. Pilkington attached the silencer to his weapon and hid it under his jacket, he walked into reception which was empty and unlocked the main door, and then carried on along the corridor to the control room. Pilkington stood outside of the room for a moment and then he knocked on the door and he entered, one of the security men turned round and recognised that it was Pilkington and smiled and said, "Hello Sir, can't you sleep, would you like a brew?"

Pilkington took out his gun and he fired into the head of the man. The second man started to stand, but he had no chance; Pilkington fired a shot into his head also. The room was silent and both men were already dead. Pilkington looked at the monitors and he could see the cars arriving at the main gate, he then pulled out the leads at the back of the CCTV control unit and also the leads out of the personal communicator control panel, the rest of the security team were now isolated from being able to communicate or being able to check the CCTV cameras. Good to his word, by 01.57 the control room was inoperable, Pilkington left the room and stood outside the security team rest room and he waited; if anybody came out he would have to kill them, but otherwise he would wait for the Al Qaeda operatives to arrive. Al Qaeda did not try to blow the gate, they simply threw over their rope ladders and climbed over it. Unlike a normal Al Qaeda attack this one needed to be as silent as possible and utilise the element of surprise, for a change it was not a terrorist attack where noise helps to add to the terror and the confusion. Two of the team went to the back of the hacienda and six of the team walked straight up to the front door, which Pilkington had unlocked on his way through reception; they quietly entered the building, they looked around the reception area and it was clear, their first target was the security team rest room and they walked along the corridor on the East Wing towards the rest room outside of which Pilkington was standing. Pilkington saw the Al Qaeda hit squad coming towards him and he felt chilled; they were dressed in black as any other elite fighting squad would be for a night operation and they were walking straight towards him, his natural instinct was to open fire, they had been his enemy for so long, but the realisation took over him that he had now switched sides, he was now working hand-in-hand with the hated terrorist group. As they approached him Pilkington lifted his right arm to indicate for them to stop, they were only one metre away from him, he then knocked on the restroom door and entered; three of the men took out their handguns from their holsters and pointed them towards Pilkington, immediately when they saw it was Pilkington they re-holstered their weapons. At that precise moment Pilkington moved to one side and Al Qaeda stormed into the room with their silenced handguns flashing out bursts of light and flame and their bullets exploded into the bodies of the security team. Without even a return shot being fired, the whole team had been put out of action and were lying there dead or dying, the operatives checked each agent and fired two bullets into each of their brains to make sure that they had finished them; they did not want a wounded agent causing them any trouble.

Annie, Joanne and Egbert were sat in Annie's room and all they could hear was the noise of the rotor blades of a helicopter in the distance, although it did sound to be getting closer, as yet Annie did not understand what it was that she had sensed, but then without warning she heard a muffled explosion close by. The two men at the back of the building had fitted an explosive device to the patio door of Joanne's room and when it exploded they ran into Joanne's room and fired into the bed where Joanne should have been sleeping; they were surprised when they pulled back the covers and the bed was empty. Desmond Williams was a light sleeper and when he heard the noise he got out of his bed and quickly put some clothes on. He knew that the sound had come from where his guests rooms were and he walked down the corridor towards room 12. As he approached the two men came out of the room and looked towards him; they did not have a chance Desmond already had his shotgun barrels pointing at them and he fired both cartridges into the two men's bodies almost ripping them apart in the process, his years in the underworld had taught him to fire first and ask questions later. Desmond quickly reloaded his weapon and walked into room 12 which he saw was empty; he came out and he banged on the door of number 15 where he knew that Annie and the Professor would probably be; he had found two glasses in there the previous morning and had already assumed that they were sleeping together, he shouted; "Open the door, quickly, it is Desmond Williams." Egbert opened the door and Desmond walked in, Joanne was stood with her weapon in her hand pointing towards him, when she was sure there was no threat she lowered her weapon and then Williams said, "Joanne, two of them just came out of your room, but I finished them, you better get out of here, I am going back to help Mr Pilkington. Make your way across the Gallops and get into the stables, I will send the security team up to you, it is made of thick timber and stone and it should give you some protection for a while."

Joanne was confident that Williams knew what he was doing and she nodded in agreement, they were on the ground floor so Egbert opened the window and the three of them climbed out and started to run through the darkness towards the Gallops and then up to the stables, there was no lighting to guide them, but Annie didn't need light; she had already taken the lead and the other two followed her.

Williams walked back along the corridor towards reception, when he saw Pilkington walking towards him, he was pleased to see Pilkington and he started to smile, he then said; "Thank God, Sir, you are alright."

Pilkington gave Williams a friendly smile and said; "Yes, thank you for your concern Desmond, what about Joanne and the other two, are they alright as well?

Williams lowered his shotgun and was about to answer, but immediately Pilkington raised his handgun and fired straight into Williams. His body crumbled and he slumped to the floor at the same time as dropping his shotgun. Pilkington walked over to the dying man who had a shocked and surprised look on his face. Williams looked up at Pilkington and although he was gasping for breath he asked; "Why Sir, why you Sir, why this?"

Pilkington looked down at him and said; "Purely for money Desmond, just money. This is not personal Desmond, just business; you have always served me well Desmond, but now it is time for you to rest." Pilkington covered Williams eyes with one hand and put his gun barrel next to Williams head with the other and then he pulled the trigger and said sincerely; "Sorry Desmond, I will miss you."

The Al Qaeda operatives rushed past Pilkington to get to room 15, they entered and it was empty, they noticed that the window was open, but before going out of it they checked the two other rooms, to make sure that they were also empty. Pilkington told them,

"They never came back this way, they must have gone through the window, and I guess they will have gone up to the stables where they will have some cover. I will go after them, I should be able to deal with Joanne and then you come and take the woman and the Professor."

Pilkington climbed out of the window and headed towards the stables. He shouted after them, but there was no response. As he approached the stables the main door opened and Egbert shouted; "James, get in here quick, are you ok?" Pilkington entered the stable and said that he was fine.

Joanne turned to Pilkington and said, "What the hell happened back there, Sir?"

Pilkington replied; "I heard a noise and I went to investigate, I checked the control room and both of the men were dead, I checked the rest room and all of the security team were dead, I came to look for you and saw that they had killed Desmond close by your room door, I saw that your window was open and I guessed that you might have come up here to hide."

"I don't know how many of them there are, but I managed to get two of them with Desmond's shotgun, we need to get down to the hacienda entrance, I have a helicopter coming to get out us out of here, listen I can hear it now."

Joanne looked outside of the stable window and she noticed movement and she told Pilkington; "We are too late, I can see at least six of them out there they look to be taking up positions to attack us. How much ammunition have you got, Sir?"

Pilkington answered; "I have twenty rounds, what about you?"

Joanne knew exactly what she had, she had kept her weapon close to her all the time she had been at the hacienda and she told Pilkington; "I have forty rounds, maybe we can hold them off until the helicopter gets here, is the helicopter bringing any cavalry to help us?"

Pilkington lied again; "Yes, there is a security team of six on board."

Egbert then spoke; "Joanne, give me your gun, I can go outside and pick a few of them off."

Joanne looked at Egbert and responded sharply; "That's crazy, I am a better shot than you, if anybody goes out there, it should be me."

Egbert replied; "That is not necessarily the case, I am guessing that they want Annie and myself alive, so I can fire at them, but they can't fire back at me, that gives me a real good chance of taking a few of them out."

Pilkington looked at Egbert and red in the face, he shouted, "No, I simply can't allow it. I am in charge here, nobody is going out there, Professor you and Annie are too important to risk, and we can hold them off until the helicopter gets here."

Al Qaeda had got themselves well-positioned to attack the stables, but were giving Pilkington every chance to get the Professor and the woman out, without them needing to attack; there was no reason to risk their lives unnecessarily.

Annie turned to Egbert and whispered to him; "I don't trust him, I have seen him before, it was him that used to shout at your father he is a liar, and he means to hand us over."

Egbert looked at Annie and replied, "He is Head of the Security Section, he reports to the Foreign Secretary, he wouldn't give us up, and he knows how important it is to keep us alive."

Annie though was insistent and said, "If you get a chance take his gun from him."

Egbert was puzzled and he had never doubted Annie's senses, but he said, "I think you are wrong on this one, we have to trust that he will get us out of this, he has looked after us so far."

Annie was not happy, but she did not say anything more, she didn't need to; Egbert could read her mind.

Joanne spoke to Pilkington, "Sir, the helicopter has arrived, but nobody is coming to help us, what is happening?"

Pilkington carried on bluffing, "It's normal, they are just checking out the enemy positions, they will engage soon and then it will all be over, we just have to hold tight."

As Joanne was speaking with Pilkington, the top of the small barn door swung open and one of the enemy reached in and fired a couple of shots towards her. Joanne leapt to her side and the shots missed, Joanne returned fire, but she did not hit anybody.

Pilkington said, "At this rate they will draw all of our ammunition and just walk in and take Egbert and Annie away from us."

Egbert leaned back and took one of the sharp pointed pitchforks off of the wall. "Well if they do, they won't find it easy."

Pilkington suddenly stood up pointed his gun at Joanne and impatiently said; "Look, I have had enough of this, Joanne, throw your weapon over to me and don't even think about trying to shoot me, I have shot a lot of people already tonight and I am quite happy to put a bullet between your pretty eyes."

Joanne looked at Pilkington and she couldn't believe her ears; Pilkington surely couldn't be on their side, but it looked as though he had to be. Joanne wondered if she could raise her hands and fire before he could fire at her, but she decided that she would have no chance and she had no choice but to throw down her weapon. Egbert looked at Pilkington and angrily asked, "What is all this about, what is going on?"

"Oh dear Egbert, nothing has changed from what you were asked to do originally, apart from you will now not be doing it for the British or American governments, but will be doing it for a far greater power and I am sure that the rewards for you will be much higher with your special skills. Come and stand beside me, there is plenty of money available for the right people and we can each have a share in some deserved wealth. I am sure that my employers would rather have you on their side than against them."

Egbert stared back and said; "You bastard, you are betraying us for money, what about your grand speeches about how important to civilization Annie's link with the NHBs will be, it was all crap."

Pilkington was in control and he knew it; he replied; "Egbert my dear man, you are as bad as your father, I tried to get him to do this around 30 years ago. You probably don't know it, but he was every bit as talented as you, he could read minds and he could hypnotize, he had a full dossier on Annie and what she knew, far more advanced than what we ever owned up to, but he would not release it to me, in fact he threatened to go direct to the Head of MI6 at the time and tell them what was happening. I had to have your father dealt with, Egbert and it was unfortunate that your mother was in the car at the same time that it happened, apparently he was on his way into Ilkley to catch the train to Leeds and then London, but somebody had cut his brake pipes and as you know, Hanging Stones Lane is a steep road to be out of control on, it must have been very frightening for them both. Of course the crash did not kill your parents, I had one of my men do that after the accident, two bullets in the brain dealt with them both and I was powerful enough at the time, just as I am now, to have the whole thing covered up and important pieces of information went missing. I thought that my chance had gone with the death of your father, but when I was contacted again recently by the powerful people, I knew that I could use you and you in your search for knowledge were easy to convince, you have helped to make me a very rich man, Egbert."

Egbert stared at Pilkington in a rage; he was so angry, he started to shake. He looked at Pilkington with hatred in his eyes and said; "You bastard, you killed my parents, you will not get away with this!"

A look of arrogance spread across Pilkington's face and he replied, "Well Professor that was some outburst, but unfortunately for you, you cannot stop me, very soon you will go with my new Al Qaeda friends, along with this unfortunate woman and you will help some very powerful people, who are more powerful than governments to take full control of the world. Then, probably when you have served your purpose you will both end up the same way that your parents did Egbert, with bullets in the brain. Joanne, my dear, would you mind stepping forward, unfortunately you will not be making the trip home, I have no further use for you and you must die sooner than you expected, if it is any consolation to you, I think that you have served your country well and that you have done an excellent job of keeping Egbert and Annie safe, now kneel down in front of me, out of respect I will make your death a quick one."

Joanne had no choice, she had realised that there was nobody coming to help them and she did not want to risk any harm to Egbert or Annie so she walked forward and knelt down in front of Pilkington who put his gun barrel at the side of Joanne's head and pulled back the trigger, the hammer cocked and he was about to squeeze the trigger, when he felt a sudden thud and a pain in his chest and then felt the warmth of blood running down from his chest to his stomach, he looked up and away from Joanne's head and he saw that he had the points of a pitchfork sticking out from his chest, the wooden handle was still vibrating from the impact, his right arm went into a spasm and he dropped the gun, which had been pointing at Joanne's head. Egbert had already leapt forward after throwing the pitchfork and he picked up Joanne's gun that was lying on the ground, Egbert aimed high enough above Joanne to make sure that he missed her but low enough to hit something vital on Pilkington's body. He fired twice, the impact of the first shot pushed Pilkington onto his back, the second one entered his lung and caused him to gasp. Joanne reached out and picked up Pilkington's weapon, but before she could do anything with it, Egbert was leaning over Pilkington and he fired two shots into his brain and as he looked into Pilkington's dying body he said, "There you bastard, you can have what you gave my parents, two shots to the brain."

Annie was stunned at how fast Egbert had reacted, first by throwing the pitchfork like a javelin into Pilkington's body, but secondly by how he had finished Pilkington off with the gun. Joanne looked at Egbert and he helped her up from the ground, she thanked him for saving her life, he kissed her gently on the cheek and gave her a squeeze, and there were no words that needed to be spoken. Egbert's emotions were high, on the one hand he had just learned that his parents had been murdered, but he had also just saved his friend's life.

Annie shouted in a friendly voice, "Oy, woman, put him down, I haven't finished with him yet and we need to sort out those bastards out there."

The Al Qaeda operatives had heard the gunfire from inside, but were waiting for what would happen next; they had no need to charge in, they had the stables well covered and the people inside were not going anywhere without them knowing about it. All of a sudden though the tables had turned and they were being fired on from the stables, Joanne was using her own gun and Egbert was using the one that Pilkington had dropped to the floor. They knew that they had to fight their way out of the barn and find some way of escaping.

The lead operative on the ground for Al Qaeda called the helicopter and spoke to Ayesha, "We need some cover fire and quickly, we need to go into the barn and finish this."

The helicopter took off and hovered close to the front of the stables. Ayesha and the armed man seated at the back of the pilot started to fire their automatic weapons into the barn, this was assisted by the six men on the ground also firing, Annie, Egbert and Joanne had no choice, they lay flat on the ground trying to avoid the hail of bullets coming towards them. Without warning and with no apparent reason Annie got to her knees and put her hands together in front of her, her eyes were tightly closed, it looked as though she was praying, miraculously no bullets hit her, although some were flying close to her. Egbert called out to Annie; "Lie down Annie, you are going to get hit!!"

Annie did not move; Joanne was some twenty feet away from her and she tried to crawl towards her to get her head down but she had to retreat back. Neither Joanne or Egbert had noticed that there was a bright light in the corner of the stable, it was about the size of a pea, and it was gradually getting bigger, it grew to the size of a golf ball and then to the size of a tennis ball and then to the size of a football before expanding to the size of a beach ball and by now Joanne and Egbert were watching it in amazement, even though the bullets flying above their heads. The light started to move towards the top half of the stable door and then it floated outside, it was at this point that Annie's eyes opened and they were staring and wide, at exactly the same time the ball of light simultaneously split into seven beams of light. The first beam hit the helicopter and the other six beams hit the six men on the ground. It was as though they were luminous, they shone brightly and did not move. They stayed shining for at least 10 seconds when all of a sudden the people in the helicopter and the six men on the ground disappeared; the only remnants of what had just happened, was that the charred helicopter crashed to the ground and the six operatives charred weapons were laying on the floor where they had dropped. The bodies had just disappeared. The light beams came back into the ball as if they were being sucked in and then it rapidly shrank back to the size of the pea before it disappeared altogether. It was eerily silent and none of the three of them spoke, until Egbert broke the silence and said, "What the hell happened there, I don't believe it?"

Annie responded; "Well, that was one of the times that my friends came to help me, they rarely let me down when I really need them."

The three of them walked outside of the stables and then down to the hacienda, they went inside the building and looked around they saw the people lying there who had been killed earlier, some of the kitchen and cleaning staff looked to be in shock, but they were covering over the dead bodies with sheets and towels. One of the waiters approached the three of them to ask if they were alright. He asked if he should call the local police, they had always relied on Williams to do what was needed, but as he was one that was being covered by a sheet, they were at a loss what to do. Joanne took charge and told them all not to worry and that she would deal with it.

Joanne called back to the UK and requested that a clean-up team should be sent out as well as forensics; she knew that there were mysteries that had happened that night and that they needed to be answered, she also asked that Phillip Joseph should get there as soon as possible to pick them up and get them back to England. It was now 03.30 in the morning and everybody seemed in a state of shock at what had happened. The staff of the hacienda were busying themselves with what they would normally do when they were working, it seemed strange because of the time of day that it was. At 04.30 a special team from the Spanish Government arrived by helicopter from

Madrid and shortly afterwards ambulances started to arrive up the long mountain road to deal with the bodies. Joanne spent some time with the senior officer who had arrived from Madrid and she told him what had happened. She said that she would file a full report for her seniors and the Foreign Secretary when she was back in England. Annie and Egbert remained silent as they drank their tea and coffee; it had been a frightening experience, but generally they were holding up well, Annie even took drinks to the hacienda staff, because she could see that they were in shock at what had happened.

At 06.55 they heard the familiar sound of a helicopter approaching and they knew that this time it was a good sound, they knew that it was Phillip Joseph. The drive was cleared to allow him to land and after saying their goodbyes the three of them were being flown back to England via Malaga airport where Phillip Joseph picked up his fully-fuelled Cessna. Inside the Cessna the mood was quiet and there was little or no conversation, Phillip tried to lighten the mood by putting on some reggae and moving his hips as he was sat in the pilot's seat, but it wasn't working, so Phillip accepted that it was just going to be a long and quiet flight.

Back in the UK

Only two and a half hours later the three of them landed at Heathrow and they were whisked passed security and into a private car to take them to SIS HQ. At SIS HQ the three of them were interviewed fully to understand what had happened from the start of the case to the end and of course their accounts were consistent with each other; even Annie said that she did not know fully what had happened outside of the stables, but that she had received help from the NHBs who had protected for all of these years. In addition to the interviews Joanne had to write a full report including her observations on James Pilkington throughout the case, and having completed her report she was again interviewed on its contents. Justin Madeley had especially returned early from his meetings in Spain about the Gibraltar issue and he visited the SIS HQ to ask Joanne personally what Pilkington had said before he died, he particularly wanted to know if he had said who he was working for and all that she could tell him was that he referred to them as powerful people, even more powerful than governments. The Foreign Secretary asked if all he had heard about Annie and Egbert's amazing abilities were true and Joanne told him that she didn't know what he had heard, but that she could vouch for the fact that their abilities were amazing. He seemed very happy with her responses and he left to go and brief the Prime Minister.

After the interviews and once Joanne's superiors were satisfied, the report was circulated with a copy also going to the Prime Minister at his request; this whole process of interviews and secondary and third interviews took place over three days and finally Joanne was told that she was in the clear and that a new Head of Department would be appointed shortly and that they would very much like her to work with that person. Joanne felt a little annoyed that she had been suspected of any wrongdoing, but she understood that it was normal procedure, especially when a senior officer is killed.

At the end of the third day Annie and Egbert were taken away from SIS HQ and were moved to an army base just outside London, it wasn't exactly a normal army base it was more like a conference centre surrounded by an army base. There was a reception area with several conference and meeting rooms, the conference rooms all had state of the art technology within them. On the second floor there were guest rooms which had toiletries and mini-bars to complement the luxury furnishings; it was just like an expensive hotel. Egbert guessed that when senior officials visited the UK on important business, that they would be hosted at this location. It was certainly very secure with the British Army surrounding the facility. They were both taken to their rooms and then were told that dinner would be in one hour in a private dining suite near to reception, they were told that there was clothing their size in the wardrobes within their rooms and that the dress code for the evening was to be informal. Egbert had a shower and got changed into a pair of trousers and a shirt and he then went down to the dining suite. He was offered a drink which he accepted, Annie followed shortly afterwards she was wearing a blouse and skirt and looked clean and refreshed, again she was offered a drink which she also accepted. A few moments later a man and a woman walked into the room; the man introduced himself as Major Greenaway and the lady was introduced as Professor Samantha Michalowski, who told everybody to call her Professor Samantha, it would be much easier. All four of them introduced themselves to each other whilst they had a couple of drinks and they enjoyed some friendly chat which had obviously been engineered to relax Annie and Egbert. Major Greenaway then said that they would sit and enjoy a nice dinner together after dinner the proceedings became more formal and the Major went on to say, "Well, I hope you have enjoyed your dinner and

I would formally like to welcome you to this superb facility, you have fully completed the debriefing process and we are now ready to continue with our original project. Professor and Miss Brown, do you feel ready to continue, I know that you have been through a lot and if you need it we can give you a few more days to recover, but we would prefer to start as soon as possible?"

Annie and Egbert both agreed that they were ready to start, with Egbert saying, "After what we have been through over the last few days I am sure that we would like to start as soon as possible, it would be nice to get back to normality as soon as we can."

The Major responded, "Excellent, then we will start in the morning at 09.00 in room 3, I am sure that you are interested to know what will happen? It is quite simple really, Miss Brown we need to make contact with the NHBs and we believe that you can help us, with Professor Egbert's assistance, you will be taken back in time through the power of regression hypnosis, which I know you have encountered before, there is a difference though Professor Egbert will be reading your mind at the same time as he regresses you, he will experience your responses, Professor Michalowski who is also an expert in regression techniques will monitor and observe the whole process and assist further if and when required. Miss Brown, both you and Professor Egbert will have wires attached to you, but this is purely to measure your heartbeat and vital organs; if at any time we feel that your health is in danger, Professor Michalowski and her team of scientists and nurses will intervene. The whole process will be recorded. Now do either of you have any questions?"

Annie looked at Egbert and then said, "Egbert, do you think that you can do this?"

Egbert replied, "Annie, it is what I am trained to do and it is what my father could do before me, Annie I promise you that you will be safe, I will not let anything bad happen to you."

Annie turned back to the Major and said, "I have no questions Major, let's get on with it."

The Major smiled and replied, "Excellent, we will start at 09.00 in the morning, now I suggest that you enjoy a couple more drinks and then get some rest, the next few days will be busy."

The four of them then continued to have a couple more drinks and the polite conversation that went with it and as they came to the end the Major suggested that it would be a good idea if Annie and Egbert had an early night; as Egbert was about to leave the room the Major called him back and said; "Professor, we know that you have become very close with Annie, but please remember the importance of what you are doing and I would suggest that for the next few evenings you sleep in your own bed. We are not prudes, but I am sure that you understand."

Egbert sheepishly smiled and then replied, "Yes Major, I understand."

Annie and Egbert each went to their own rooms and as they were walking Annie sent a message to Egbert's mind, *"Egbert, Samantha told me that I have to sleep alone tonight, bloody spoilsports."*

Egbert mischievously thought back, *"Annie, I know, I asked her to, I thought she might pop round and keep me company."*

Annie thought back, *"You lying bugger, you just wait until all of this is over."*

Annie smiled to herself as did Egbert and they both continued to their own rooms and had their early night sleep that had been suggested to them.

The Regression

The morning came around very quickly and at 08.00 the two of them were called on the room telephone's to advise them that their breakfast would be in their rooms at 08.15. Annie wasn't happy with this she liked to stay in bed for as long as she could, and she certainly wouldn't rush to get out of bed for food, but she did as they asked and by 08.50 she was ready to go down and be regressed, which she guessed would take the best part of the day. When Annie was in the room, she noticed that there was a mirrored glass wall and she was sure that they would be observed from the other side of the glass, just as she had seen on the American cop programmes on TV. Egbert walked into the room and smiled at Annie; Annie replied with a smile and in a half singing, half speaking voice she said, "Morning."

It always made Egbert smile when she did that and he then asked her, "Are you ready for this?"

She looked back at Egbert and said, "Yes I am, let's to do it."

Egbert pointed to the bed and said; "Ok Annie, please lay on the bed."

Annie sent out a thought to Egbert; *"Are you going to take advantage of me, Professor?"*

Egbert thought back, *"Behave yourself woman!"*

Annie lay on the bed and a nurse attached sensors to her. Egbert sat in a reclining chair next to her and the nurse also attached sensors to him. Their heart rates were checked from the other side of the mirrored wall and all was fine. Egbert switched on a metronome and then he spoke softly to Annie, "Annie, I want you to listen to the beat of the metronome and I want you to match your breathing to the beat, can you do that for me Annie?" Annie nodded and gradually her breathing slowed and she matched the slower beat of the metronome.

Egbert continued in a quiet and gentle voice. "Now Annie, you should start to feel very relaxed, listen to the beat and clear everything else from your thoughts, can you hear the beats between the silences?"

Annie didn't answer, but she nodded in the same way that she would if she was dozing off to sleep.

Egbert could tell that Annie was going under and he said, "I want you to remember the first time that you saw the light orb and I want you to describe it."

After a few seconds Annie replied, "It is in the corner of the room, it is floating and very small, so small like a pea, I can see it, it is getting bigger and bigger and it is coming towards me, I want to shout and wake my sister and brother, I want to get out of bed and run downstairs to my mum. I can't move, I can't speak, and it is over the top of me, why can't anybody else see it? Please leave me alone, go away, go away! It's not listening, it is getting bigger, what is it doing?"

Annie started sobbing and continued, "It hurts, it is going into me, into my stomach, aargh, somebody stop it aargh, it is killing me, it is stretching my whole insides, get out of me you bastard. I can't move, it is inside me it is moving from side to side and up and down, from my toes and up into my head and from my fingers into my body, I am dying. Oh God, please help me, I am only little."

Annie went quiet and she was breathing deeply and then her breathing became normal and she said; "It is leaving my body, I don't know if I am dead or alive, I think I might be dead. No, I am alive, I can feel my heart beating, I can see it in the corner of the room, it is getting smaller like a pea, it is going, it is going, it has gone. I am lying in my bed and I am covered in sweat, I feel so weak, I am going to sleep, sleep, sleep."

Egbert sensed that Annie really was going into a sleep and he said, "Annie, you are not alone, tell me did it happen the same the second time?"

Annie replied, "Yes"

Egbert went on to say, "How many times were there, Annie?"

Annie drowsily said, "There were many times."

Egbert wanted to push Annie and take advantage of her relaxed state, so he continued; "Tell me about when it changed, Annie?"

Annie started to speak again. "I am lying in my bed and the light is in the corner of the room, it is coming to me again and this time I don't fight it, I am too tired. The light is getting bigger, it is coming into my stomach, I can't move, but it is not hurting me as much, it is moving up and through my body and into my head, it is talking to me. I can't hear the words, but I know what it is thinking, it wants me to go with it, back to its home, I am frightened, I don't want to go with it, it asks me again and it tells me not to be frightened, it says that we will only go for a short while and then it will bring me back, it is not hurting me now. I want to go but I am scared."

Egbert interrupted and asked, "Annie, do you ever go with it?"

Annie drowsily replied again, "Yes, it keeps asking me each time and eventually, I say yes to it."

Egbert now saw that this was his opportunity to interact inside of Annie's mind and he asked, "Annie, I am coming into your mind so that we can see it together?"

Egbert tuned into Annie's mind and he could feel everything that she was feeling; it was as though he was lying on her bed all of those years ago and he could feel the Light Orb's presence, he could hear the orb talking to her and it asked, *"Annie, Professor Egbert is in your mind, do you want him here?*

Annie replied, *"Yes, I want him here and I trust him, can he come with us?"*

The orb responded, "Yes Annie, if you trust him."

In the observation room Professor Samantha was seeing fluctuations in Annie's heartbeat and she could also see Egbert's heartbeat mirroring Annie's. Professor Samantha cannot hear what the Orb is saying but whatever is happening she knows that Egbert and Annie are on a journey together and Egbert is now as much on this journey as Annie is.

Egbert suddenly speaks out loud, "I can see the all the colours of the rainbow, it is beautiful we are going through them all, where are we?"

The orb replies to Egbert, *"We are in my world, Professor Egbert, and look down, you can see our lights occupying the shapes that we want to be in."*

Egbert was there on the journey and he looked down and again he spoke out loud, "I can see human shapes and animal shapes and light balls travelling around, everything is so peaceful, everybody is happy, I feel happy, I can hear music, I can hear children laughing, I can see people and animals eating food from the fields, they are eating straight from the fields or picking food straight from the trees, birds are flying, human shapes are flying alongside them, dogs are flying next to the humans, tigers are flying and everybody is happy, nobody is angry."

The orb decided that their journey had been long enough, especially for the Professor and it cast its thoughts into both their minds. *"Annie and Professor Egbert, it is time for you to go back now, because if you don't go back now, you will never want to leave."*

The next thing that Egbert knew was that there was a nurse next to him, checking his pulse whilst he was being woken up, he looked around at Annie and she was already awake and sitting up on the bed. Annie spoke to Egbert, "How did you like that, then?"

Egbert was very drowsy but he asked, "Did we really go there?"

Annie was smiling and then she said, "Ask your colleagues Egbert, they recorded what you said, but yes we did go there."

Egbert was curious and he asked; "How did it happen though, I was regressing you back in time, when the past became now?"

Professor Samantha came into the room and interrupted the conversation, she asked, "Are you both alright, we thought we had lost you there?"

Egbert looked at Professor Samantha and said; "I feel ok, but I feel shattered, why did you think that you had lost us?"

Professor Samantha looked back at Egbert with concern on her face and then said, "Professor Egbert for 15 seconds both you and Annie flat-lined, both your hearts stopped beating, yet you were still speaking. Your hearts stopped beating at exactly the same time and then both re-started at exactly the same time; I have never seen anything like it."

Egbert replied, "I can't explain it, but I can assure you, I was very much alive, maybe there was some problem with the equipment?"

Professor Samantha answered, "I checked the equipment and it was working fine, the nurses were just about to start applying CPR to you both when Annie sat up on her bed and your pulse came back. I can't explain it either, but I am not sure that we can proceed any further with this, it is too dangerous."

Egbert snapped out of his drowsiness and replied firmly, "Professor Samantha, that is out of the question, Annie and I have been through too much to stop now, it is our choice and we will continue, just give me thirty minutes to allow me to rest."

Professor Samantha looked at both Egbert and Annie and then she reluctantly agreed to continue, but she said; "I will agree to it continuing, but I want the CPR equipment put on standby and I want my two nurses in the room when you are doing it."

Egbert looked back at the Professor and again firmly said, "You can have the equipment on standby, but you can only use it if my heart stops and I am not speaking and only after you have waited for ten full minutes, and I will not allow nurses in the room when I am carrying out the regression; there can only be Annie and myself, in the room."

Professor Samantha looked fiercely at Egbert and was just about to speak when Egbert raised his hand and said, "Enough Professor, that is enough, we are doing this my way, it is clinically proven that the heart can be stopped for at least 20 minutes without any major problems and I am prepared to take that risk, we are on the brink here of achieving what we set out to achieve!"

Professor Samantha turned around indignantly and she left the room to go back behind the mirrored wall; she realised that any further discussion with Egbert about the subject was futile. She walked over to the telephone and she made a call to the Major and she said, "Major, I would like you to come to the observation room, Professor Egbert is adamant that we carry on with the regression, but in my personal and professional opinion he is putting their lives at risk."

The Major replied back with a question: "Why is that Samantha?"

Professor Samantha answered; "Well he was able to enter Annie's mind and he described what he was seeing, which was amazing, but both of their hearts stopped for 15 seconds during the process, at precisely the same time, it is too dangerous."

The Major, thought about what he had just been told and then asked, "Samantha, was he in contact with the NHB?"

Professor Samantha responded to his question, but still with a concerned voice, "It would appear so, Major."

The Major was pleased to hear this and he then said, "Then I agree with him, we shall continue, but I will come over, I would like to witness it."

Professor Samantha could not believe that the Major would not back her judgement and she replied, "But Major, I strongly disagree."

The Major knew that he had to placate Professor Samantha, so he reached out to the scientist within her, "Samantha, if you were on the edge of discovering something fantastic, would you stop?"

Professor Samantha thought about what the Major had just said and she was forced to back down and then replied to his question. "Well, when you put it like that, you know that I would continue."

The Major was happy that she had conceded and then said, "Exactly Samantha, now let him continue. When is the next session?"

She replied, "In thirty minutes Major, he is resting now."

"Ok, I will see you then."

The call ended.

The professor started to check that the equipment was working and she played back the recording, what Egbert was describing was, she must admit, fantastic; but she wondered how much further he could go and she did have concerns that the only voice that she could hear was Egbert's, which made the evidence inconclusive. The 30 minutes passed and the Major arrived, the sensors were still attached to both Annie and Egbert. The Major, Professor Samantha and her technical team along with the nurses were observing behind the mirrored wall. Egbert sat up and he felt refreshed, he turned to Annie and he asked if she was ready to go again and Annie replied, "Yes Egbert, this is exciting, let's do it."

Egbert started the metronome and started to speak in his gentle and quiet voice; "Annie listen to the metronome, listen to the silence between its beats, now breath in time with the beats, can you feel the silence Annie?"

Annie replied; "Yes, I can."

Egbert went on to say in a very gentle manner, "Well done Annie, now you are drifting back to the second time that the light orb took you to its world can you see it Annie?"

Annie was drowsy now and it was clear she was back under again, "Yes, it is beautiful."

Egbert was excited and anxious to be in her mind with her and he then said, "Annie, I am coming into your mind now, I am going on the journey with you."

Annie drowsily replied, "Yes, come with me."

Egbert felt so at peace as he entered Annie's mind, he described the colours and the happiness and every being living in perfect harmony but then suddenly Egbert started to convulse slowly at first, but then his movements became quicker and stronger, the sinews of his muscles were tightening and then relaxing, his body was contorting and his face was etched with pain he then collapsed back into the reclining chair and he was motionless and now he has stopped speaking.

Professor Samantha said to Major Greenaway, "We have to stop this, he is in trouble."

The Major replied, "Wait Samantha, he said to leave him for ten minutes and that is what we will do, put your nurses on standby though, in case we have to go in there quickly, are their heart beats normal?"

Professor Samantha checked the monitors and replied, "Annie's is slower but still strong, Egbert is slower but becoming weak."

All of a sudden, Egbert sat bolt upright in his chair and he looked towards the mirrored wall. He started to speak in a voice which was not his own, it was deep and it echoed; "Major Greenaway, Professor Michalowski, do not worry about Egbert he is fine, his heartbeat has slowed because I have slowed it to protect him from this experience. Annie is also fine, we know that you want to have contact with us but there is little point in you continuing to regress Annie, as I will speak to you directly through Professor Egbert."

The Major was amazed by what he was witnessing, but quickly regained his composure and turned to David John of Professor Samantha's technical team and he asked him to compare the voice coming from Egbert to his normal voice.

The voice coming from Egbert continued, "Yes Major, that is good, you must do your voice test, because you must believe that this is not Professor Egbert who is speaking to you. I am using him to communicate with you, I could do it telepathically which is the normal way that I would communicate, but it is important that you are able to record what I say, so that you are in no doubt about what is happening."

Both the Major and Professor Samantha and her team watched and listened and they were truly amazed.

The voice went on; "We selected Annie many years ago because she is strong of spirit and she is strong of mind and we knew that one day she would lead us to this moment. In your Earth time this has taken over 30 years, but in our time it has been much, much less as time is not as relevant. Major, we know that your world is in trouble and it is time for us to help you; we can introduce you to technologies which are ancient for us but which are way beyond anything that you have ever imagined, Annie has seen these technologies because we have shown them to her, but more than the technology, your world must learn to live in peace, you must stop fighting and killing each other, you must stop destroying your planet and its atmosphere, you must make a mind shift and you must learn to live in harmony with your fellow men, you must stop killing what you call animals who are really your brothers just to eat them, we can show you many new ways, but you must trust us and follow our direction. I know, Major that you alone cannot do this, but you do have people on your planet that we can work with, to get help you. In my world we do not fear natural disasters, we use their power to make our world stronger, we do not fear being hit by asteroids which could wipe out a civilization, and we can divert the power of the galaxy to a positive energy, not a negative one. We do not make weapons to destroy each other and the planet, we do not need to. Our people are superior in knowledge to your people, but you could become equally as strong and knowledgeable, you are like children that need to be taught, we have tried in the past, but you have not changed your ways, it cannot and must not continue like this. Your people believe in many gods but they are all the same one, and it is the same one that we believe in, which is the God of goodness. Now

Major, I must leave Professor Egbert soon, as he will need time to recover, but make sure that my messages, which you are recording, are taken seriously and make sure that your world leaders, your people that can make the right decisions are aware of my visit. Annie and now Professor Egbert can help your leaders to understand and we will give you what you need to survive and flourish."

The Major then spoke, "Wait, before you go, if you do not believe in killing, why did you kill the soldiers that were trying to take Egbert and Annie in the mountains of Spain."

The voice coming from Egbert responded, "We did not kill them, we took their consciousness and we will repair them, so that they can be reborn into another carbon body and they will learn to live in peace as they should; the ashes that were left behind were their old carbon bodies that they no longer require. They believed in evil, but they will be reborn and will be good. We believe that everybody has the right to be good. We stopped them because we knew that their leaders would not listen to us in the same way and Annie and Professor Egbert would have been in great danger as would your entire world. Now Egbert will sleep for seven days after this, but he will recover. Do not fear for him and do not fear for Annie, we have already given her special gifts, but they are not unique to her, your people and your animals already possess these gifts albeit not yet all in one body; we can teach you to develop these gifts for each and every one of you on your planet, if you have the desire to learn. When your leaders are ready I will reappear, but do not leave it too long."

With that Egbert slumped back into the chair and his heartbeat started to return to normal. The Major looked at Professor Samantha and they were both stunned. David, the technician had carried out his tests on the voice match and he spoke out, "The voice was not Egbert's, there is not one matching pattern, the voice came from somebody or something else."

The Major replied, "Are you absolutely sure, David?"

David was confident and he replied; "Yes Sir, I am 100% sure, believe me I have worked with this technology now for many years and I am sure."

By now the nurses were at Egbert's side and Annie was again sat up on the bed. Egbert's pulse was back to normal, but he was sleeping in a comatose state.

Annie said, "Don't worry about him this normal, the Light Orb would not hurt him, take him to his bed and let him recover, I will stay with him until he does."

The nursing staff and Professor Samantha carried out a few more routine tests on Egbert, but all of his body was functioning as it should, he was simply in a deep, deep, sleep. They moved Egbert on to a trolley bed to take him back to his room, but before they took him, they also checked out Annie and everything was as normal as it should be. In Egbert's room they transferred him from the trolley bed to his own bed; they then connected vital organ sensors to him and they left him to sleep, albeit he was under constant monitoring. Annie sat next to him for a few hours and just watched him, the nurse told Annie that she should also get some rest, and that she would tell her if Egbert's condition showed any sign of change. Annie felt tired and so she agreed and went back to her room. Back in the observation room the Major spoke to Professor Samantha and David the technician; "What we have just witnessed is absolutely 'Top Secret' it must not be mentioned to anybody, I need you to compile full reports of what has happened today and I want them on my desk by 17.00, along with all of the recordings. I will ensure that the report is forwarded to the powers that be."

The Seventh Day

On the seventh day Annie was sat at Egbert's bedside as she had been every day when suddenly Egbert sat up and said to her, "Wow, that was fantastic, did all of that really happen, did the Orb really speak through me, or was I dreaming?"

Annie looked back at Egbert and she smiled, she was happy that he had woke up just as the orb said that he would. "Egbert, you know that it happened, how do you feel?"

By this time Egbert was sitting up, he replied, "Annie, I feel like I have been asleep for a week, but I feel fantastic, I feel that I could run to the moon and back."

Annie laughed and she replied, "Steady down, Superman."

They both laughed, and within minutes the Major and Professor were at Egbert's bedside, the Major spoke to Egbert, "Egbert, how do you feel?"

He replied, "Major, I feel bloody fantastic, you can get these sensors off of me now."

The Major shook his head and said, "All in good time Egbert, we just need to run a few tests on you and then you can get up, you know the drill though, we do need to debrief you about what you remember."

Egbert looked back at the Major and said, "I have no problem with that, I remember it all."

The Major was pleased with Egbert's response and said; "Good, then we will get it over with as quickly as we can, the Foreign Secretary has asked that I make him aware as soon as you are passed fit."

All of the tests and the debrief took place and Egbert was found to be in amazing shape, his tests actually showed him to have the body of a 20-year-old; the debrief was carried out and Egbert repeated word for word exactly the words that had come from his mouth whilst the Orb was present. Egbert and Annie had dinner that evening at the conference facility and they were told that the following day they would be meeting with a high-ranking individual who was looking forward to meeting them. With that in mind they had an early night in their own beds and had a good sleep.

The next day came around quickly and they were collected by a driver and another man in a black, top-of-the-range Jaguar, which was preceded by another black Jaguar and followed by another black Jaguar. Annie looked at Egbert and said; "They must have got a good deal on Jaguars. This is the life Egbert, I wonder where we are going?"

Egbert smiled and said; "Well, judging by all this attention, maybe we are going to see the Queen."

Annie sat next to the rear, nearside passenger window and whenever the car slowed down she practiced her royal wave to the onlookers, she said; "Look Egbert, they think I am royalty."

Egbert couldn't hide his smile as he shook his head and said; "You will be having us done for treason, if you are not careful."

They were both in high spirits and their faces were smiling for nearly all of the journey. The cars eventually pulled up outside number 10 Downing Street, London and the two of them were taken inside and into a grand reception room. Moments later a familiar figure came to greet them; it was Major Greenaway, who said, "How was the trip, you two?"

Annie replied; "It was bloody fantastic, certainly better than when I was tied up in the boot of a car."

The Major smiled and responded; "Well, I think you might need to start getting used to it, I think your life will now have changed for ever."

Annie pointed to Egbert and then said, "That's good, I must admit, it was getting a little bit stale before I met this man."

A few moments later another familiar figure walked in; it was the Prime Minister, David Cameron. Annie was almost speechless, she never expected to meet the Prime Minister, and she didn't know whether to bow, or courtesy, or what she should do. She finished up doing both. The Prime Minister smiled at her and said, "Please, please Annie there is no need, after what you have done and what you have been through, I should be bowing to you."

She looked at the Prime Minister and smiled and then said, "Well, you can if you like."

Cameron gave an uncomfortable bow, although he was smiling and he then moved over to Egbert and he shook his hand and said, "Thank you Professor, we owe you a great debt. Now please, if you would both follow me."

The Prime Minster led the way and as they were walking Annie whispered to Egbert; "Do you think I should tell him that I never voted for him?"

Egbert replied, "What he doesn't know won't hurt him."

The Prime Minister led them into another grand room and there was somebody sat in a large leather swivel chair; he was looking out of the window and onto Downing Street. Prime Minister Cameron then said; "Annie, Professor, there is somebody that I would like you to meet; the chair swivelled around and sat in it was a smart-looking black man, who smiled at them both, he stood up and he walked over to greet them and then he said, "Good morning Miss Brown, good morning Professor Janus, I have heard so much about you, it is a real pleasure to finally meet you."

Annie looked at the man who was instantly recognisable as President Obama, but she couldn't help herself, and she replied with a half-speaking, half-singing voice, "Morning!"

Annie had not been able to help herself, it was part nerves and also because of her excitement at seeing both Cameron and Obama in the same room. Obama started to speak, "Miss Brown, may I call you Annie and Professor, may I call you Egbert?"

They both nodded their approval and the President continued, "I believe that I need to spend a great deal of time with you both, and I have diverted Air Force One from Berlin to London just to meet with you, I have to leave for the G20 Summit, where I will be discussing what you have both achieved, but I wanted to ask you one favour? When the G20 Summit has finished in Berlin, can I divert back to London and collect you both to fly you back to Washington and the White House with me in Air Force One?"

Annie looked at Egbert and then looked back at President Obama, before saying, "President Obama, are you asking me or are you telling me that I have to come with you to Washington?"

The President smiled at Annie and then replied, "Annie, you should only come if you want to, but it is very important that you do."

Annie smiled and then replied, "President Obama, I accept your invitation, I would be delighted to attend the White House with you, and it is much nicer to be asked than to be told, that is where people have made mistakes with me in the past."

President Obama smiled and said, "Thank you both very much, Annie and Egbert."

Annie looked at Egbert and said, "Egbert, it looks like our adventure hasn't run its course yet, I wonder what the future holds, for us both?"

Egbert simply shrugged his shoulders and said, "Whatever it is, I am sure it will not be dull."

Meanwhile, only a short distance across London in his office at the Palace of Westminster the Foreign Secretary Justin Madeley had his office door closed. He was contemplating the events of the last few weeks, which had been hailed as a successful operation; it had been his responsibility to ensure that Annie Brown and Professor

Egbert Janus had been safely delivered to the British government and that their experts had gathered enough information to try and make contact with NHBs. Not only had they gathered the information, but actual contact with NHBs had been made through the body of Professor Egbert and now the president of the USA was taken the contact a stage further and he, through Egbert and Annie was aiming to speak direct to the NHBs and that would bring massive benefits to the world. Justin Madeley should be a very proud man because of his success in making this happen and on the outside he was, but on the inside he was very disappointed.

Madeley took out his mobile phone, but this time he didn't bother with his voice-changing application, there was no need; he was calling one of his associates, Congressman George Machin, when Machin answered, Madeley went on to say, "Hello George, we have missed the opportunity, your President has now met the woman and the Professor and they will be going back to Washington with him. The security around them will be too tough for even our people to deal with, my guess is that once Obama has made contact with the NHBs that he will appoint somebody to lead a NHB contact team; that will be our opportunity, we need to make sure that we have one of our people leading that team, George, I will now hand the project on to you, for you to make that happen."

Machin responded, "I agree with your assumption Justin, I have the very man in mind, he is greedy just as your man Pilkington was, I will position him with Obama when he returns, I have his ear and I am confident that he will take my recommendation, I will speak with you soon, don't worry we the Illuminati will prevail as we have done for hundreds of years.

The call ended; but the mission had not ended it had just moved onto its next phase.

End

Annie's Lights/Pitts

Lightning Source UK Ltd.
Milton Keynes UK
UKOW04f2227251115

263547UK00005B/348/P